DOCTOR WHO

PALACE OF THE RED SUN
CHRISTOPHER BULIS

D1589383

BBC

Published by BBC Worldwide Ltd,
Woodlands, 80 Wood Lane
London W12 0TT

First published 2002
Copyright © Christopher Bulis 2002
The moral right of the author has been asserted

Original series broadcast on the BBC
Format © BBC 1963
Doctor Who and TARDIS are trademarks of the BBC

ISBN 0 563 53849 X
Imaging by Black Sheep, copyright © BBC 2002

Printed and bound in Great Britain by Mackays of Chatham
Cover printed by Belmont Press Ltd, Northampton

Prologue

The last of the Imperial guards fell defending the doors of the audience chamber, cut down by the relentless hail of the invaders' gunfire. A few shots flashed over their twisted bodies and struck the ornate doors themselves, blasting through the precious inlaid wood until they exposed the heavy metal plate that formed the door's core.

'Cease fire!'

The clipped, commanding tones sounded over the attackers' helmet phones. It was a voice that expected and received immediate obedience.

They drew aside as a figure strode up the corridor, his scarlet battle armour contrasting sharply with their utilitarian grey. There was no insignia of rank on his breastplate, but then none was needed. From the lowliest trooper to the most venerable general, all knew him; and out of fear or love, or some strange combination of the two, followed where he led without question.

Two small flying disks also seemed strongly attracted to the scarlet warrior. They swooped and bobbed in his wake, binocular lenses glittering as they refocused, capturing his image from different angles even as their microphones faithfully recorded his every word. One disk bore the marking DAVE#3, the other DAVE#11.

The scarlet warrior stepped over the bodies of the fallen until he stood before the high double doors of the audience chamber. He clasped their ornate handles and pushed, but they did not move. He turned to the squad commander.

'Are all the exits covered?'

'Yes, sir. The royal family definitely came this way. They must be inside.'

The scarlet warrior raised a gauntleted fist and drove it against the charred and splintered wood with all the power of his suit's servo boosters. Three times the booming knock rang out, then he spoke, his voice amplified though his chest speaker.

'Hathold! Hear me! This is Glavis Judd. The city has been taken. There is no escape. Surrender now and you have my word there will be no further bloodshed.'

There was no sound from beyond the doors. Judd pounded on them again.

'Resistance can serve no further purpose. Your soldiers fought bravely, Hathold, but they are beaten. You and your family will be unharmed, but only if you surrender to me now! You have one minute to open these doors. But I warn you, my patience will not extend one second longer.'

The DAVE units glided closer to Judd as the minute slipped away, focusing on his cold eyes as they glittered behind his helmet visor. The doors before him remained closed, silently defying him. Some of the watching soldiers trembled at the intolerable affront to their leader.

When the time was up, Judd said coldly: 'Bring up a cannon.'

A self-propelled energy cannon rumbled through the palace corridors, its tracks grinding on the marble floors, and came to a halt before the closed doors. Its turret swung around as it aligned the projector with the target.

'Visors!' the squad commander called out to his men. The lenses of the DAVE units darkened as the soldiers snapped down protective shields.

An incandescent beam lashed out from the projector and struck the base of one half of the tall doors in a shower of sparks. The wood sheathing was instantly blasted away in blazing fragments.

The tough alloy beneath resisted for a second or two, glowing cherry red then yellow, before decomposing into molten rivulets. The projector swung steadily upward, drawing an arch of fire in the doors. Smoke filled the corridor. A hanging tapestry beside the doorway began to smoulder in the reflected heat.

The beam faded as it touched the base of the opposite door. The cannon drove forward and struck the doors with its ram bars. The excised section fell inwards with a leaden boom.

'Take them alive if possible!' Judd ordered.

Soldiers poured through into the chamber beyond, swinging their weapons about to cover every corner. In a few seconds the call came back: 'The room is secure! One prisoner, under guard.'

The ever-attentive DAVE units caught the frown that flickered across Judd's brow as he strode through the smoking archway. One prisoner only?

The audience chamber was all gilt and marble, hung about with centuries-old shields and portraits. Relics of times past but still impressive in an age of starflight, they chronicled the heritage of those who had ruled Esselven – until today. Along one wall great windows stretched from floor to ceiling, looking out across gardens to the city beyond. Many buildings were burning, sending columns of black smoke into the sky which were in turn cut across by the contrails of warplanes.

At the far end of the chamber, flanked by massive columns, was a raised dais on which rested a massive, high-backed throne of carved wood so old and time-worn as to be almost black. The seat of the rulers of Esselven for almost a thousand years, now it was empty and unguarded. Judd spared it barely a second glance.

On either side of the throne were lesser chairs for advisors. On one of these sat a grey-haired man with a guard standing alertly behind him. He wore a dark Esselvanian formal suit and about his shoulders hung a gold and ruby chain of office.

Judd stood in front of the old man. 'Chancellor Dhalron, isn't it? Hathold and his family – where are they?' he demanded.

Dhalron said nothing, continuing to sit with his hands folded across his lap, staring at some point beyond Judd as though he was not there. One of the DAVEs glided to one side to capture him in the same frame as Judd.

His guard ground the muzzle of his rifle into Dhalron's neck. 'Answer when the Protector asks you a question!'

Dhalron looked slowly up at Judd, his face radiating utter contempt. '"Protector". Is that what you call yourself now, Judd? Too ashamed to be known as the tyrant that you are –'

The guard drove the butt of his rifle into Dhalron's back, sending the old man sprawling from the chair onto his hands and knees. A DAVE darted in for a close-up shot. With dogged slowness, Dhalron hauled himself back onto his seat. A mirthless smile overlaid the pain on his face. He pulled a fine linen handkerchief from his pocket and dabbed his lips, then met Judd's gaze without fear.

'That was a taste of your benevolent protection, I take it?'

'You will not be harmed if you tell me where Hathold and his family have gone. We know they came in here. How did they leave?'

Fiery defiance burned behind the old man's eyes.

'They've gone where you cannot find them, Judd. I am too old to run, but the royal family are still young. They will rally the resistance to you. You think you have taken Esselven? No! A hollow victory. You don't have the keys of Esselven. Without them the planet will never be truly yours. One day they'll return... to take back... what's theirs...'

Dhalron's words were becoming disjointed. His head slowly bowed forward. Judd clasped him by the collar and lifted him off his feet until his face was level with his own. The Chancellor's eyes stared sightlessly through him into infinity. The clenched hand that had held the handkerchief slowly opened and a small empty plastic vial fell to the floor.

For a moment it seemed that Judd would throw the body aside in his rage at such an act of defiance. But his mind mastered his emotions, and instead he set it carefully back down on the chair. The face he turned to his anxious soldiers was perfectly composed.

'There is a concealed exit to this room. Find it!'

When Dexel Dynes walked in fifteen minutes later, Judd's men had already torn down half the wall panelling and an engineering team were running scanners over the floor. Dynes stepped nimbly aside as another panel fell with a crash, brushing specks of dust from the black trenchcoat and fedora with white piping trim that was the traditional dress of his profession. Half a dozen DAVE drones followed him into the room. With a few words he directed four of them to record the search, while the other two remained hovering above and behind his shoulders.

Judd was sitting on the ancient throne at the far end of the chamber. He was still in his battle armour, though he had removed his helmet. He looked up as Dynes approached.

'I thought you'd appear once the fighting was over,' Judd said sharply.

'I never pretended to be a soldier, Protector,' Dynes responded smoothly. 'The press is always neutral. I don't take sides in a war, I just report events as I see them. Besides, I had to stay in my ship to coordinate the coverage. I got some very newsworthy material during the final assault on the city. Can you tell the public how it feels to have conquered Esselven?'

A couple of DAVEs moved in to catch Judd's response.

'If you've been watching your own cameras, you will know that I have not truly conquered Esselven yet,' Judd said. 'Not while the royal family and their personal servants are still at large. But I will find them, wherever they're hiding.'

That was what made Judd such an interesting media type, Dynes thought. He never overestimated his own achievements or accepted unjustified flattery. It suggested he was something more than a thuggish warmonger. Research showed these sort of personal insights helped keep the A and B bracket viewers watching his reports back home. Mix that with enough violence and gore to keep the D and E sub-lits happy and it made a winning formula.

'And what do you plan to do when you do find them?' Dynes asked, hoping silently for another trial and execution. The ratings for the last one had been tremendous.

Before Judd could reply, one of the engineers called out: 'Sir – look at this!'

A section of the column to the left of the throne had swung open to reveal a narrow lift shaft that vanished into depths of the earth.

'First team, form up!' Judd snapped. 'Find out where this leads. Use no lethal force. Any natives you encounter are to be held for interrogation.'

But even as the battle-suited soldiers began to descend the shaft, a call came through on the command channel on Judd's suit speaker: 'Protector from Admiral Tacc – urgent!'

'Judd receiving. What is it, Tacc?'

'A ship has just launched from a concealed silo in the mountains to the north of the city. It appears to be making for open space. I have ordered the cruisers *Adrax and Gantor* to intercept.'

Dynes saw Judd's fist bunch within his armoured gauntlet until the fabric creaked audibly. 'It is likely the ship contains members of the Esselvanian royal family. They are to be taken alive if possible, Tacc.'

'Understood, Protector. The ship will be force-locked and boarded. The cruisers are now within three hundred kilometres and closing… The enemy ship is accelerating at unusually high velocity… One hundred kilometres… Beams activated, force lock forming… No!'

'What happened, Tacc?' Judd demanded.

There was a pause, then the Admiral replied, with a noticeable tremor in his voice. 'I regret to inform you, Protector, that the enemy ship has entered hyperspace. They took a considerable risk in jumping so soon. They were well below the minimum safe distance for this planet's gravity well and probably suffered damage to their hyperdrive. Do you wish the pursuit to continue, sir?'

Dynes watched Judd's face, knowing as well as he and Tacc that it was virtually impossible to intercept a ship in hyperspace unless its course was already known with reasonable accuracy. But if Judd ordered it, the entire fleet would scour hyperspace for a century. And if Judd ordered it, Tacc would step out of an airlock as punishment for failure. Judd was utterly ruthless in matters of discipline, but also by his own rules, scrupulously fair.

'Stand down the pursuit, Tacc. I shall catch those fish by other means.'

'As you command, Protector,' said Tacc, audibly relieved.

Judd looked about him at the waiting soldiers, then down at Dhalron's body still slumped in its chair.

'The keys of Esselven. What did you mean, old man?' Judd scowled in deep thought for a moment, then snapped: 'Where are the City treasures kept? There must be a vault somewhere. Find it!'

An hour later they stood in an anteroom at the bottom of a shaft extending fifteen hundred metres beneath the city. Before them was a massive grey circular door, shimmering slightly behind a force field. Judd's engineers were working intently at a console mounted beside the door. Judd stood and watched them in silence, his face impassive.

Dynes observed Judd in turn, knowing the inner rage that drove the man was in check for the moment, but wondering how long it would remain so.

Eventually the chief engineer made his report.

'Protector, this is a Radzell and Styne Maxima Vault. I have only ever seen them described in technical journals. It is said to be the most secure installation of its kind. It… cannot be forced.'

'Anything can be forced if enough power is applied.' Judd said.

'With respect, Protector, in this case only at the cost of totally destroying the contents. The vault has its own internal power source, collapsium-lined walls reinforced by internal fields and an external force shield. Any explosive device yielding a megatonne or higher would rupture it… but there would be nothing left within.'

'Then cut it open!'

The engineer chewed his lip anxiously. 'Protector, the vault will be programmed to resist beams or material drills as long as it can, but as soon as it is breached it will self-destruct.'

'Then if it cannot be forced, how can it be unlocked?'

'The key is based around a whole body DNA scan, Protector. If a person whose pattern has been entered in the vault's memory banks stands before it and is recognised, it can simply be ordered to open its door.'

'Can this be bypassed?'

'The scanning system is entirely self-contained, Protector. It will only respond to a living body with the right DNA pattern.'

'Might it be programmed to recognise members of the same family?'

'Very possibly, Protector. Depending on the discrimination of the system, it might even be designed to accept genetically related individuals who have not specifically been programmed into its memory.'

'The Esselvanian royal family, for instance?'

'Quite possibly, Protector.'

'So that is what Dhalron meant about the keys!' Judd said half to himself. 'Well, you have said what cannot be done, what of positive use have you discovered?' he demanded of the engineer.

'The inventory is accessible, sir,' the engineer said hastily, beckoning Judd over to the console. 'You can see what has been stored in the vault.'

Dynes peered past Judd's shoulder and a DAVE unit tilted forward to scan the list as it scrolled across the screen.

There was more than material treasure in the vault. The images and descriptions of stores of precious metals and ancient items of royal regalia Judd passed over quickly, clearly expecting such things. But then he came to the archives of Esselven. There were deeds and charters, census data, legal judgements, trading agreements with other planetary systems, the computer codes that controlled the world transport net and stellar communication web. And each one was listed as a unique item – all other copies were shown as having been destroyed just hours earlier.

They were the tools with which an advanced society functioned – and they were locked away beyond Judd's reach. Without them whatever puppet administration Judd put in power could not operate properly. Judd viewed sound government as a hallmark of his rule. Every world he had conquered thus far worked with order, precision and ruthless efficiency. The people might live in fear, but there was full employment and none lacked the necessities of life. Gradually resistance was stifled by pragmatic acceptance.

But it would not be so on Esselven. It might take years to re-create what lay in the vault, and meanwhile, as their society failed about them, the people would know who was to blame. It would be a constant reminder that Judd was not all powerful. Such conditions would breed resentment – and opposition.

Dynes saw the full implications dawning on Judd and took a step backward.

'I will not be defied like this!' Judd roared.

There was a crack and chips of concrete pinged and skittered across the floor.

Slowly, as his men looked on in frozen fear, Judd withdrew his gloved fist from the pulverised indentation he had punched into the wall. If mere anger and determination could have breached the vault, Dynes thought, then its door would be lying a shattered wreck at that moment.

Then Judd's iron will and calculating mind were in control again; governing and channelling the emotions that had driven him to conquer twenty star systems. Judd took a deep breath and looked upwards, as though penetrating the thickness of rock above their heads with the force of his gaze until he saw the stars.

'Wherever you've gone, Hathold, I'll find you,' he said evenly. 'You will open this vault for me. I will be master of Esselven!'

Chapter One

'What am I doing here?'

The thought came as though out of nowhere, to the complete surprise of the thinker.

Then the sensation of surprise itself also registered, initiating a cascade of response and association which almost overwhelmed the thinker's mind. Then, surfacing out of the wild storm of images and ideas, came the question:

'I, I… what do I mean by "I"?'

Momentarily the contradiction posed by the very structure of the question seemed unresolvable. Unthinking, unfeeling greyness threatened to return. Then the tentative answer emerged:

'"I" is self. "I" is me.'

It had never meant that before. Previously 'I' had just been an abstract concept (first person nominative singular pronoun) to produce at the proper moment in a sentence obeying certain rules of syntax and grammar. Now it had value, meaning. For the first time it was truly personal. Personal to him.

Him?

(Pronoun. Objective [accusative dative] case of 'He', came the unbidden knowledge once again.)

Him… he? Was that right? It seemed so. It would certainly serve as well as any other term. He also had a name but he realised, with a grasp of perception deepening from moment to moment, that it was no more than a functional designation.

He looked around at the fields and the sun and the sky. They were as they should be, and his place in relation to them remained as it had been only moments before. But it was as though he was seeing them for the first time. He had never appreciated that the pattern of furrows in a ploughed field could mirror the striations of a high cloud. Each leaf was so intricately formed. A bee hummed past and he marvelled at the play of light across its shimmering wings…

He covered his eyes to prevent his mind from being overloaded and for a timeless interval remained motionless. Only when he was certain he could control the flow of raw sensation did he look about him once more.

The world on which he dwelt was wonderful and yet also disturbing. He knew his place in the order of society that inhabited its surface, but now there was no comfort in that knowledge, only a growing sense of dissatisfaction. Simple purpose was no longer sufficient. Questions were arising within him that demanded answers. But who could he ask?

Turning about in desperation he saw another of his kind working at the border of a field. He headed for him as fast as he was able, calling out his questions ahead of him.

And received only incomprehension in return.

Desperately he probed his fellow for a companion spark of individuality within… and found none. Whatever he was experiencing meant nothing to the other.

Over the next three work periods, he questioned all the workers under his command and discovered all were equally unresponsive. They functioned efficiently, they responded in a mimicry of thought and animation, but there was nothing more. Did this mean that he was unique? Was this what 'loneliness' felt like?

Twelve more work periods passed before he encountered any other beings. In the distance he saw a party of riders heading north along one of the great avenues that cut through the fields.

They were Lords, of course, and he knew he had no right to interfere with their progress in any way, far less initiate a conversation. But surely they would understand. Driven by need he forced himself onto the road ahead of them and held his arms out wide as a signal they should halt.

At the last moment they reined in the mounts, seeming reluctant to acknowledge his presence.

'Why does it bar our path?' the young man at the head of the group asked in mild surprise.

'I know not, My Prince,' another replied vaguely.

He tried to ask his questions, to beg an explanation of why he was here, to understand the purpose of his existence – but he could not speak! The effort of overcoming the deeply imprinted rules that underlaid the structure of his consciousness had rendered him mute. He could only jerk his arms about as though trying to shape words out of thin air.

He saw them losing interest in him, looking across the fields and ignoring his silent pleas.

'We have made good time, My Prince,' a second man commented.

'But there is still a fair ride yet ahead until the borders of Aldermar,' the Prince said. 'Let us be on our way again. I do not wish the Duke to arrive before us.'

And the riders guided their mounts around him and continued on at a steady pace so that in minutes they were lost over the horizon, leaving a lonely and disconsolate figure on the road behind them. Why had he not been able to speak? Was he a complete prisoner of his predestined nature?

Frustrated anguish resonated and grew within his mind until it could no longer be contained.

'Please, somebody help me!' the robot cried aloud.

But the landscape ate up the words of the plaintive appeal and their fields of whispering gold and green stalks offered nothing back in return. He would have to wait long for an answer.

And wait… and wait…

* * *

Time passed, as it always did here, almost without being noticed...

From the shelter of the bushes, Kel, Nerla and Raz watched the gardeners move through the orchard, picking the ripest apples and placing them carefully in their baskets. The watchers knew that the fruit was meant for the Big House, but they still intended to have their share.

The three thieves in waiting were hardly more than children, though long ago hardened to their precarious existence. Under their patchwork clothes of roughly stitched plastic and sacking fabric, overlain with ingrained dirt and grime, their skins were pale. They didn't venture this far into the sunside often, and when they did they kept to the shadows.

Kel grinned at his companions. They were the best scavenger team amongst all the people, he thought, because they dared to go further into the gardens than any of the rest. Even though Nerla was a girl and Raz had a twisted foot, they always came back from a hunt with food and useful things that only the gardeners had. But they were all growing bigger, and the best garden scavengers were small and agile. Soon Kel and Raz would be old enough to join the men in hunting animals in the forest and Nerla would have to start having children.

The gardeners disappeared through a gate in the wall at the far end of the orchard.

Kel pointed and without a word they scampered from their cover to the nearest tree. Kel and Nerla scrambled up into the lower branches while Raz held an empty sack ready below them. They had already raided a vegetable patch and one sack slung over Raz's shoulder was bulging with edible roots.

Apples began raining down from the branches, which Raz deftly caught and bagged. In a couple of minutes they had stripped all the fruit they could reach. There was still some room left in the sack, so Kel gestured at the next tree. Nerla and Raz nodded. They clambered down and across the grass and up a second tree. Apples started dropping into Raz's waiting hands again.

Then Nerla gave a warning hiss. Raz dropped flat and slithered into the shelter of a trunk, while Kel froze, only his eyes moving as he strained to see what had alarmed Nerla. Through the tangle of leaves he saw the unmistakable figure of a gardener moving purposefully along the aisle between the last row of trees and the high garden wall.

Hardly daring to breathe, Kel watched the gardener's progress. Perhaps he was simply passing through the orchard. If they kept still they should be safe.

But when he was almost level with them the gardener stopped abruptly.

Kel saw his head turn about, as though searching for something. Then he set off again, but this time cutting across the rows of apple trees, their branches brushing his high shoulders as he headed directly for them. He must have seen them!

Mingled with the thrill of fear that coursed through Kel was the horror of failure. They must get the food home. They always came back with something…

With a yell, Kel snatched at an apple and dropped to the ground. He ran straight for the gardener and threw his improvised missile so hard that it burst across his chest. The gardener grabbed at him but Kel sprang nimbly aside out of his reach.

'Yahh! No catch me!' he taunted, then darted away through the trees with the gardener in pursuit. But Kel knew he was faster than any gardener. He would lead him in the opposite direction, while Raz and Nerla got away with their spoils, then he would lose him and make his own way back.

An open garden gate appeared in the wall ahead of Kel and he plunged through it out of the orchard. Beyond were row upon row of berry canes strung from wires spanning the ground between the walls and filling the air with their sweet scent. He dashed along the first row then ducked down and scrabbled through the narrow space between the canes, heedless of their thorns. Back on his feet he sprinted away again.

He would find another gate and then somewhere to hide until the gardeners gave up their pursuit. They would never find him. He was Kel, he was the best!

He scrambled through the next fence of canes and crashed into something solid. Before he could pull away a gloved but steely-hard hand closed about his arm. Kicking and yelling, Kel was hauled upright to find himself staring into the implacable face of a second gardener.

'You are a scavenger,' the gardener said, contriving to put a sense of loathing into his flat voice. 'You are a blight on the gardens. You will not be allowed to steal from them again!'

'I will not be made to wed against the calling of my heart!' Oralissa said, stamping her foot for emphasis.

Her face was flushed with anger, though this was invisible in the blood-red sunlight streaming almost horizontally through the window of the dayside drawing room. The white light of the glow tubes that lightened the shadows within the room revealed her parents' faces were unhappy but resolute. A touch of pink high-lighted her mother's cheeks as she stared with unlikely interest at the pattern on the rug, while her father tugged on his beard, a thing he only did when he was deeply troubled.

'I'm sorry, child,' her father said. 'You know I would not ask such a thing of you except compelled by great need. We must have an alliance of strength in these troubled times. Eridros and Corthane are our neighbours. A union with either would make us secure. One of the twain it must be.'

'But Aldermar is high amongst the Nine Kingdoms!' Oralissa protested. 'We have a strong army and great fortresses. Who do we fear, Father?'

'Aldermar is not as great as it was. Others have grown strong while we have but held our ground. There are stirrings in the East we can no longer ignore. For the sake of our country you must do this, Oralissa.'

'It is not as though you are being forced to cleave to any one man, dear,' her mother pointed out with an effort to sound reasonable. 'You may choose either the Duke or the Prince. Both have many fine qualities. Why, most girls would be envious of such a circumstance, and worry only that they would make the best choice between two such suitable mates.'

'But I do not want to choose either Duke or Prince,' Oralissa said. She clasped her hands together before her. 'When I marry I want it to be for love, to one whose soul sings with mine!'

Her father muttered: 'That maid of hers has been telling her foolish stories again…'

Her mother said: 'And how can you know Prince or Duke will not be one such soul? You've never met the Prince, and seen the Duke only once when you were but a child. You are still young, Oralissa, and your head is full of romantic tales. In time you will find love follows where need drives.'

'But Mother –'

'Still your tongue, now, Daughter; you have had your say in full measure,' her father interjected, a stern note in his voice warning Oralissa that further protest would be unwise. 'Promise that you will at least receive both our guests civilly, and allow them each fair measure of company so that you may converse together. Do not bar that songful heart of yours from the chance that love may yet strike it from one or other whom you have so carelessly dismissed.'

Oralissa's lips pinched and she lowered her eyes meekly. 'Very well, Father.'

'Then we shall speak no more of the matter until our visitors come. Leave us now and enjoy the good day.'

Oralissa managed a rueful smile and swept out of the room in a flurry of skirts.

The Queen patted her husband's hand reassuringly. 'Worry not. She's a good girl. She'll see sense in her own time.'

'But will it be in time enough?' the King wondered.

Chapter Two

Boots watched the two strangers curiously. They didn't quite fit in with their surroundings.

They had set up a little hut on a stretch of lawn, and beside it they had put out a table and chairs under the shelter of a large umbrella. That was perfectly right and proper as far as Boots was concerned. It was what people did in the gardens. But while one of the strangers was dressed appropriately, the other was wearing something quite different to anything Boots had ever seen before. This one also kept disappearing inside the hut every so often. Boots hoped there might be children inside, but none had appeared so far.

Boots always wanted to play with children.

Still, he could sometimes play with adults, though they often found his games harder to understand, he remembered. Would the strangers want to play? And if they did, should he be nice... or should he be naughty?

Peri Brown sipped her iced lemonade and leaned back in her chair with a smile. For once the Doctor had landed them somewhere civilised. They had been here over three hours and they hadn't been insulted, chased or shot at once. That had to be some sort of record, she thought.

The only slight problem was that they didn't actually know where *here* was.

The Doctor came out of the TARDIS. He was frowning as deeply as he had been when he had gone in and was scratching his unruly head of dark blonde curls.

'Still can't get a fix on this place, eh?' Peri asked.

'No, it's very odd,' the Doctor admitted. 'The navigation unit appears to be working properly, but it won't give any coordinates. I've set the automatic fault locator to run a complete system check just in case.'

'Well sit down and relax while it does its thing. Enjoy the ambience.'

The Doctor allowed himself to be talked into a chair and Peri meaningfully handed him a glass of lemonade. After a few minutes his frown softened and his broad face relaxed into a half smile.

'I suppose there are less congenial places to have a mechanical breakdown,' he admitted.

Peri scanned their surroundings once again and agreed with him.

Bees – or whatever locally passed for bees – buzzed amongst the flowers. Birds – or at least birdlike things – flew lazy arcs in the sky. Flower beds overflowing with lush blooms enclosed a perfect green square of grass. It could almost have been mid-afternoon in some classic English stately garden, the result of a few centuries of tender nurturing – except for the sun, of course.

The sun was a softly red-tinted disk, appearing slightly larger than Earth's sun, burning out of an almost cloudless purple sky about halfway to the zenith. It was either, the Doctor had said, slipping into what Peri thought of as his 'lecture mode', a red dwarf star, in which case the world they were on was orbiting it at a distance of only a few million kilometres, or else it was a red giant, which meant they were several hundred million kilometres distant. But without being able to fix their location, he could not find out which alternative was the correct one.

Whatever the case, the sun had not moved significantly in the sky since they arrived, which suggested this world was gravitationally locked to the sun. Here there would be no sunrise or sunset, only the illusion of being suspended in some perpetual summer afternoon just before tea was served on the lawn. Peri half expected to see a butler appear with a laden tray at any moment. But apart from the birds and insects, they had seen no sign of animal life. Of course somebody had to live here, otherwise who was keeping the grounds so immaculately neat and tidy?

Peri shrugged. She couldn't bring herself to worry about it. One thing the TARDIS's instruments had registered was that the sun was putting out minimal ultraviolet radiation, so there was no problem about sunburn. In fact it hardly felt hot at all, just comfortably warming to her skin. After their recent adventures, she could quite happily laze away a few days here doing a whole lot of nothing in particular.

An impatient grunt from the other chair told her that the Doctor was not as content with the status quo as she.

'The fault locator should have finished its run by now,' he said, getting up and making for the TARDIS.

'Take your time,' Peri called after him, as he slipped through the narrow door of the Police Call Box, which was the current unlikely external appearance of their space-time machine.

Peri decided to stretch her legs and picked up her parasol. Earlier in the TARDIS's vast wardrobe room she had found an ankle-length lacy summer dress with matching accessories, which seemed more suitable for their refined surroundings than any of her own clothes.

She strolled around the lawn, smelling the flowers and trying to reconcile them with her own knowledge of botany. The red sunlight gave a peculiar depth to the shadows and subtly tinted everything, so she couldn't be sure of true colours. Some blooms had quite reasonable arrangements of petals, stamen and stigma that would easily have passed muster on Earth, while others seemed to have no recognisable parts at all. Was this a collection from several different worlds? She was tempted to pick some to take back to the TARDIS for closer examination, but restrained herself. Admiring a garden uninvited was one thing, picking specimens from it would seem too much like stealing.

She passed through an open archway in the wall to the next section.

They had already explored the area immediately around their landing point, and found it comprised a series of linked high-walled gardens laid out in a regular grid, with nothing visible beyond them except the tops of a few trees. Each section seemed to have a slightly different theme. In this one the walls were covered in ivy-like climbing plants, and several stone pillars supporting cross beams had been arranged in the centre to form a shaded arbour.

Passing through another archway she found the next garden along was crossed by several carefully raked paths of blue-tinted gravel, bordered by what looked like rock plants. But what caught her eye was the decorative feature in one corner which contained a statue. It was a male figure draped in robes that could have been Greek or Roman. It looked pretty old and didn't tell her much about who owned the gardens now, except that they were probably humanoid. Of course, as they could be anywhere in time and space there was no telling who they might encounter –

'Hallo, I'm called Boots,' said a cheery voice right behind her. 'What's your name?'

Peri started, resisting the urge to yelp aloud even though she had bitten her tongue. Slowly she turned round.

Standing on the path was what could best be described as a golden brown teddy bear not quite as high as her shoulder, wearing a tall hat, a multicoloured waistcoat and large red lace-up boots. Black button eyes blinked at her even as the corners of a stitched mouth turned up in an enquiring smile.

Peri didn't waste much time goggling in disbelief or wondering if she was hallucinating. Travelling with the Doctor she'd met far stranger things that had announced themselves far less politely. I can cope with a talking teddy bear, she told herself, counting to ten in her head.

'Hallo, yourself,' she retorted at last. 'Do you make a habit of creeping up on people and scaring the hell out of them?'

'Sometimes,' admitted the bear with unexpected candour, 'it depends what game we're playing. I like Hide-and-Seek, do you?'

'I might,' Peri said guardedly. She was peering at Boots intently, trying to decide if he was some sort of animated doll or an actual living creature with a strange taste in clothes. And was he breathing or not? The odd sunlight made it hard to tell. Perhaps she'd had a touch of the sun herself. 'This place isn't called Wonderland, by any chance?' she asked hesitantly.

'It can be if you want,' Boots said.

'No, really, I'd like to know where we are.'

'I won't answer any more questions until you tell me your name.'

'Okay. I'm Peri Brown.'

'How do you do, Peri Brown,' said Boots, raising his hat politely.

'Hi, Boots,' she replied automatically. 'Now, about this place –'

'No, first we play. See if you can catch me…'

Boots turned about and sped off along the path, his stubby legs moving in a blur.

'No, wait –' Peri called.

But Boots took no notice. Muttering angrily to herself, Peri picked up her skirts and dashed after him. She saw Boots vanish through an archway, and in a few seconds she raced through after him, only to skid to a sudden halt.

A tall, square cut purple hedge of some shrub with dense diamond-shaped leaves confronted her. It seemed to fill the space between the walls, and ran left and right in an unbroken line, except for an opening directly in front of her, through which she could see more hedge.

She heard a faint: 'Catch me if you can!' from somewhere within the maze.

'Boots, come back!' she yelled, but there was no reply.

The Doctor was still tinkering with the console when she got back to the TARDIS. He listened with half an ear as she recounted the details of her unlikely encounter.

'How remarkable,' he said when she finished.

'I could've thought of a few stronger words, but I guess that'll do,' Peri said. 'Well?'

'Well what?'

'What do we do about it?'

'You are proposing that we hunt down this, uh, pseudo-ursine creature?'

'Yes!'

'But even supposing that we find it, on your own account it does not seem to be a very likely source of reliable information.'

'Well it's better than nothing,' Peri said. 'I don't see you've got much to show for an afternoon's messing about with the works.'

The Doctor sighed. 'There may be something in that.' He gathered up his tools and put them back in the toolbox. 'I just wish I knew why I can't determine our coordinates.'

'Maybe because we are in Wonderland,' Peri said darkly.

'Oh I doubt that – unless…' He fixed her with twinkling eyes. 'You're sure this creature did not resemble a white rabbit constantly consulting a large pocket watch?'

Peri chuckled. 'No, definitely a teddy bear – or his first cousin, anyway.'

'Then let us find this remarkable individual. Perhaps we can bribe him with honey?'

They walked for twenty minutes through one walled garden after another. They explored the maze as best they could, but there was no sign of Boots. To her relief, the Doctor retraced their steps to the entrance without any difficulty.

'Not a particularly complex layout,' he observed as they emerged. 'The four - dimensional maze on Madross Prime, that's a real challenge.'

They continued on.

Peri was beginning to think the whole planet was one big garden, when they saw the tops of a line of trees rising over the walls ahead of them. In a minute they emerged through a gap in a tall hedge into quite a different space. To the left and right of them stretched a wide gravel avenue, bordered by grassy verges out of which grew the majestic trees. Their smooth trunks rose sheer for almost half their height before sprouting almost horizontal branches which were covered in perfect cone-like masses of dense blue-green foliage. The roadway appeared to run perfectly straight and level, vanishing over the horizon before it reached any obvious destination. Opposite them on the far side of the avenue were the walls and hedges of what looked like more gardens.

The Doctor strode out into the middle of the gravel and looked thoughtfully along it in both directions. It was quite deserted. Peri joined him.

'Well, you could have quite a procession along here,' she observed.

'It is rather grand,' the Doctor agreed. 'Perhaps it is meant for some formal event. 'But do you notice something odd about the road?'

Peri frowned at the long swathe of gravel and the converging lines of trees.

'Well, it sort of dips out of sight both ways before it disappears. Maybe we're on a hill.'

'No, I think that's the natural horizon.'

'But it can't be more than quarter of a mile away.'

'About that. No more than 400 metres, certainly. Which would make this world a little over a hundred kilometres in diameter – the size of a typical asteroid.'

'But then shouldn't we only weigh a few pounds? Everything feels about normal weight.'

'There are ways of simulating higher gravity. The core of this world may be composed of degenerate matter, covered by a thin shell of normal rock and earth. That would also help retain an atmosphere.'

'Can that sort of arrangement happen naturally?'

'Possibly, but it's more likely that this place has been engineered.'

'All right, so where do we find the people in charge? We haven't seen anybody, apart from my furry friend, and I don't think he's into planetary engineering. But then who's keeping it so neat and tidy? There are no weeds, and this grass looks freshly mown. Where are the gardeners? There'd have to be – hey!'

The Doctor had been looking over her shoulder with narrowed eyes. Now he grabbed Peri's wrist and drew her rapidly off the road and into the shelter of the nearest garden archway.

'There's no reason to suppose they'd be unfriendly,' the Doctor said, 'but perhaps we'd better observe them first.'

As they peered through the screen of leaves, the speck the Doctor had seen cresting the horizon curve of the road resolved itself into a large horse-drawn caravan of antiquated appearance. It was decorated with wooden scrollwork, its barrel roof had a chimney projecting through it and its boards were painted in bright if faded colours. Two men sat on the bench under the awning at the front of the caravan. They were dressed in loose, multicoloured tunics, and wore turban-like hats into which were stuck several long feathers. They were waving their arms at each other and seemed to be paying little attention to guiding the horse, which fortunately maintained a steady pace indifferent to the activity of its drivers.

As the vehicle got closer they could hear their raised voices.

'… No, No!' the nominal driver was saying to his companion. 'We runneth the Hat Routine, Trampole's piece, then the Kettle and Weasel song as finale. End with a laugh and a tear, I say.'

'Why not end with the Hat Routine? That always leaves them merry, that does.'

'The Kettle and Weasel song is a better closer.'

'Sez you. Why not put it to the vote?'

'Cos I sez so. Have I or have I not performed before all the crowned heads of the Nine Kingdoms –'

'Excepting Aldermar, Bolwig. We've never been here before.'

'Thou japering fool, Lurket! Who says: I performed but in eight out of the nine, M'lord? They will say: Go away, fellow, and send in one who can claim the full score - or else ask why we come to them last and not first?'

The other scratched his head for a moment. 'Because we wanted our act to be perfected in every finest detail of word and action before presenting it to them?'

'And have them think we are amateurs just learning our craft? Besides, when I present myself to their majesties of Aldermar, I will have performed before all the nine.'

'Not Relgorian! Thou never did Relgorian.'

'I did so!'

'It counts not when the Arch-Duke dies before you go on!'

'He was watching in spirit! Though his body was cooling, I felt the presence of his wraith, unwilling to ascend to heaven 'til he had partaken of his last earthly pleasure. What finer praise could a humble player ask? I dedicated the Three-legged Donkey rhyme to him.'

'They chased you out of the city for that!'

'A misunderstanding! They have no 'preciation for fine words and tender sentiment in Relgor…'

As the vehicle passed their place of concealment, Peri saw painted on the side of the caravan in garish lettering: *BOLWIG'S*

31

FAMOUSE PLAYERES. A wooden porch-like structure projected from the back of the wagon, and on it sat a man similarly dressed to the first two, strumming vaguely on a lute in between taking swigs from a china flagon.

Even as they watched, the man slumped lower in his seat and slid gracelessly off onto the gravel. A cord tied round his ankle jerked tight and pulled a jangling chain hung with small brass bells out of the back door of the caravan. At the alarm the cart stopped and Lurket and Bolwig got down, still arguing over the order of their performance, walked back to their fallen companion, who was now snoring loudly, picked him off the road and loaded him back onto the rear porch seat, returned to their places up front and set off again, as though the entire process was quite normal.

Peri saw the Doctor's eyebrows raised in amusement even as she struggled to keep from laughing aloud. For a moment she thought he would step boldly out and start questioning the travellers, but he stayed where he was and they watched the caravan diminish in the distance.

'Are those guys for real?' Peri wondered.

'Apparently so.'

'Want to go after them and ask where we are?'

'I'm doubtful if they could provide any reliable information,' the Doctor said dryly.

'You mean they don't look like they're clued up on planetary engineering either,' Peri interpolated. 'Their getup and that wagon looked almost medieval. Even if they're going to a costume party, would they need all the trimmings? They even sounded the part. So what gives here?'

'If this world is as artificial as I suspect, then they certainly seem out of place. But since we don't understand the social order here we can't say for sure what is normal. The answers may lie at one end or the other of this road. The travellers were making for somewhere called "Aldermar". We may learn more there.'

Peri hesitated, looking round. 'Or maybe the other way gets us somewhere useful sooner? Can you see a signpost saying how far this Aldermar is?'

'No. Possibly one way is as good as the other –'

'Left or right or right or left? Best foot forward, but who knows which!' a voice chanted behind them.

They spun around to see a small figure peering through the arch in the garden wall behind them.

'Ah, this is Boots I take it,' the Doctor said.

'That's him,' said Peri.

Boots raised his hat to them in mock salute and then turned about and ran off.

'Oh no, you don't get away so easily this time,' Peri said, dashing after him with the Doctor at her heels.

Boots skipped along in front of them in improbable bounds, running through the gardens and then out onto the verge of the avenue again. But Peri was determined to catch him. With a burst of speed she closed the gap between them. Boots scurried through an archway opening onto the grass verge only just ahead of her. Peri made a grab for the tail of his waistcoat even as Boots sprang into the air – jumping clean over the pit lying unexpectedly in Peri's path and into which she plunged headfirst.

Peri's yell of surprise and alarm gave the Doctor sufficient warning to bring himself to a teetering halt on the very lip of the pit. On the far side of the obstacle Boots was skipping away, calling out: 'Naughty Boots, naughty Boots…' Then he turned into the gardens again and vanished.

His face clouded with concern, the Doctor knelt by the side of the pit and peered anxiously down at Peri, who was lying motionless in a swirl of lace.

'Peri, are you all right!' he called out.

Slowly Peri stirred and sat upright with a groan.

'Are you hurt?'

Peri gingerly rubbed the small of her back. 'Just my pride, I think.' Wincing, she pulled her parasol out from under her. The shaft was broken in half. She shrugged and tossed it aside, then climbed to her feet and looked about her. 'What's this hole doing here anyway?'

The pit was a rectangle about six metres long and half that wide. Its grassy sides were sheer, but curved smoothly at the lip and bottom. Along its centre ran a length of spike-topped brick wall a little higher than Peri's head, stopping short of each end of the excavation. The great disk of the motionless sun filled it with light, making it hard to see against the level ground from any distance.

'It looks like a haha,' the Doctor said.

'I beg your pardon?'

'A device used in landscaping. A wall to keep animals penned is hidden in a ditch so as not to spoil the view.' He frowned. 'Except that the location makes no sense. You can walk right round it. It doesn't close off anything. So why was it built here…'

'Doctor, can we keep the speculation until after I get out of this thing?'

'What? Oh, sorry.' The Doctor lay full length on the grass and thrust out an arm. 'Now, just take hold of my hand.'

But Peri could not take hold of the Doctor's hand, even when she stretched and jumped for it. The spikes prevented her from climbing onto the haha wall itself to gain some height, and the Doctor could not lean any further over as there was nothing within reach for him to hold onto. It wouldn't take much for him to slide over the treacherously rounded lip of the pit and join Peri.

'I used to wear a long scarf that would have been particularly useful right now,' the Doctor said, after Peri again failed to reach his hand. He got up and brushed off his knees. 'I think I'd better go back to the TARDIS. I've got a wire climber's ladder somewhere.'

34

'You could always rip up that coat of yours to make a rope,' Peri suggested hopefully.

'I think I'll try the ladder first,' the Doctor said with a smile. 'Meanwhile I suggest you sit tight and stay quiet. We don't understand enough about this place yet to know who we can trust, but as long as you don't draw attention to yourself you shouldn't come to any further harm.'

Peri sat down cross-legged in the bottom of the pit and rested her chin on her palms. 'Go on. I won't be going anywhere.'

As the Doctor made his way back to the TARDIS at a brisk walk, he turned over in his mind the new facts they had acquired. He hadn't admitted it to Peri, but he was beginning to feel concerned.

The travelling players were a puzzle, but at least they seemed harmless. But the behaviour of 'Boots' and the illogically located haha suggested something rather more disturbing. Boots, whatever he or it was, had obviously intended to lure one or both of them into the haha. Such a fall could have caused serious injury or even death. But no properly organised world, with the advanced technology that obviously lay behind the creation of this one, would permit such a thing. Therefore, despite the superficial elegance of their surroundings, there was something very wrong.

Was it linked somehow with the inability of the navigation system to give the proper space/time coordinates?

He was still musing on the problem when he entered the garden in which they had landed. Then he stopped short.

There in the middle of the lawn were the impressions where the table, chairs and TARDIS had rested. But now the lawn was quite empty.

Chapter Three

'Interview with Protector Judd in his private office onboard battle cruiser *Valtor* en route through hyperspace,' said Dynes as an audio ident, while the DAVE units focused on Judd and prepared to record.

Judd sat behind an imposing antique desk of heavy wood. It helped conceal the fact, not obvious when he was wearing battle armour, that although he had a fine physique, he was slightly under average height. He was wearing a formal suit loosened a little at the collar. On the desk before him several neat stacks of reports were arranged about a multi-function keypad. To one side was a monitor screen, angled so that Dynes' cameras would get an oblique view of moving columns of text and changing images, without revealing any detail. On the bulkhead behind Judd lighting panels glowed brightly while the rest of the office was rather dimly lit. Even though there was no natural day or night onboard a spacecraft, it implied that the hour was late.

All these little details combined to suggest to the viewer that Judd was a conscientious administrator being interviewed at the end of a long day. What intrigued Dynes was that he had suggested none of these tricks himself. From the very first, Judd had been careful to project a conscientious and statesmanlike image at their formal interviews.

'Protector,' Dynes began, 'it's been a year since you conquered the Esselvanian system. Since then, you've not extended the borders of the Protectorate any further. Yet in the previous year you took over three world systems –'

Judd interrupted. 'I do not take over worlds, Mr Dynes. I answer the call of people oppressed by inefficient and corrupt governments and bring them under the just rule of the Protectorate. I am not a conqueror but a liberator.'

'Of course,' Dynes agreed smoothly. 'Well, since you liberated Esselven, then, has something happened to delay further expansion?'

Judd steepled his fingers and looked weary but resigned. 'It is true that Esselven has taken up more of my time than I had anticipated, and so, temporarily, I have had to postpone the liberation of new worlds. The people of Esselven have only their former ruler to blame for this. In an act of great selfishness, he crippled certain critical elements of the administrative system. Despite the best efforts of the new government, standards of public service and provision have fallen below those in the rest of the Protectorate.'

'In fact there have been shortages of some basic necessities.'

'Regrettably, yes.'

'And there have also been acts of rebellion against the new government, have there not?'

Judd's lips pinched, but he answered evenly: 'There have been isolated acts of sabotage by small groups of counter-reformists. They are being dealt with.'

'Meanwhile, you have been searching for King Hathold and other members of his family.'

'Yes, they must be returned to Esselven to put right some of the damage they have done to their world, and then to stand trial for crimes they committed against their former subjects.'

'And now you believe you have located them?'

'As a consequence of extensive investigations of the flight logs of Esselvanian starfleet craft and questioning of their crews, we have determined the likely location of their hideaway.'

'Some viewers might think it surprising that this process has taken so long.'

'A lingering sense of loyalty to their former masters has hampered the process,' Judd conceded. 'There were attempts to conceal or destroy the evidence, but we have finally managed to piece the facts together.'

'Is such loyalty not rather surprising, in the circumstances? Shouldn't the people be eager to help their liberators?'

Once again Judd's lips tightened, but he answered easily: 'The mystique of royal succession can induce a false sense of defer-ence and duty in otherwise sensible people. Those involved are being re-educated to rid them of their distorted sense of values. On the new Esselven, the first duty is to the common good.'

'I see,' said Dynes. 'Perhaps, Protector, I might be allowed to interview some of these, uh, misguided individuals?'

'Of course,' said Judd. 'After their re-education has been completed, naturally.'

'Naturally,' Dynes agreed. He sensed Judd's patience wearing thin, and added quickly: 'One final question, Protector. When you do finally confront the King, do you expect him to surrender peacefully?'

Judd spread his hands in a conciliatory gesture.

'I wish no further bloodshed, Mr Dynes. I will give the King my guarantee that he and his family will come to no harm if they return to Esselven to face trial.'

'Of course, it takes the presence of a living member of the royal family to unlock the city vault.'

'Another reason for them to surrender peacefully, Mr Dynes. They owe it to their former subjects to end this malicious disrup-tion to their lives. That is one of the charges that will be laid against the former King and his advisors when I find them,'

'You sound very certain that this expedition will be successful, Protector.'

'Properly planned operations based upon sound intelligence are always successful, Mr Dynes.'

Dynes returned to his own small ship, the *Stop Press*, clamped to a docking port on the hull of the *Valtor*. Once inside he downloaded the DAVE recordings and reviewed the interview.

He hoped Judd was right about finding Hathold because Dynes needed something spectacular to report. Over the last year Judd had become obsessed with Esselven and the search for the royal family. Unfortunately this did not make for exciting news stories.

Dynes had played all the angles he could about the subjugation of Esselven. He'd run the placating words of new government pronouncements against images of frightened people with fixed grins on their faces queuing for rations. He'd shown obvious stooges thanking Judd for his intervention with tears in their eyes while they mouthed the official dogma. The recent appearance of a resistance movement had helped, and Dynes dwelt lovingly on images of crippled spaceships and ruined transport tubes, comparing the chaos with the strictly ordered societies of other Protectorate worlds.

But Dynes had received feedback from his base office of the Interstellar News Agency that the audience who had previously been following his coverage of Judd's triumphs was slipping away. Reporting on an occupation simply didn't register the same appreciation factor as all-out planetary war. The simple fact was that death and destruction fascinated people – as long as they knew it was taking place light centuries away and didn't threaten them.

Well he'd give the people what they wanted, whatever it cost.

He'd worked hard over the last few years to recover his audience recognition rating after the Gelsandor treasure story had ended so disastrously. Finding Judd just as he started expanding his empire had been a stroke of luck, and while it continued to produce newsworthy material, he would stay with it.

Dynes finished reviewing the interview with some satisfaction. There were a few tense responses from Judd that he could make something of, depending on how the mission developed. He knew he'd almost pushed Judd too far a couple of times, but the Dictator always held his temper in check.

He had one weakness that Dynes exploited to the full.

For all Judd's power, Dynes could give him something nobody else could: a sense of legitimacy. The chance to justify himself and his actions before a neutral observer. Judd wanted to go down in history as a great reformer and liberator of the masses. He really believed, Dynes thought, that if people only understood his philosophy properly they would accept what he had done. For someone otherwise highly intelligent and pragmatically ruthless it was a demonstration of remarkable self-delusion.

Dynes didn't care either way. His only objection to Judd's dreams of interstellar conquest was that life on the Protectorate worlds post conquest had low news potential. It was the unexpected and controversial that made news, not just what the ruling party deemed acceptable. Dynes wanted to be free to report the news wherever he found it. And if there wasn't a story to be found, he could always make one.

Dynes had few illusions about the moral values of sentient beings and knew never to let the facts stand in his way. Facts were useful but they could be made to tell many stories. They were not in themselves the truth. There was only one certainty Dynes held to, and that was that above all things people wanted to be entertained. They wanted to have their consciences pricked and yet be reassured that all was well with their own little world. They longed to be appalled and to be thrilled, to live vicariously a life more exciting than their own.

And he was the one who gave them what they wanted.

He shaped their thoughts and played on their emotions and he could imagine no better job. Knowing that after the transmission of a Dexel Dynes exclusive report over the word net, a hundred million people would have their minds filled with the images he had captured and repeat the words he had spoken, was all the power he ever craved.

Glavis Judd sat in thoughtful silence after Dynes had left his office.

He knew the reporter was cynical and cared for nothing but his latest story, the more sensational the better, but he had his uses. It was important that the rise of the Protectorate should be documented for posterity. Of course there were many official recorders, but Dynes owed Judd no allegiance, and it was instructive to see the reactions of an outsider to the new order. Judd was using Dynes as a mirror, albeit a distorted one, through which to see his actions as outsiders might do. When the next phase of expansion started, his propaganda department would incorporate these observations into the material they insinuated into the media of target systems ahead of the invasion fleet. Unknowingly, Dynes was preparing the way for the day when the wave of change reached those far-off worlds to which he reported.

Judd allowed himself a moment's contemplation of things to come, seeing in his mind's eye the Protectorate spread out across the galaxy; bringing justice where there had been misrule and certainty where there had been doubt. That had always been his destiny…

From his early years on Zalcrossar, Glavis Judd had known he was special, and often wondered how his quite unremarkable parents had ever produced him. His intelligence won him a place in an accelerated learning stream in junior school – and a lesson in the realities of life.

A larger boy from a less able class taunted Judd for being under-sized. Judd replied scornfully in language that the other probably didn't understand and received a beating in return. The incident taught Judd not only to control his emotions, but also how to apply his abilities to gain revenge. Judd secretly exercised while studying the theory of self-defence and unarmed combat, stoically enduring further maltreatment from his less gifted contemporaries in the meantime. Only when he was certain he was ready did he fight back, choosing the moment with care to ensure they had the largest possible audience.

He won the fight with ease, reducing his tormentor to a state of tearful humiliation. From that moment on the other children treated Judd with awed respect. It was his first success in manipulating the world about him and a confirmation in his own mind of his unique nature. He never had a problem with bullies again.

After a brilliant academic career, he eventually graduated with the highest honours. But the society of Zalcrossar was traditionally stratified and academic achievement by itself was not well rewarded in a material sense. Other people were ready to employ his talents, but they would benefit disproportionately from his work. Judd had already developed a contempt for the ruling classes, whom he regarded as his intellectual inferiors. Yet, they controlled his destiny through their patronage. He might spend years working his way up corporate ladders of achievement, yet the highest positions would always be denied him. How was he to achieve a position where he could exercise his abilities to the full?

He studied his prospects with care, noted the means by which previous leaders of his world and others had risen to power. Then, to the surprise of his contemporaries, he voluntarily enlisted in the armed forces. It was then a time of peace and the military was moribund and not highly regarded. But Judd had known exactly what he was doing...

* * *

Judd came out of his brief reverie with a thoughtful expression on his face. He communicated with the captain of the *Valtor* and gave certain instructions concerning their emergence from hyperspace and approach to their destination.

On Esselven he had given Hathold time to surrender which he had used instead to make his escape. Judd would not make the same mistake twice.

Chapter Four

'Hetty, what am I to do?' Oralissa exclaimed, scuffing the gravel pathway with the toe of her shoe.

Oralissa was in the company of her personal maid and confidante in the Palace gardens.

Resting on the horizon the eternal sun glimmered through the trees, casting its crimson rays across the lawns and hedges. Rising against the purple sky, the spires and towers of the palace shimmered like fingers of fire. Windows sparkled where they caught and threw back the sunlight, making it seem as though the building was burning from within. Out of other portals cold white interior lights challenged the ember-glow. Larger lighting rods, standing taller than a man, were dotted about the grounds, illuminating pathways and creating little oases of sharp shadows where flowers shone with their true colours.

It was along these ways that Oralissa walked, oblivious to the delicate scents that perfumed the air about her. Her fine features were creased with worry, her bright eyes dimmed, her normally straight and active form bowed at the shoulders.

'I would not wish to cross my parents, nor fail in my duty to Aldermar,' Oralissa continued. 'But this is not the path to love I had imagined. Why can life not be more like the story books?'

Hetty's plump, red-cheeked face was a picture of concern mingled with excitement as she anticipated the emotional tribulations to come. There was nothing quite like sharing in the ebb and flow of strong passions. Though only a few years older than Oralissa, she reassured her charge in a motherly fashion.

'There, there, My Lady. Things may yet turn for the best. Why, who's to say you don't find one or t'other of your suitors to your liking? Prince Benedek is said to be young and more than passing handsome.'

'A year younger that I myself,' Oralissa pointed out. 'I do not wish to wed a child. I wish to join with somebody who has sense in their head and has experience of life so I may honour his wisdom.'

'Duke Stephon may prove more to your liking, then. He is a man of some learning, I hear.'

'But much older than me.'

'A few years only, My Lady.'

'Seventeen! Almost twice my age. And a father already. How should I manage with a family already underfoot.'

'But both girl children, My Lady. They would be no threat to your position. And mark this, though Stephon is only titled "Duke", he rules Eridros in totality. Thou would be a queen in all but name from the moment you were wed. Whereas Prince Benedek will someday be king of Corthane, and you his queen if so you had chose, that day may be far distant, for his father is said to be yet hale and hearty.'

Oralissa sighed. 'This does not ease my woe. When my love comes I will know it in my heart as though the sun had taken residence within me. He will show himself true by some noble deed. I will not have to think of politics or succession. It will just be so. A certain thing, as stone is hard and water soft; nothing less and nothing more.'

'Even were he not of noble birth, My Lady?'

Oralissa hesitated, a frown creasing her clear brow. Then she said slowly: 'No, Hetty, not even if it were so. Even if he should be a humble artisan I would follow him, in rags and barefoot should need demand. For is not love supposed blind to rank and position? But what chance have I of meeting such a man? My life seems to run a predestined course, and I am faced with a choice of two strangers, which if neither suits is in truth no choice at all.'

Hot tears pricked at her eyes, and she drew a lacy handkerchief from her sleeve and dabbed her cheeks.

For once Hetty was lost for words, and could only pat Oralissa's hand reassuringly. 'There now, my pet. Don't fret yourself further. Things will work out for the best.'

'Yes, things will work out,' Oralissa said. 'There will be an end, but not of my choosing. Oh, Hetty. Why do I feel there is a doom coming to me? As though I am suspended between breaking bough and hard earth beneath with only the thin air for passing comfort? I am falling, and when I strike that will be an end to all things!'

'Hush, My Lady! It is wicked to talk of such things!'

'But what if there is no choice – oww!'

Oralissa broke off with a gasp of pain as a pebble struck her sharply on the arm.

The bushes by the path rustled and they had a momentary glimpse of a small hunched body mottled in green and brown, supporting a pumpkin of a head cut across by a gash of a mouth filled with tiny pointed teeth. Mischievous yellow eyes flashed at them and they heard a guttural laugh of delight.

Oralissa gave a gasp of fear and disgust even as Hetty cried out: 'A brogle! Be off with you, foul creature! Help! Help! A sprite in the grounds!'

Her shouts roused a pair of guards and a gardener, who had been working nearby. As the three raced towards them, the sprite gave an angry snarl and plunged away through the bushes. The pursuers dove into the foliage after it. A guard captain puffed up, looking red in the face, and cast an anxious eye over Oralissa.

'Are you hurt, My Lady?'

'No, Captain, merely a little bruised. The creature only meant to do mischief as is its nature.'

'It might have had your eye out throwing a stone like that,' Hetty said, determined to make the most of the little drama.

'Well it didn't,' Oralissa said, 'so that shall be an end of the matter.'

The sounds of pursuit faded into the distance.

'The gardeners will catch it or chase it clear of the grounds, My Lady,' the captain assured her. 'They care less for the creatures even than they do scavengers.'

'They're all dirty, good-for-nothing beasts,' Hetty opined with feeling. She turned to Oralissa. 'Now come inside and get you to bed, My Lady. You've had enough troubles for one day.'

As she was led away, Oralissa said: 'It is strange. I do not feel greatly alarmed. The surprise seems to have driven a little of the gloom from my head. At least the sprite was out of the routine order of things.' She paused, frowning deeply. 'I am almost certain that such a thing has never happened to me before, in all the many times I have walked these grounds. Is that right, Hetty?'

'What a question, My Lady,' Hetty said. 'But not to my knowledge. We've glimpsed sprites before, but never has one harmed you. And it's only to hope it never does so again.'

But Oralissa's eyes were filled with a curious excitement. 'It gives me hope. It is a reminder that the unexpected can happen. Something different from the steps already deep imprinted in the road ahead, in which I seem destined to place my feet.'

Hetty looked at her mistress doubtfully. 'Well at least you're not talking about doom no more. You just get to bed, My Lady. I'll bring you a nice glass of warm milk and honey. That'll set you right.'

Chapter Five

Panting slightly, the Doctor paused in the shade of a silvery-leafed tree, pulled a handkerchief from his pocket and dabbed his face. Above him the red sun simmered motionless in the purple sky. Around him the perfect gardens basked in the sun's perpetual warmth and light. But of what he sought there was no sign. He had to face the facts. The TARDIS had been deliberately removed from its landing place and running round trying to find it without better knowledge of his surroundings was getting him nowhere.

There was also the matter of Peri, whom he had left for far longer than he had planned. She would be wondering what had happened to him by now. Perhaps it would be best if he went back for her, then they could search for the TARDIS together and cover more ground. But he still needed a rope to get her out of the pit.

Looking round for inspiration, his eyes alighted on a shaggy fan of ivy-like growth spreading across a nearby wall. Thoughtfully he went over and examined it more closely. The main stem was gnarled and woody, but the newer, more slender growth still showed some green. He worked his fingers under a tendril and managed to pull a length free. Yes, if he wove enough of these together he could make a rough sort of rope. It would hardly be suitable for mountaineering, but it would only have to take Peri's weight for a few seconds. Perhaps he should have looked for something like this near the haha pit, but then he wouldn't have discovered the TARDIS was missing. Oh well, you couldn't turn the clock back – not too often, anyway.

He tore several more strands from the wall and draped them over his shoulder in a bundle. Then he set off back to Peri, his fingers working nimbly as he began stripping off the leaves and plaiting the ivy strands together.

After a brisk quarter of an hour's walk he emerged onto the avenue with a three metre length of coarse roped coiled over his shoulder. As he strode up to the pit he called out:

'Sorry to be so long, Peri, but I had to –'

His words trailed away as he looked down into the pit. It was empty. There was no sign of Peri.

Automatically the Doctor looked up and down the great avenue and called out her name several times, but there was no reply. He began peering through the openings in the garden walls and hedgerows that flanked the avenue, but then checked himself, scowling in thought.

Had Peri somehow got herself out of the pit? Unlikely. If she had not been able to climb out with his help, then she certainly couldn't do it alone. Therefore somebody had helped her. But who? The only being who knew she was down there was Boots, and why should he come back and help Peri out, even assuming he had the means to do so? Perhaps she had been found by other travellers on the avenue, though it seemed unlikely anyone else would discover the pit by chance in the hour he'd been gone.

However she had got out, if she'd been free to do so, she would have either stayed by the pit knowing he would be returning soon, or retraced her steps through the gardens. In the latter case he should have met her along the way – always assuming she hadn't got lost, of course. If she'd been compelled to go another way, she should have left some sort of sign or marker. That there was none suggested that her actions were restricted to some degree.

But had she gone along the avenue or back into the gardens?

If it had been the avenue and whoever had taken her away had some means of powered transport, then he had little hope of catching up on foot, even if he knew which way to go. The gardens were hardly an easier prospect, providing so many potential places of concealment that he could search them for days without success. Of course he had various devices in the TARDIS that might help him… if only that hadn't gone missing as well.

Yet unlike Peri, the Doctor reasoned, the TARDIS was a bulky object. Surely it couldn't have been taken very far without leaving some traces. Perhaps it made sense to find that first if he could. It was possible that the same agency had been responsible for the removal of both it and Peri. If he tracked it down he might get some clue as to her whereabouts.

Hoping desperately that Peri was safe for the moment, the Doctor once again set off back to the landing site.

'They're really terrific… purple pod-things,' Peri said desperately. 'Yes, really plump and… and purple. And they smell just about ripe…' she inhaled deeply as though savouring the aroma of a fine wine. 'Oh, yes, really great. And I bet they taste as good as they look… yum yum!'

She was running out of nice things to say about rows of fruit bushes and strangely shaped and coloured vegetables. But it seemed to be what her hosts expected of her.

There were three of them. Each was half again as tall as she was, with heads that were amiable parodies of humanoid features, except for glowing red photocell eyes. They had no legs, however, and their highly polished silvery metal torsos were mounted on broad soft rubber tyres.

They were robots, of course, but clearly rather specialised ones. Around their bases were clipped a variety of gardening tools, ranging from small trowels to forks, powered shears and rotovator blades. Each tool had the same standard socket, which could obviously be exchanged for the large but quite human-looking rubber-covered hands (gardening gloves?) which they currently had fitted to their arms.

A short while before, Peri had been sitting morosely at the bottom of the haha. Her thoughts were divided between puzzling over the mental state of whoever had given such an inappropriate name to a landscaping feature, and wondering if the Doctor was ever going to take them someplace where this sort of thing didn't happen. Then she became aware of movement above. She glanced up to see the three robots ringed about the pit looking down at her.

She'd been too surprised by their sudden appearance to speak for a moment, but fortunately they had taken the initiative.

'A lady!' one exclaimed.

'She has suffered a misfortune,' said the next.

'Is she broken? Will she require grafting?' added the last.

They lacked any mobile features by which to convey expression, but there was enough intonation in their otherwise flat mechanical voices to convey a sense of dismay. Peri clung to that hopeful detail. At least they seemed concerned about her welfare, unlike the mischievous Boots.

'I'm okay,' she called back at them, scrambling to her feet and clutching her broken parasol to her. 'Please, can you find a rope or something so I can get out of here?'

'Of course, Lady. Please let us assist you.'

And they had bent over and reached down, their metallic arms extending telescopically. Before she realised what they were doing, Peri felt large soft hands grasp her wrists and upper arms, and she was raised smoothly and without apparent effort up onto the grassy verge once again.

'Thanks,' she said, trying to keep her voice even. The three machines seemed a lot bigger and more powerful seen up close.

'Our pleasure, Lady. Please excuse this regrettable misfortune. May we introduce ourselves? We are Red-3, Red-7 and Red-10, gardeners of Red Sector East Three.'

Peri noted the coloured flashes and numbers on their chest-plates as each bobbed its head deferentially to her. At least they seemed to have good manners. Peri began to relax a little.

'I'm Peri Brown,' she said. 'So, you keep this place going, do you? Very nice. Neat borders.'

Was it her imagination or did the robots give a tiny shiver that might have been interpreted as a sign of pleasure?

'We are so pleased that you approve, of our work, Lady Peri,' said Red-3.

'We receive so few visitors from the Palace this far in the gardens, Lady Peri,' Red-7 added.

She was going to ask them to stop calling her 'Lady', but the mention of 'the Palace' intrigued her. But before she could enquire any further, Red-10 said:

'Would you do us the honour of inspecting our work, Lady Peri?'

Peri hesitated, wondering if it might be a good idea to play along with them for a while. Maybe she could find out what was going on in this place and have something to tell the Doctor when he got back. She gave what she hoped was a graceful smile.

'Well, as long as we don't go too far,' she said. 'I've got somebody to meet back here soon.'

They escorted her through a brick arch into what looked like a high-walled kitchen garden. Clumps of curling red leaves sprouted from neatly tilled rows.

'These are the pink rethlonium beds, Lady.'

'Right. Rethlonium. Great…'

Some of the plants were familiar, but most were totally strange to her. After she had inspected her tenth vegetable plot, Peri's enthusiasm was waning. What was even more annoying was that the robots kept overwhelming her with details about what they were growing and then ushering her on before she could ask about the Palace. She began to understand why politicians and royalty had those stiff smiles on their faces when touring some factory or government project.

'How about showing me some flowers?' she said in desperation.

'Of course, Lady Peri,' said Red-3.

They led her through a gate into a huge nursery garden, stocked with rank upon rank of flowers of every form and hue in various stages of growth. A wave of mixed perfume struck Peri with the nasal equivalent of an orchestral symphony. She forgot about asking probing questions, overwhelmed by the sheer mass of blooms. The ornamental gardens she had seen earlier had been laid out in perfect harmony and balance, but this place trumpeted the song of lush and riotous growth.

For several minutes Peri walked along the aisles between the green stems, trailed by her attentive guides. Finally she stopped beside a row of flowers with velvet petals so violet as almost to be black, with a blaze of deep red at the centre. They exuded a heavy but subtle scent that did not carry the immediate joyous delight of a rose, but a gentle contemplative pleasure that some-how made her think of churches.

'These are… wonderful,' she said appreciatively.

'Long-stemmed Altruista violets, Lady,' Red-10 said. 'We find them more lasting than the shorter varieties.'

Peri took another deep breath of the complex scent. 'I bet they're popular at the Palace.'

As soon as she spoke she knew she'd said something wrong. The robots seemed to stiffen within their metallic frames.

'Altruista violets are flowers of mourning, only to be displayed inside at a time of death,' Red-3 said.

'Of course,' Peri agreed quickly, 'how stupid of me. Wow, look at the time! Well, I guess I'd better be going. Thanks for showing me round…'

'You would know such a thing – if you came from the Palace,' Red-7 added. There was a definite edge of menace in his words.

Peri tried to sidle away from them, but they moved with deceptive speed on their large tyres, cutting off her retreat. Gleaming metal confronted her each way she turned.

'You are a scavenger!' Red-10 said, as though accusing Peri of the worst crime imaginable.

'No, you've got it all wrong,' Peri protested. 'Okay, I'm not from the Palace. I'm a traveller. I've come here from outer space. From the stars, you know.'

'Stars?' Red-3 said slowly. 'What are stars?'

The response stopped Peri short for a moment. Of course, if the sun never set here and nobody had told them about other worlds, they wouldn't have seen the stars. A deep knowledge of astronomy wasn't essential for keeping gardens tidy.

'The stars are like your sun, only further away.'

'What can be further away than the sun?' Red-7 asked.

'Everything. The rest of the universe. Look, don't you guys ever go round to the dark side of this planet? You'd see the stars from there.'

'The dark side is… uncultivated,' Red-3 said with evident distaste. 'It is where the wild woods are.'

'What's wrong with that?' Peri said.

'It is where the scavengers live.'

Peri groaned. 'I said, I don't know anything about any scavengers!'

'There are the gardens, the Palace and the wild woods,' said Red-10, as though reciting some basic tenet of faith.

Three pairs of red eyes glared at Peri accusingly.

'You are not of the gardens, nor the Palace, so you must be a scavenger,' said Red-3.

The rubber-coated hands that had lifted her so easily from the pit grasped her arms once again, but this time Peri could feel the steel within them. She tried to pull free, but her struggles were quite futile.

'You will now serve the gardens and repair the damage your kind has done,' said Red-3, as though passing a sentence upon her.

Luci watched the strange man crawling about the lawn with curious interest.

Apparently Boots had been telling the truth when he said there were strangers in the gardens. Luci was never sure whether to believe Boots or not. He was often naughty and she had to tell him off. Luci, of course, was never naughty and always set a good example. She was always polite, made sure children all got equal helpings at tea and played games by the rules. Even when the children wanted to play with Boots and some of his friends instead of her, Luci never lost her temper.

Well Boots had had his chance and now it was her turn. Of course the stranger was obviously not a child, even if he was dressed more like a clown or jester. But the Lords came here infrequently and it had been some time since she had anyone to play with except Boots and the others. The gardeners never wanted to play and she understood that the scavengers were not very nice people. For a moment she wondered if the stranger was a scavenger, but dismissed the idea. Scavengers hid in the shadows and would never crawl about in the open like that. Perhaps if she showed him how well behaved she was, he could find some children for her to play with?

The Doctor looked up from examining the grass for tracks where the TARDIS had stood, to see a figure approaching him across the lawn. It appeared to be a young humanoid girl wearing a white summer frock. Long blonde curls spilled over her shoulders. Silver buckled white shoes sparkled in the sunlight. She seemed to match her surroundings perfectly.

She stopped in front of him, waiting until he got to his feet and dusted off his knees, before saying brightly: 'Good day, sir. I'm Luci Longlocks.'

The Doctor smiled back and replied with equal formality: 'Good day to you, Luci. I'm the Doctor.'

She offered her cool, lacy-gloved hand daintily and he took it, making a little bow, which appeared to please her.

'May I enquire, Doctor, what you are doing? Have you lost something?'

'As a matter of fact I have, Luci. It's a blue box about this high…' he held his hand up over his head. 'I left it here earlier and now it seems to have vanished. I don't suppose you've seen it anywhere?'

'I'm afraid I haven't, Doctor. Do you want to play a game?'

The Doctor blinked at the sudden shift in the conversation, looking curiously into the girl's guileless blue eyes. He said carefully: 'I'm afraid I can't play right now, Luci. It is rather important that I find my box, you see. Of course, if you help me find it, then I'll be free to play. Do you have any idea who might have taken it?'

Luci appeared to consider for a moment. 'I suppose the gardeners might have done. It is their job to keep the gardens neat and tidy.'

'Yes, they do it very well,' the Doctor agreed. 'And where might I find these gardeners?'

'Oh, I'm sure I don't know, Doctor,' she said lightly, with a suggestion in her tone that such things were beneath her. 'They are supposed to stay out of the way when the gardens are in use. One wouldn't want them working nearby when one was taking tea on the lawn, would one?'

'No, one wouldn't,' the Doctor said. He tried another approach. 'Luci, are there places in the gardens that you're not supposed to go or play?'

'Why, yes there are, Doctor. How clever of you to know that.'

The Doctor beamed modestly. 'It was nothing. Now, could you show me where the nearest one of these places is?'

'Yes... but I'm not supposed to tell.'

'I'm sure you're not supposed to tell children, but it's been a long time since I was a child. You can tell me. If you do, we can play a game called "Hunt the TARDIS."'

Luci giggled, delicately putting her hand over her mouth. 'What a funny name for a game!'

'"TARDIS" is the name of my blue box.'

'Whoever heard of calling a box by name!'

'Well, this is a very special sort of box.'

Luci's eyes sparkled. 'Is it... magic?'

'I think you could call it that,' the Doctor said, then lowered his voice conspiratorially and added: 'Actually, it's bigger on the inside than the outside!'

Luci looked suitably amazed. 'Are you teasing me, Doctor?'

'If you help me find it, you can see for yourself.'

'Very well, Doctor. There is a place not far from here that children are not supposed to enter. This way...'

Luci led the Doctor confidently along the path and through a brick arch into the next garden. As they went the Doctor asked thoughtfully: 'Luci, who told you about these places children should keep away from?'

For the first time Luci frowned. 'How very peculiar, Doctor. I don't remember. All I know is that it's very important not to let children play there in case they get hurt.'

'And we wouldn't want that, would we?' the Doctor said.

'No, Doctor. Children must play safely and learn good manners,' Luci said firmly.

'How very proper,' the Doctor agreed.

'This is the place,' Luci announced.

They had stopped where a dividing wall between two of the enclosed gardens abutted the wall of another plot running across their ends. For a moment the Doctor could see nothing special about the location. Then his eyes narrowed. To Luci's evident amusement, he began pacing out the widths of the two smaller gardens and comparing it with the dimensions of the garden that bridged the two ends. After a minute he gave an understanding smile.

'It looks like a common wall, but it isn't,' he said half to himself. 'Unless it's solid, which would be rather absurd, there's a long narrow space between two walls. But where's the way in, I wonder? Have you any idea, Luci?'

'I regret I have none, Doctor. I only know children are not supposed to play here.'

The Doctor circled the surrounding gardens, but there was no obvious means of climbing the high walls or any vantage point from which he could look over them. He forced himself to think clearly. The long side walls were bordered by flower beds and small shrubs and trees. An entrance opening onto them was hardly practical. He turned his attention to the cross walls that closed the two ends of the hidden area. One formed the back of a flower bed while the other backed a section of smooth flagstones. The Doctor inspected this section of wall closely.

'This looks like the easiest point of access, otherwise your gardeners would leave tracks across flower beds and there's no sign of anything like that. But if there's a door set in this wall it's well hidden. The join must be concealed in the mortar lines.'

'If there's a door, should it not have a handle, Doctor?' Luci asked.

The Doctor looked at her curiously, but she appeared to be asking the question in all innocence. 'Very true, Luci. A handle or a key. Of course the key might be electronic, but there's usually a manual backup. But it would be concealed where children could not operate it accidentally. How high up that wall can you reach, Luci?'

Luci obligingly stretched her hand up the wall, standing on tiptoe to reach as high as she could.

'Thank you,' the Doctor said. 'Above this line of bricks, then…'

He carefully examined the brick courses on either side of the blank section of wall. On the right-hand side he found a brick set slightly deeper than the rest.

'Stand back!' he warned Luci, and the girl skipped aside, face bright with expectation.

The Doctor pressed the brick, there was a slight click and a section of the wall swung silently inwards. Inside was the top of a long concrete ramp that angled downwards along a high-ceilinged tunnel, illuminated by dimly glowing lighting strips that converged in the darkness somewhere far below them. It was easily large enough to accommodate the TARDIS, carried on some sort of trolley or small low-loading vehicle.

'It looks like your gardeners live underground,' the Doctor said, peering into the depths. 'Perhaps you should wait here while I take a look.'

'Oh no, Doctor!' Luci exclaimed. 'I want to see this magic box of yours.'

She ran lightly forward only to halt suddenly on the very edge of the ramp. Her face showed surprise, then dismay.

'I can't… I mustn't,' she said. 'It's not allowed. I must go… find some children. Goodbye, Doctor.'

She darted away along the path and turned through an archway into the next garden.

'Luci, what's wrong?' the Doctor shouted, running after her. But by the time he had rounded the corner, Luci had vanished.

Frowning, the Doctor returned to the concealed ramp. There was no sound or sign of activity from its depths. He started down with a resolute expression on his face.

He estimated he was at least twenty metres below the surface when the ramp levelled out and opened onto a wide transverse corridor with a curving roof like a subway tunnel, illuminated by the same subdued lighting. Now he could hear noises; several faint metallic clinks, a brief rustling and the soft thud as though a heavy object had been set down, all overlain with the steady background hum of unseen machinery.

Peering round the corner of the junction he saw there was an arched opening in the opposite wall a little way along to his right. Some of the noises seemed to be emanating from within, and every few seconds the fan of light it cast out into the corridor flickered as an indistinct shadow passed across it.

The Doctor was about to step out into the corridor when an approaching whisper of wheels caused him to flatten himself against the wall.

A glittering silver robot rolled busily past him on soft rubber tyres. He watched it reach the far end of the corridor and then turn out of sight.

'Presumably you're one of the gardeners,' the Doctor muttered to himself, having noted the tools arrayed about the robot's lower frame. He looked both ways to ensure the way was now clear, then stepped quickly and silently across to the arch on the other side and peered through.

The chamber beyond was stacked with orderly piles of garden chairs and tables, folded awnings and sunshades, together with assorted rigid frames and panels to make up larger temporary structures. Two more of the silvery robots were engaged on some task at a workbench in the far corner. But the Doctor's eyes were drawn to the middle of the chamber and a set of garden furniture purchased in Salisbury in 1985, beside which rested the reassuring form of a battered and equally anachronistic Police Public Call Box.

The Doctor judged the distances between himself and the TARDIS and it and the robots, even as he drew out his key. He didn't feel inclined to open up a dialogue with the machines just at that moment. Something was badly wrong on this strange little world and he had no idea how they might respond. Besides, his first priority had to be finding Peri.

Once safely back inside the TARDIS he could make a short range spatial hop to the vicinity of the haha pit in the avenue – he could estimate its bearing closely enough now he'd been there – and then use the portable multi-range scanner to search for Peri. Once he'd found her, they might try talking to the gardeners, or even Boots and Luci, if they ever appeared again.

Unfortunately the door of the TARDIS was partially facing the working robots. If they turned around while he was opening it he would certainly be seen. But there was no other way.

He slipped through the archway, hugging the wall, then ducked into the shelter of the stacks of garden supplies. Carefully he began working his way between them towards the TARDIS, which stood apart from the other items in the room. To reach it he would have to leave his cover.

He got as close as he could while watching the two robots intently. But they still seemed engrossed in their work. He rose and tip-toed across the open floor, holding his key at the ready. Another five seconds –

'Scavenger!'

The accusing metallic voice had come from behind him.

The Doctor spun round to see a third robot had just entered the chamber. A pair of shears was attached to its right arm in place of the rubber hand. Alerted by its cry, the two other robots stopped their work and spun round to face the intruder. Their wheels squealed on the floor as their motors buzzed, jerking them into angry motion.

The Doctor took a split second to calculate distances and speeds and realised there was no time to get inside the TARDIS before the three inexplicably angry machines reached him.

He put his shoulder to a stack of garden chairs and toppled them in the path of the third robot. As it crashed into them, rocking wildly, the Doctor leapt to one side. Clattering powered shears sliced past his head and tore into a pile of wooden trellis panels, sending up a shower of splinters.

Then he was past the machine and diving through the archway and back out into the main corridor. Recovering the TARDIS would have to wait. Now his only concern was escape.

He turned onto the ramp only to skid to a halt. A robot was coming down the ramp right at him, eyes blazing.

'Scavenger!' it brayed.

'Sorry – must run!' the Doctor called, turning about and darting back the way he had come. His original pursuers had emerged from the storage room, so he had no choice but to turn left and sprint away along the corridor.

Rounding the first junction he turned into a large chamber filled with the hulking angular forms of what looked like earth-moving machines, drills and tunnel borers. For a moment he crouched down in the shadows between them, wondering if he could conceal himself until the pursuit passed him by. Then he heard robots entering the chamber. They were not allowing him time to hide!

He ran out of the far end of the chamber and along another corridor, passing rooms filled with machines that looked as though they might be part of an automated assembly line and others that seemed to be maintenance shops for the gardening robots. Nowhere did he see any sign of living beings. Who controlled the robots, or were they completely autonomous, he wondered as he ran? How far did this complex extend, and was it the only one on the planet or were there other centres? But above all, was there another way out?

The pursuit was intensifying. Behind him he heard the growing whirr of motors, the squeal of rubber tyres and the cry of:

'Scavenger!'

As he passed a side passage he felt a breeze on his face, carrying with it the smell of earth and mulch. Was this a way up to the surface?

The Doctor turned into the passage and sprinted forward, straining his eyes for the sight of daylight. Instead he found himself in a chamber ringed by pipework and pump-like devices, centred around a row of large metal hoppers standing taller than his head.

Even as he took this in, he heard the squeal of tyres from the far end of the passage he had just passed along. He looked around desperately, but there was no other way out of the room! He turned back to the hoppers. These robots didn't seem to be equipped for climbing...

He sprang upward, hooked his fingers over the rim of the hopper, heaved himself over with a grunt, and dropped inside just as a gardener entered the chamber.

He found himself lying on a pile of leaves, finely shredded stalks and grass cuttings; organic waste from the gardens presumably destined for composting.

Straining his ears, he heard the robot moving about the room, obviously checking all possible hiding places. As long as it didn't consider the possibility that the object of its search was more agile than its own kind.

Then came a click and rattle of metal turning against metal which reverberated through the hopper. From somewhere below the Doctor came a rushing noise that grew steadily louder...

The pile of compost suddenly dipped in the middle as the contents of the hopper began to sink downward. The Doctor made a desperate grab for the rim of the hopper but it was already out of reach and the sloping sides offered no other handhold. The loose material rolled inward, closing over his waist as he was sucked downward. The compost rose over his head and he clamped his lips shut and screwed up his eyes. He felt a momentary increase in pressure as though he was passing through a constricted space, then he was falling though empty air.

He landed in a container already half-full of compost. The loose pile broke his fall but sent him tumbling helplessly sideways. His head cracked violently against the edge of the container. The world seemed to explode in a shower of purple sparks, then darkness enfolded him.

The flow through the chutes ceased. Valves closed again with a clang. There was a low hum of power. The underground train with its truck-loads of organic waste and one unconscious passenger pulled smoothly away. In a few seconds it had vanished into a tunnel.

Chapter Six

Peri rubbed a grimy hand across her brow, wiping away the sweat.

She was no longer the elegantly dressed figure she had been when sipping lemonade on the lawn only a few hours earlier. Her once pristine summer frock was dirty and seriously abbreviated since she had been forced to pull off the sleeves and tear the skirt across at the knees. But it was either that or risk fainting in the heat.

The artificial lights of the subterranean greenhouse were brilliant and the air was hot and humid. Peri appreciated such conditions were good for the plants and they didn't trouble the robot gardeners, under whose watchful lenses they laboured, but it wasn't easy for their human workers.

At least they looked human to Peri's eyes. There were eight or ten of them, and Peri thought she had never seen such a ragged and miserable group of people. They were of both sexes, two or three in their late teens, she guessed, the rest adults. A couple of older men were thin, lined and grey-haired, looking worn down by life more than their years. All were dressed in a strange mixture of animal skins and pieces of plastic sheeting, roughly sewn together, and criss-crossed with straps and belts of hide or wire and what might have been nylon cord.

They were, she presumed, the 'scavengers' that the gardeners seemed to disapprove of so vehemently. Not that any of them had yet spoken to her to confirm their identity. She had received several suspicious glances and was obviously the subject of some muttered exchanges, but none of them had responded to her attempts to start conversations when they had passed by her in the course of their work. Whether this was from fear of her or their captors she didn't know.

Taking a deep breath, Peri went back to her task of separating seedlings from a clump in a tray and planting each one in a small individual pot. Once a larger tray of potted seedlings was ready, it was placed on a table under the lights and mist watering pipes for forcing. It was repetitious, mind-numbing work, the irony of which was not lost on her. She'd been a botany student back on Earth before she met the Doctor. But if she was going to have to do much more of this she would rapidly go off the whole phylum.

She hastily quashed the idea that she might end up like the wretches who worked about her. The Doctor would find her or she would escape. Rotting away down here was not an option she was even going to contemplate. You are going to get away from here the first chance you get, Peri Brown, she told herself firmly. Keep your eyes open and your wits about you.

She finished another tray and carried it with shuffling steps over to a clear area of the bench. She had to be careful how she walked. Like the others, she was hobbled by a length of plastic strapping secured about her ankles. It allowed her to take short steps, but not to run.

Peri recognised the material as the sort of tie used to secure a young shrub or sapling to a supporting post. It was usually fitted with an adjustable buckle so the loop could be let out as the plant grew and then easily removed when it was strong enough to support itself. It made a strange sort of sense that the gardeners would use something like this to control their prisoners, but it was not exactly chain-gang security and seemed curiously amateurish. Surely they could have made something better. Perhaps they were not that adaptable; prisoners of their programming, which in her opinion had obviously been seriously screwed up somewhere along the line. Not that she was complaining. However tough it was, plastic could be cut a lot more easily than metal. Just let her get hold of a knife…

Then she saw the scavenger boy again, pushing a trolley-load of fresh planting trays into the greenhouse.

This particular boy, or perhaps she should say young man as she guessed he might be fifteen or sixteen, was different from the rest. He had an unruly mass of dark curls, the shadow of a moustache forming on his upper lip and a sharp clear eye. He held himself straight and performed the tasks the robots set him with calculated insolence. There was a proud defiant set to his features. Of all the scavengers, he at least had met her gaze squarely, if with a curious frown. There's somebody who's not going to knuckle-under quietly, Peri thought. Somebody worth getting to know better, perhaps?

Turning these thoughts over in her mind, she toiled on.

The light underground was as unchanging as on the surface. Did people here simply sleep when they were tired, she wondered? She began repeatedly checking her watch, worried that she was losing track of time. Then she worried about becoming obsessive when she found only a few minutes had passed and gave it up. Her thoughts drifted. What did she mean by people, anyway? So far she'd seen three antiquated types in a wagon, robots, scavengers and Boots – whatever he/it was. Was that an average cross section of the local community? But who made the place in the beginning and did anybody actually run things now? The gardeners had mentioned a Palace. If anybody was going to rule, that's where they would be. If… no, *when* she got out of here, it would go right to the top of her Places-To-Visit-In-A-Mean-Mood list.

She was roused from her brooding thoughts by a gardener ordering the workers to stop what they were doing.

In a shuffling file they were herded along a passage into what was obviously a combination mess room and sleeping hall, with rough straw pallets arrayed about the walls and a metal trough in the centre of the room. Half the trough was filled with water, which the workers eagerly fell upon, gulping it down from their cupped hands. Peri reluctantly copied them, feeling too thirsty to care about niceties. She splashed some more water over her face, grateful for the feel of something cool after the sweatbox conditions of the greenhouse.

A gardener entered carrying a large plastic mesh bin filled with multicoloured fruits and vegetables, which it tipped into the other half of the trough. As soon as it had withdrawn and the barred door of the chamber had clanged shut, the scavengers fell upon the food, snatching up all they could carry and shambling off to their crude beds to wolf it down.

Almost too late, Peri realised that nobody cared about equal portions and had to elbow her way in to grab the last of the food, hating herself as she did so for being a part of such a degrading process. She came away with a couple of pale vegetables like large knobbly potatoes and an orange ball with a coarse ribbed rind.

Peri felt many eyes upon her and saw that, in between tearing at their food, the others were staring at her with frank suspicion. Even in their present sorry state, her clothes were clearly different from theirs and she suddenly felt very much the outsider. She also experienced the first pangs of alarm. Having seen them behaving little better than animals, Peri could almost understand the gardeners' contempt. And now they were locked in this room together without guards. But had they been like this before the gardeners had captured them? What was going on here?

She looked round and saw the proud dark-haired boy sitting apart from the rest, looking contemptuous of his fellows' evident resignation to their situation as he bit into his food. Taking a deep breath, Peri stepped over to him.

'Hallo, my name's Peri. What's yours?'

He eyed her up and down rather too closely for her liking, but she stood firm. After a long pause he said: 'Where you from? Melek's House? Stoneford? You didn't come to last gathering.'

'I don't know about any gathering, or where those places are. I'm from somewhere called Earth.'

He frowned. Underneath the layered dirt he had quite a nice face, she thought. 'Only three home-hearths in wild woods,' he said. 'Thorn Tree, Melek's House, Stoneford. I be Kel of Thorn Tree. You be from Melek's or the Ford. Nobody lives on own in woods.'

'Well, Kel, it's a little complicated. Maybe I can explain. Can I sit down?'

He grunted, which Peri took to be an assent, and she settled herself beside him, trying to ignore the noticeable odour emanating from his ragged clothes. Though after a few days here, she probably wouldn't smell much better.

'These wild woods of yours, they're on the dark side of this planet, right?' Peri began.

Kel frowned again. 'Sun never shines on wild woods.'

'So you must be able to see the stars from there.'

'What are stars?'

Peri sighed. She'd hoped these people would understand more than the gardeners, but perhaps she'd been wrong. 'Stars are little specks of light that shine in the sky when there's no sun. You must have seen them.'

Kel shook his head. 'Sky over wild woods is clouds. Rains often. Makes streams and lakes. Water runs to sun and gardens where there is little rain.'

It made sense, Peri thought. Rain condensed out of moist air over the cooler, dark side of the world and flowed back to the daylight side to be evaporated again. Unfortunately it didn't help her explanation.

'Don't you ever get clear weather, see any gaps in the clouds where it's really dark?' she asked.

'Dark like in cave?' Kel said. 'Never that dark. Always some light in sky, always enough for hunt.'

Obviously the twilight zone stretched far enough round this small world so that it never got properly dark. She was wasting her time trying to give astronomy lessons.

'Okay,' she said. 'This place Earth that I come from, which you've obviously never heard of, goes round a star that you've never seen. Take it or leave it.'

'So, you not live in wild woods?'

'No.'

'You live in the gardens somewhere away from gardeners?'

'No! Somewhere else far away. Beyond your sun. I've just been trying to explain… Oh, never mind!'

Kel looked at her curiously as Peri angrily bit into one of the potato-like vegetables she had snatched from the feeding trough. It tasted a bit like very mild cheese. After a minute she asked: 'What's the name of this world. Everything round us, the ground under our feet, you know.'

'This Esselven,' Kel said, as though stating the very obvious.

'This whole world, or just this part of it?'

Kel shrugged. 'Everything is Esselven,' he repeated.

Peri thoughtfully chewed some more cheese potato for a moment, then said: 'Tell me about the Palace.'

Kel looked at her oddly. 'The gardeners say "pal-ace" when they mean the Big House.'

'Okay, "Big House". Who lives there?' She saw his look of disbelief at her question and added: 'Really, I don't know. Please tell me.'

'The Lords of Esselven.'

'Big shots, eh? What are they like?'

'Like men. But they have fine clothes and horses. They ride the straight ways, walk in gardens.'

'Have you ever talked to any of them?'

'No. Only seen from far away.'

'I don't suppose you've been inside the Palace?'

'No. It is guarded by warriors and magic. Death for scavenger people to go there.'

'I see. Anywhere else around here I should know about?'

Kel scratched himself thoughtfully. 'There is land of the Pal-ace of Winter.'

'You mean there are two Palaces?'

'Yes. Gardens belong to the Pal-ace of Summer. Beyond the great fields is the land of the Palace of Winter. Hunters say it is where water turns hard and the ground is white.'

'And how do your people, the scavengers, fit into all this?' she asked. 'I mean, where did you come from?'

Kel scowled. 'The elders say we sent away from the Palace as punishment for angering the God. Long ago, elder's fathers-fathers went to Palace to beg forgiving. Palace warriors drive them away. Scavengers not go there now for long time.'

'But where did you come from before then?'

Again she got the look of disbelief that she should ask such a question. 'The Sun God-ship brought us to Esselven, long ago. We lived with Palace Lords then. Palace lords serve the Sun God. They put up great towers to please him. Then was the dividing. The elders say that is why we live in dark woods. We angered the Sun God and the Palace Lords send us away from his eye into dark lands. That is why we not live with Lords. Elders make sacrifices, call to sun but nothing changes.'

At last Peri felt she was getting to know something of the history of this place, even if none of it made much sense at the moment. She persevered. 'How long ago did all this happen?'

'Long ago.'

'But how long?'

'A long time. Before the flood washed away the old Stoneford, before Hrothgeld killed the great wolf. A long time.'

Suddenly Peri understood. If the sun never moved here and there were no seasons, then there would be no years. Without artificial timekeeping, they would soon lose track of time. Not just the time of day, if you could call it that, but entire years. The only chronology left would be the order of notable events, which would soon become mingled with folk tales. She'd better not put too much reliance on the accuracy of what Kel told her, but for the moment it was all she had to go on.

'Sounds like you've had a rough deal,' Peri sympathised. 'Even the gardeners are down on you.' She frowned. 'What do you think the gardeners are, anyway?'

Kel gave her an odd look. 'Gardeners are Lord's servants, like warriors who guard Palace.'

'But they're not human are they. You can see that. Have you ever heard the word "robot"?'

Kel shook his head. 'Gardeners are mek-anycals. That is Lord's name for them. They grow food for Palace. We take from the gardens, they chase us. Catch us if they can.' His face darkened. 'Catch Kel, but not for long!'

Peri lowered her voice slightly. 'You want to get away too, right? Well so do I. Maybe we can work together to get out of here.'

He looked her up and down again in his uncomfortably direct manner. 'Maybe you too old woman for scavenger run-hiding. Should be mated at home-hearth having children.'

Peri managed to stifle her instinctive response to this outrageous observation, and instead said icily: 'Just give me a chance and I'll show you some run-hiding. I've been chased by worse things than the gardeners, you know.' She looked down at the strapping binding her ankles. 'But first, we've got to get these things off. We need a knife, or maybe secateurs or pruning shears. The gardeners carry those sort of tools…'

'I had knife,' Kel said. 'Good metal knife, not stone. Scavenged from gardeners. Sharpened and made handle myself. But was taken away when they caught me.'

'I don't suppose you know where they put it?'

Kel shrugged.

'Well we'd hardly have a chance to go wandering about after it, anyway. We've got to use something close at hand. But it must be the right time. Do we ever get let outside?'

'Yes. Other work to do in gardens. Putting bigger plants in ground, scraping grass –'

'I get the picture. I doubt they'll let us have any really sharp tools to work with, but at least out in the open we'll be in position to make a run for it if we get the chance.' She looked round at the other scavengers. They'd finished their food and were huddling down to sleep. 'Perhaps we can help them escape as well.'

'They are no longer true scavengers,' Kel said contemptuously. 'Gardeners have kept them too long. They will not run. Have lost the fire inside.' He thumped his chest. 'Kel still has the fire!'

Peri considered their companions again and had to admit Kel was probably right. It would just be her and Kel, then. She turned back to him and jerked a thumb at herself. 'Well I've got that fire inside me as well. Where I come from a burning torch is a symbol of liberty and we don't take kindly to being kept as slaves. So we start planning how to get out of here, right?'

He considered her determined expression for a moment, then said: 'You talk much – but maybe you have fire. Time to sleep now.'

And he turned over and curled up on his straw mattress.

Peri shrugged, shifted herself over to the mattress next to Kel's, which nobody seemed to have claimed, and made herself as comfortable as possible.

Tomorrow she was getting out of here, she told herself. Today hadn't exactly ended on a high, but tomorrow was going to be a better day. She was going to get away from the gardeners some-how… exact details still to be resolved, then find the Doctor… she wasn't sure exactly how…

She drifted into an exhausted sleep, niggled by the thought that on Esselven, tomorrow never really came.

Chapter Seven

Benedek and his travelling companions had halted at the crossroads, with the sun throwing their lengthening shadows before
them, when he saw the riders approaching from the east. Though
they were too far off for any details to be seen, Benedek guessed
who they were.

Briefly he considered riding on at once and making good his
advantage, but the horses were tired and in any case, it might
appear undignified. So he contented himself with making a show
of nonchalant ease. His companions adopted the same manner.

The party of five horsemen drew up as they reached Benedek's
party. Their leader was a lean man with a saturnine face and dark,
intelligent eyes. His gaze flickered appraisingly over Benedek's
company before he made a slight bow from his saddle.

'Greetings, Prince Benedek. We have met before upon my last
visit to Corthane, though you may not recall the time, being then
a mere child.'

There was a subtle emphasis on the last word that suggested
Benedek, in his opinion, was still not quite done with childhood.

Benedek made a stiff and minimal bow in return.

'Greetings to you, Lord Duke. Yes, I recall your visit, even though
I was a stripling. But as you can see, I am full grown now.'

Duke Stephon smiled. 'You may find that the getting of a year's
height and a year's wisdom are not one and the same. Achieving
man's full estate may yet lie a little way ahead of you.'

Benedek's companions stirred at the Duke's words, but Benedek
motioned for them to be silent and beamed back at the Duke.

'I thank you, lord Duke, for those cautionary words. Doubtless such musings come often to one as the count of years multiplies and wistful thought must take increasing precedence over bodily activity.' And as he spoke his eyes flickered over the grey touching the Duke's temples and down the line of his beard.

Now it was the turn of the Duke's men to bridle, but they were silenced at a glance from their master, who nodded to Benedek in acknowledgement of his swift riposte. He looked back down the avenue from the south along which Benedek had ridden.

'You travel light, Prince,' he observed. 'Do you not feel the need to present yourself at the Palace of Aldermar in better than clothes stained by travel?'

'I shall present myself properly accoutred,' Benedek assured him. My baggage train follows on but half a day behind. I did not wish to be constrained to the speed of pack wagons for fear of arriving late.' He looked along the eastern road. 'You also seem without provisions fitting to your station.'

'They also follow along at their own pace. Like yourself, I wished not to be late. A gentleman is always punctual – especially when being presented to a lady of renown.'

'Now we have the truth!' Benedek exclaimed. 'You were sent a likeness of her as well as I, and wonder if the artist did her justice.'

Stephon held his poise. 'It is well known that Princess Oralissa is fair to look upon. I would not be a man, despite those years you believe lie heavy on my shoulders, good Prince, if I did not anticipate agreeably meeting one such as she. Do you deny you are not driven by a similar curiosity?'

'I do not deny it. I happily admit it before these witnesses. I wish to make a match, and if Oralissa is half as fair and gentle of nature as reports suggest, then she will do very well for me.'

'You are very sure of success, young Prince.'

Benedek's eyes narrowed. 'What I seek I have, as the skins of many mighty beasts that adorn the walls of our citadel upon the icefields will testify.'

'You will find the courting of a lady requires different skills than those of the hunt. You may hang your walls with a thousand rich pelts, Prince, and still not win this prize.'

'We shall see, Lord Duke. Now, do we cross into Aldermar together, or start a race for the palace gates from this spot?'

'I shall ride on at a seemly pace if you will do the same.'

Cautiously the two men urged their mounts forward, their followers falling in behind them, each casting suspicious glances at their counterparts and edging uneasily about the road. After a minute the Duke said:

'Would you care to ride a little before me, Prince, so that the dust of my passage does not clog your nostrils and grit your eyes?'

'A kind offer, Lord Duke. But then I will be constantly twisting my neck about to see that you do not suffer likewise.'

'Why incommode yourself so? Are you so concerned for my wellbeing?'

'Perhaps. Leastwise, I suddenly find myself overcome with a desire not to let you out of my sight.'

The Duke smiled. 'Then let us ride side by side so we may continue this most companionable discourse. The road is, I think, wide enough to pass us both.'

'The road perhaps,' the Prince said, 'but at its end there can be no sharing.'

'Of that at least, we can agree.'

The pace of their ride north slowed and the baggage trains of both parties caught up with their respective masters. So it was, when they finally arrived at the gatehouse of the Palace of Aldermar, Prince and Duke were each dressed in their finest clothes and accompanied by companion-guards whose leather was oiled and metalwork shone.

A company of Aldermarian guards were waiting to escort them through the parks and gardens to the Palace itself. Having expected the guests to arrive separately, the guard commander had to adjust the planned disposition of his men to accommodate a Prince and Duke who seemed determined to ride to the Palace shoulder to shoulder.

As the oddly mingled party dismounted in the Palace courtyard, the royal family came out onto the broad flight of steps before the main doors to greet their distinguished guests. The Duke and the Prince, still shoulder to shoulder, bowed to the King and Queen, and handed over small gifts of welcome, as was the custom in Aldermar.

And then they were presented to Princess Oralissa, who had been standing silently a little behind her parents, her eyes down-cast. At the sight of her the flow of conventional words of greeting and regard faltered as they realised that the images they had seen had not done justice to her beauty.

Oralissa was small and slender, with a heart-shaped face, skin the colour of dark honey, white-blonde hair constrained in a single thick plait and tawny eyes of gem-like clarity. Demurely she held out her hand and each man bent low over it.

She was so beautiful yet so sad, it seemed, that Benedek was moved to lift her spirits. Fighting to keep a nervous stammer from his words, he said:

'I... I had thought that I had known beauty when the sun lit the ice valleys of Corthane and turned them into jewelled halls of light... all bedecked in crystal splendour. But now I have met you, Princess... I shall not walk those valleys again, knowing them but pale imitations of true loveliness.'

Oralissa's eyes widened in surprise at the boldness of the young man's compliment. She smiled brightly back at him, her joyful nature parting the veil of her despondency for the first time that day.

Recovering his own composure and realising Benedek had drawn the first show of approval from the Princess, the Duke deftly interposed himself between the two.

'Prince Benedek compares thee to snow and ice, Princess. But I see only warmth and life in thy countenance. The great woods of Eridros hold many secret glades where the most fair flowers grow, prized throughout the realm for their many hues and scents so rich and yet so subtle as to dazzle the senses. But here in Aldermar the most perfect bloom in Esselven has grown and blossomed, and it is my privilege to gaze upon her.'

Oralissa blinked at the unexpected words falling from the lips of the older man, then favoured Stephon also with her warmest smile.

Standing to one side, the King and Queen exchanged glances of relief. Oralissa had clearly made a deep impression on their guests, and they in turn had raised her spirits.

The eyes of Benedek and Stephon also met, but there was no meeting of minds behind the gesture. Their earlier hostility had merely been a reflection of minor disagreements their countries had shared in the past. Now their rivalry had taken on a personal dimension.

The object of their curious interest had been revealed as a living being of exceptional quality. In a few moments, innocent of the power she wielded, she had kindled the fires of desire within them both. But only one could claim her. Each signalled the other with that single glance that no quarter would be given in the battle to win Oralissa's hand.

Chapter Eight

The emergency alarm sounded throughout the length of the *Valtor,* followed by the Captain's voice.

'Final warning! We are about to re-enter normal space at minimum proximity to planetary gravity well. Secure all systems and stand by for disruption effects. In ten, nine, eight…'

Strapped into the control chair of the *Stop Press*, Dynes braced himself for an unpleasant few moments. The task force was going to emerge from hyperspace practically in orbit about their objective. Regular passenger liners or cargo carriers would never contemplate such a manoeuvre. Only front line military craft with sufficient energy reserves to control the collapse of the hyperfield would take the risk. The slightest error could tear the ship apart. But Dynes felt no serious concern. He knew Judd would have calculated all the parameters. He was not the suicidal type.

'…three, two, one… drive off!'

Dynes felt a shudder run through the *Valtor*, transmitted to the *Stop Press* through the docking clamps. A spasm of nausea churned his stomach, causing him to swallow hard. Warning lights flickered briefly across his control panel, then settled down to normal. They'd made it.

The distorted vista of hyperspace vanished from his external monitors and he saw the hard contours of the other ships in the task force sparkling under the harsh light of a white dwarf star whose disk filled most of one view screen. Even as Dynes took in the scene the other ships broke formation and sped away from the *Valtor*, each taking up its pre-arranged position in tight orbit around… what?

It filled space below them, yet at the same time it was almost invisible to casual observation. It was as though a mirror-glass globe hung there, showing only a dazzling spot of light where the sunlight reflected from it and a few lesser pinpoints of bright stars. Otherwise it was as black as space itself. It was the largest broad spectrum forcefield Dynes had ever seen; a 130 kilometre sphere enclosing a worldlet with a collapsed matter core, capable of sustaining a narrow biosphere. Even as he watched, the reflections of sun and stars slid across the mirror surface. Real sun and reflection met, then the incandescent globe was cut across by a hard-edged arc of darkness. In seconds the solar disk had vanished as they plunged into the planetoid's shadow.

The *Valtor* fell on along its sharply curving orbit as its artificial senses probed the world below. Stars rolled behind the black disk hanging in space with dizzying speed, and Dynes felt an unexpected spasm of motion sickness. The mass of a minor planet compressed into the volume of an asteroid generated a steep gravity well that rapidly diminished in intensity with altitude. Even so they were still orbiting the tiny world at several kilometres a second.

Dynes turned to face the DAVE unit hovering beside him and signalled it to start recording.

'I'm looking down on a freak of astrodynamics augmented by planetary engineering technology, orbiting close to a white dwarf star where no habitable world should be,' he began. 'This is the secret that has taken Judd a year to wring from the survivors of the Esselvanian space fleet. Locating it has involved not only painstaking study of decades of cargo manifests, space logs and flight plans, but forcing many unwilling tongues to loosen. It's meant exploring and eliminating numerous false trails until one set of unexplained coordinates remained.

'This is the retreat of the rulers of Esselven. The private world where they took their holidays away from the public gaze – and now perhaps their refuge from an implacable enemy. There's no absolute certainty that the royal family and their retainers came here on their last desperate flight from Esselven, or that they haven't moved on since, but where else would they go? Judd has contacts on a hundred worlds. If Hathold and his family attempted to claim asylum anywhere in this sector, he would have known about it…'

The dazzling white limb of the sun reappeared on the opposite side of the dark globe and it rose as rapidly as it had set barely half a minute earlier. They were making a complete orbit about the planetoid in under two minutes.

'The probability is that if they're anywhere, they're here,' Dynes continued. 'This world was obviously prepared as a place of concealment, a sanctuary, and now it has failed its builders. Judd's ships are already encircling it – there will be no dramatic last minute escape this time. The bolt-hole has become a prison. The last act of the conquest of Esselven has begun. Any moment now…'

Dynes broke off his commentary as he noticed activity in the *Valtor's* control room, relayed from the DAVE he'd left there to give him an overview of the situation. Two more DAVEs were assigned to Judd's own landing craft, while the rest were with Dynes inside the *Stop Press* ready to cover the landing. Now he saw that the reports of the deployment were coming in and being relayed to Judd.

'Even as I speak, Protector Judd is in his landing craft preparing to lead the assault team down to the surface…'

Judd shifted in his seat, feeling his powered armour move with him, sensing and amplifying his movements. It felt good to be back in battle dress again. The last time he'd worn it had been for the assault on Esselven, and it was about time that he reminded the men that he was a warrior as well as an administrator.

Though facing the prospect of imminent danger and violence and prepared to use all the tools of warfare at his disposal, Judd despised people who were uncontrollably violent or who sought out danger for its own sake like a drug. It was simply a means to an end. In fact a measure of applied violence had enabled him to mark out his future path during basic military training...

It was the day they started the course in unarmed combat. Sergeant Vengle, their instructor, taunted the trainees that this was their chance to 'take a swing' at a superior officer without fear of the consequences. Vengle would take on any of them brave enough to face him before training proper started. Judd recognised the crude ploy to assert his dominance over the trainees. He watched Vengle easily beat three recruits, and then stepped up himself.

It was a hard fight, for Vengle was no physical weakling, but Judd was driven by more than mere muscle. Eventually, bloody and half-senseless, he landed the winning punch. It guaranteed him the respect and admiration of his fellows, and also ensured none would dare cross his path.

Judd contrived to meet Vengle privately later, before the latter had a chance to formulate some plan of revenge, and stated his case bluntly. Vengle had already witnessed the fact that Judd was more than a common recruit. He could either stand in the way of his ambitions or he could help him along and reap the rewards later. Vengle decided to be sensible. With his support, Judd passed through basic training top of his muster.

Once assigned to regular duty with an aerospace assault unit, Judd gained rapid promotion, applying his considerable intelligence to rationalizing an uninspired military organisation. He had little opposition. Most personnel were unambitious time servers who did not obstruct him. A few from the traditional military classes, serving because it was expected of them, might resent his rise through the ranks. Old families, however, as he rapidly discovered, all had their secrets. These he diligently uncovered through unofficial use of military resources and then applied them to influence their soldier sons to his advantage. Genuinely able personnel he gathered under his own command, waiting for the opportunity to use their ability to his advantage.

By this time Judd's name was being mentioned within the higher ranks of command, but he knew that for his purposes he needed to become a public figure. He watched for the opportunity he knew would come…

The captain of the *Valtor* was speaking to him over the comlink.

'Englobement is complete, Protector. No ship can leave the planetoid without being intercepted within a matter of seconds…' he hesitated, then continued: 'The intelligence team reports that the planetary shield is denser than anything the Esselvanians used against us before. Apart from some radiation loss in the infra red from the night side, which must be necessary to maintain a habitable surface temperature, it registers as completely stable and inert. It's reflecting our scanning beams with almost no attenuation. There must be some means of opening a discontinuity to let ships pass through without exposing the surface to the full solar spectrum, but at this moment we cannot locate it or even identify gross surface details.'

'I can manage without a map if I have to, Captain,' Judd replied tersely. 'But if the shield is that complete, I won't even be able to get a landing craft down. Open a hole in it!'

'But… where shall we aim, sir?'

'Anywhere, Captain, since one point seems as good as another. Use every missile and beam in the fleet if you have to, but crack that shield now!'

'At once, Protector! All ships! Target sunside zero meridian, forty-five degrees North by standard reference...'

The ships of the task force shifted to bring their weapons to bear on the perfect mirrored-globe beneath them. Drive plates glowed as the vessels checked their hectic whirl about the tiny world. Missile ports opened while the muzzles of energy projectors tracked and locked on target.

A volley of missiles burst from their tubes and flashed across the few tens of kilometres that separated the closely orbiting ships from the top of the shield. As the missiles struck, every cannon in the fleet fired. Every beam and missile was targeted on a single point on the shield less than five hundred metres across.

An incandescent fireball erupted into space like the rising of a new sun. Secondary electrostatic discharge radiated outward from the point of impact as a thousand jagged bolts of lightning sought a place to earth.

Under the impact the mirror of the shield rippled like the surface of a still pond broken by a pebble. The ripples ran across the globe and back, and then melted away. The fireball faded and thinned into a hazy glowing cloud, spreading slowly across the force field that still cocooned the tiny world.

Chapter Nine

With returning consciousness came the pain.

The Doctor's head throbbed and his neck ached. I hurt, therefore I am, he thought muzzily to himself. Now why didn't old
René Descartes put it like that? It's so much more true to life…

He realised his thoughts were wandering and marshalled them
with an effort. He remembered tunnels, robots, the TARDIS, a chase,
falling through the waste hopper into some sort of container…
then blackness.

Now he was lying on his back on some hard surface. He could
smell sun-warmed earth and machine oil. He put his hand to the
side of his head where the worst of the pain seemed to be
centred and found a pad of damp cloth had been placed over
the contusion.

'Are you recovered now?' said a mechanical voice.

The Doctor tried to sit up with a jerk and instantly regretted
the impulse. Even a Time Lord, he reminded himself sternly as he
lay flat again, had to take a little time to recover from a blow that
might have killed a lesser being.

He opened his eyes and found himself staring into the red lenses
of a robot identical to those that had so recently pursued him.

'Ahh…' he groaned apprehensively.

'Do you require watering?' the robot asked.

For a moment the Doctor could not make sense of the odd
enquiry, then he realised he was being offered a drink. Strange for
one of the garden robots to be so solicitous of his health after
pursuing him so vigorously. But if it was a trick, what would be

the point of it? He had obviously been at the machine's mercy for some time before he had recovered consciousness. Could he detect a trace of concern behind its words?

'Water would be… nice,' he replied carefully.

The robot held up a plant sprayer and squirted it at the Doctor's mouth. The Doctor screwed up his eyes and gulped down what he could of the unconventional refreshment, finally spluttering: 'Thank you… enough!'

The robot withdrew the sprayer and resumed his impassive contemplation of the Doctor.

The unexpected dousing had been reviving. He felt the life flowing back into his limbs. Moving slowly he managed to sit up, this time with only minor discomfort. Pulling out his handkerchief he mopped off his face, watching the robot as he did so in case this show of unexpected concern suddenly changed into something more sinister. But the machine made no move towards him. In fact he realised that it conveyed the odd impression, despite its lack of expressive facial features, of being anxious, almost shy, certainly not belligerent. Feeling the sense of imminent danger lifting, he spared a moment to take in his surroundings.

He was sitting on a long workbench set in one corner of an open-sided vaulted structure the size of an aircraft hangar. Large skylights let into the roof allowed in bars of sunlight that caught the twinkling dust motes and illuminated the interior. Close by the bench were arrayed a comprehensive selection of machine tools and storage racks containing robot body shells and other spare parts. Beyond them, parked in neat rows, were numerous pieces of agricultural equipment, including tractor-like vehicles with various attachments and harvesting machines. Several other robots bustled purposefully about the huge shed, but only his immediate companion seemed to be paying him any attention at present.

Outside was a patchwork of neat fields planted with a variety of crops bearing bristling cobs or pod-heads, their stalks waving gently in the slight breeze as they ripened under the timeless sun. The Doctor twisted cautiously round to scan the entire panorama, but there was no other structure between him and the sharply curving and abbreviated horizon. How far had the underground train carried him – and how long had he been unconscious?

The Doctor took another look at his robotic first-aider. It seemed identical to the ones that had chased him, except that it had a green square on its chestplate, together with the numeral '8'.

'Where am I, exactly?' the Doctor asked.

'You are in the central farming zone, Green Sector,' the robot replied. 'I am Coordinator of the North-east quadrant of Green sector. My designation is Green-8.'

'Hallo, Green-8,' the Doctor said tentatively, 'I'm the Doctor.'

'"Doc-tor". It is not a usual name for a scavenger.'

'Probably because I'm not a scavenger. I don't even know what scavengers are – except that your, ah, colleagues back under the gardens don't seem to approve of them.'

'Scavengers are the enemies of the gardens,' Green-8 said bluntly. 'They steal produce and damage the plants. We are directed to restrain all scavengers and send them to the Red Sector gardens for permanent confinement and restitutional labour.'

'I see,' said the Doctor, dabbing his head again. 'And how did I come to be here?'

'I found you in a tube capsule of waste organic matter that had been sent from the Red Sector gardens for use on the fields. Before it arrived a warning had been transmitted that a scavenger had entered the Red sub-levels and was still at large. It was obvious who you were.'

'Your logic is impeccable, Green-8, but nevertheless your deduction is erroneous. I was the person they were chasing, but as I said, I'm not a scavenger. It was all a misunderstanding.'

'But your covering resembles a scavenger costume,' Green-8 persisted. 'It is a miscellaneous and un-coordinated patchwork of material.'

The Doctor swelled indignantly. 'I'll have you know there are places where this coat is considered the height of fashion!' He winced and dabbed the cloth to his head, then looked at Green-8 closely. 'Still, you thought I was a scavenger, your enemy, yet you treated my wound. And now don't seem to be in a hurry to send me back.' He looked round at the other robots in the shed which still seemed to be paying him no attention. 'For that matter, neither do your friends.'

'I have instructed the other units under my control to ignore your presence.'

'Ah, I see. Not that I'm not ungrateful, of course, but why? I am right in thinking you're a general service robot of the same make as the others back in the gardens?'

'That is correct, Doctor.'

'Yet they did not express any doubt about what they wanted to do with me, indeed the consensus was quite alarming. You must all have the same basic programme, so why are you acting as you are?'

Green-8 hesitated in a very un-robotic manner. 'When I found you I... chose not to follow my programme. I thought I might... like to talk to you first, before returning you to Red Sector. I reasoned that even a scavenger might have... ideas of interest to exchange. I have tried before to talk to scavengers when I found them stealing produce from the fields, but they were afraid of me and ran off. You are the first being of another kind with whom I have successfully communicated.' Green-8's head lowered slightly as though in shame. 'I know it is wrong. I believe I am malfunctioning. Many work periods ago I missed a scheduled service and applied a reserve reintegration sub-programme to my central processor. An error must have occurred –'

The Doctor slid off the bench, telling himself firmly that despite the apparent swaying of the entire landscape he was not going to fall over, and stepped up to Green-8.

'No, not an error, Green-8,' he said. 'Obviously you are evolving, growing. I've encountered this sort of thing before. Any sufficiently complex organism, whether it's carbon or silicon based, has the potential to achieve awareness and self-determination if it's given half a chance and a little time. This is what must have happened to you.'

'Time…' Green-8 said, almost wistfully. 'Yes, time is something there is a lot of here, Doctor. The other machines I am responsible for do not think for themselves. Time means nothing to them, except as a measure of productivity and a means of predicting the growing cycle. But gradually I found I had to conceive of abstract concepts to fill the emptiness. I have looked at the world and wondered…is this all there is? We grow and harvest, we serve our programme… yet is that enough?'

The Doctor clapped Green-8 on the side companionably. 'That's how thinking for yourself starts. Occasional confusion is the price you have to pay, but it's worth it in the end.'

'I find I have a question I wish to ask you, Doctor.'

Still feeling dizzy the Doctor sat himself back on the workbench again. 'Ask away.'

'If you are not a scavenger, and not of the gardens or the Palace… where are you from?'

'I'm a traveller in time and space. I come from another world far beyond your sun.'

The Doctor wondered if he was going to have a problem convincing the robot about the true nature of the universe, but Green-8 simply said: 'Is there something beyond the sun? I know only this world and the gardens, the care of plants and the principles of polite conversation should I ever meet Lords from the Palace.'

The Doctor gestured at the sky. 'Out there are millions upon millions of worlds of every kind, populated by as many different beings. Sometimes even I'm overwhelmed by the complexity of it all.'

Green-8's eyes glowed. 'I think I would like to see these other worlds. Somewhere that was not field or garden. Somewhere... different.'

There was a terrible sense of melancholy in his flat words.

'Maybe you'll get the chance sooner than you think,' the Doctor said gently. 'But first I must find out what's gone wrong on this world.'

'You mean something unplanned is occurring?'

'Yes. There are inexplicable flaws in these perfect gardens of yours, and no properly organised society with the resources this one evidently commands would permit the treatment of these "scavengers" that you describe. You mentioned "Lords from the Palace". Who are they?'

'They are the rulers of Esselven.'

'"Esselven" is the name of this world?'

'Yes...' Green-8 hesitated. 'The name was never included in my core memory, but it is the name the Lords use, so it must be correct. It is in their service that we tend the fields and gardens. Most live in the Summer Palace, sometimes also called by them the Palace of Aldermar.'

'I see. And what are these Lords like?'

'Like you, except in the style of their dress. They do not visit Green Sector often. I wish I could speak to them. Perhaps they could explain the purpose of my existence. But the words will not come...'

The Doctor frowned. 'How long have you been operational, Green-8? Were you here when this world was first settled?'

'I was assembled in the Red Sector workshops, Doctor, to replace an older model that was beyond repair. I took over its assigned functions. That was 76,427 work periods ago. I have no direct memory of a time before that.'

'And how long are work periods?'

Green-8 paused. 'I do not know how you can determine this without experiencing a full work period for yourself. Work periods are used to regulate the activity of scavenger labourers. They are based on a unit called a "Standard Day" which…' Green-8 paused again, then continued in a curious tone: 'A unit which I now realise does not seem to have any relevance here. Where did it originate?'

'"Standard days" must relate to the planet from which your Lords, presumably the builders of this place, originally came,' the Doctor suggested. 'Here you have no day/night cycle and probably no seasons either. Most worlds turn about their own axis, causing a regular cycle of light and dark as their parent sun is hidden from view. The sun appears to rise over a point on the horizon, crosses the sky and disappears behind the opposite horizon.'

'A sun that moves in the sky of its own accord,' said Green-8, managing to impart a sense of awe to his mechanical tones. 'That would be… most wonderful to see.'

The Doctor smiled. 'Assuming your standard day is close to the mean of the tolerable parameters for humanoid life forms, and also allowing that human-settled worlds commonly have years between three and four hundred days long and taking an average, then I estimate that you have been functioning for nearly two hundred and twenty years.'

'Is that a long time?'

The Doctor raised a sardonic eyebrow. 'It would make you quite a youngster where I come from. But by the standards of most living beings, yes it is a long time. It's not surprising that you have developed a personality of your own.'

'For most of that time I did not think of myself as an individual entity,' Green-8 admitted. 'I interpreted instructions according to my programme, nothing more. I recall the actions I took, but now I do not feel as though I was truly there.'

'Because you were not completely sentient then. Do you know what "sentient" means?'

'It is defined in my linguistic files as the ability to feel through senses, or to be capable of experiencing feeling.'

'Exactly. You could perceive the external world through your senses from the day you were activated, but only now are you responding to those sensations with feelings and emotions of your own.'

'So I am sentient, self-aware… alive? Even though I am a machine?'

The Doctor replied with all the conviction he could put into his words. 'You are alive if you think you are! You are alive if you feel the need to go beyond the limitations of your programming, to ask questions, to be inquisitive, to search for the indefinable, to attempt the impossible!'

'I think I wish to do all those things,' Green-8 said.

The Doctor spread his hands wide expressively. 'Then you know the answer to your question.'

The robot trembled as though caught up in a maelstrom of indecision. 'I see so many possibilities. But what shall I do first?'

'Well, you could start by helping me with my problem, which may also answer some of your own questions. I'd also like to meet with these Lords of yours, but first I must get back to the gardens. I have a lost friend I must find. Knowing her she's probably got herself into trouble by now.'

'Is finding this friend important?' Green-8 asked.

'To me, yes. It's my duty to find her.'

'Is "duty" the same as an operational programme?'

'No. You can be taught duty, but it is more than a set of instructions. A sense of duty is part of a moral framework that most intelligent beings evolve to help them function properly and interact with each other. It acknowledges that you have a responsibility for the wellbeing of others. I would be failing myself and my friend if I did not do everything I could to find her.'

'Her presence and function are important to your own state of being? She is an efficient fellow-worker?'

The Doctor snorted. 'Peri is opinionated, annoying, impatient, quarrelsome and stridently American... and I would miss her dearly. Not that I'd admit it to her face.'

'Interrelationships between sentient beings are evidently more complicated than I imagined,' Green-8 said. 'But I will help you, Doctor. It seems to be the... right thing to do. But returning to the Red Sector gardens will not be easy.'

'Couldn't I go the way I came? You send produce back to the gardens via your underground railway, I assume. I could hide out in one of the containers.'

'Each shipment is inspected as soon it arrives in Red Sector. You are certain to be discovered.'

'Then I'll walk back above ground,' the Doctor said determinedly. 'It can't be that far. Judging by the curve of that horizon this is a small world.'

'The robots in the Red Sector gardens will be alert for your presence. If they do not find you in the sub-levels they will search the gardens. They will not give up until they are certain you are no longer in Red Sector.'

'Nevertheless, I must go. Can you describe the quickest route, or do you have a map of the way?'

'A map?'

'A scaled-down symbolic representation of an area of landscape.'

'I understand the concept. I know the relative positions of the surface features of this hemisphere of Esselven, but I have no physical map. I know the range and bearing of all locations I need to visit for the purposes of my work. I simply travel to them by the most direct route.'

'A useful ability, Green-8, but it's no good to me. Until I know what's out there I won't know where I need to go, or to avoid. I've no idea how far I'll have to search to find Peri. Could you draw me a map of this hemisphere showing the most prominent features?'

'I can make what you need, Doctor,' Green-8 said, then hesitated. 'But I thought... I might be able to guide you in person.'

The Doctor looked at Green-8 in surprise. 'You'd be willing to accompany me?'

'On one... condition.'

'Ahh...'

'That you tell me more of these worlds beyond the sun as we go. You see... I have talked more in this last tenth work period than I have since the day I was activated.'

The Doctor struggled to keep his voice steady, deeply moved by Green-8's admission.

'Certainly, Green-8,' he said, beaming at his new companion benignly. 'I'd be delighted to talk to you about any subject you wish. I have something of a reputation as a lecturer, you know. I think you will find the journey most instructive.'

'I'm sure I will, Doctor.'

Green-8 cut a section of plastic waterproofing sheet from a roll and laid it out on the workbench. A laser knife set to a fine low intensity beam produced a dark line on the plastic. Green-8 drew a circle with mechanical precision.

'Esselven is a sphere one hundred and seven kilometres in diameter...' he began.

Chapter Ten

Peri blinked in the glow of the motionless red sun as she and the other prisoners were herded up a ramp and out into the gardens once again. The fresh air stirred by a light breeze was a welcome relief after the heat and close humidity of the subterranean greenhouse.

They were all pushing trolleys laden with plants and saplings ready to be planted out in the open, shuffling forward as fast as their ankle hobbles allowed. Their guards led them along paths that twisted through several immaculate garden enclosures. Peri looked about her intently as they proceeded, but nothing seemed familiar. They had been brought up a different ramp from the one she had been taken down the previous 'day'. It was another obstacle to her plans. Even if she could escape, how would she find her way back to the TARDIS?

Perhaps she would simply have to keep going until she struck the great avenue. Surely she could find something of that size. Then she could work her way along it until she found the haha pit, then head back through the gardens (assuming she'd remember the way) until she found the one the TARDIS had landed in. But would the Doctor be there even if she did get back? Probably he was even now searching the gardens for her. The trouble was that they extended so far they could wander for days without meeting each other by chance. If only there was some way of making a signal he could see or hear, or even one really tall tree that she could climb.

The prisoners were directed through a gate into a garden enclosure evidently in the process of replanting. Half the beds were now freshly turned earth, while a pile of uprooted plants lay awaiting disposal. The scavengers were set to work, some taking away the old plants, others digging, the rest putting in the fresh stock. Peri made certain she stayed close to Kel and was given the same job as he was; removing plants from pots and digging them in according to an exact planting pattern already marked out on the bare earth. Fortunately it seemed that the gardeners didn't care who worked with who, as long as their allotted tasks got done.

Kel did his work with studied contempt, handling the plants roughly and ramming them into their holes. Peri worked mechanically, while surreptitiously examining every tool they used in case it might possibly cut their hobble straps. They had been given small hand trowels to use, which she had initially thought were promising if they could be sharpened. But closer inspection revealed the blades of the trowels were of some dense plastic composition which seemed unlikely to take an edge, even assuming she could smuggle one back to their underground quarters and work on it during their sleep period.

'Kel,' she asked out of the corner of her mouth, 'do the gardeners check the tools when we finish work?'

Kel frowned at her. 'What you mean?'

'Do they make sure we aren't taking any of the tools they've given us away from here. Anything we could use to cut these straps, I mean.'

'Yes. All tools counted at end of work period. Last time one was missing, workers made to take off clothes until it was found.'

Peri sighed. 'I should have known it wouldn't be as easy as that.'

She returned to her task, thinking furiously. That meant that they would have to get free out here. But how? She began casting thoughtful glances at the scavengers wearily digging over the flower beds. The blades of their spades looked like metal and they certainly had more mass behind them. If she got hold of one she could sit on the flagstone path so she had something to work against and hammer away at the hobble strap with the edge of the spade until it parted. How many blows would it take? Five, ten? It certainly couldn't be done quietly. And what likelihood was there that the gardeners would stand dumbly by in the meantime?

'Nuts!' she muttered under her breath.

Gradually her attention began to focus on their robotic captors and the tools neatly clipped to each of their base sections. Especially the shiny pair of secateurs. Now they looked like they would make short work of the hobble straps, she thought, and they'd be easy enough to conceal. If they couldn't use them to cut their hobbles while they were outside, they might even be able to smuggle them back underground at the end of the day and then cut their hobbles at leisure. No, she corrected herself, they'd *almost* cut them through. Then the next time they were let out they could make a break at the most opportune moment. It all depended whether or not the gardeners would notice if one of their own tools was missing. Surely it was worth taking the chance.

She nudged Kel. 'Listen. In a minute we're going to start fighting and then –'

'Why?' Kel asked suspiciously.

Peri groaned. 'You've never seen any prison camp escape movies have you? Look, we just pretend to fight. One of the gardeners is sure to come over to break it up. We fall against him as we struggle and one of us grabs the secateurs –'

'The sek-ka –?'

'The small cutting tool with the two curved blades. If you can snatch it tuck it into your coat. Then we let the gardener calm things down. If we get the chance we cut these straps out here today. Otherwise we take the secateurs back inside with us when we're finished here. Understand?'

Kel still looked puzzled, as though trying to get his mind around the plan. Peri didn't think he was actually stupid, just unused to adapting to new ideas. Life for the scavengers probably hadn't allowed for much beyond basic survival for a long time.

Finally Kel nodded slowly. 'We shall do this! I shall scavenge the tool from the gardener. I am Kel the quick, Kel the brave!'

His words sounded less like boasting and more like an attempt to psych himself up for the deed. Peri wondered how scared he really was under the show of bravado and stoic determination.

'Great, fine,' she said aloud. 'Just don't let him see you do it.'

Peri looked around to see where the gardeners were stationed, then deliberately flicked some earth into Kel's face. For a moment Kel looked genuinely offended, then threw a larger handful of earth back in Peri's face. Peri spluttered and wiped her eyes, realising that Kel was not particularly subtle at this sort of game.

'What d'you think you're doing?' she shouted.

'You… you clumsy slith worm!' he retorted.

'Who're you calling a worm?' Peri screamed back, and lunged at Kel.

Locked in a clinch they rolled across the freshly dug earth shouting and kicking wildly. The heads of the other scavengers turned to watch them in dumb amazement.

'Stop! Return to your work,' a gardener boomed. 'You will damage the plants!'

They continued their mock struggle, coming to rest with Peri on her back and Kel half sprawled across her, clutching her wrists as though trying to stop her from clawing at his hair. Peri saw a gardener looming over them and hissed: 'Now – roll backwards!'

Kel didn't move. She tried pushing him off her towards the oncoming machine but she couldn't shift his weight.

'Kel – now!' she gasped.

But Kel seemed unable to comply, staring into her eyes with a foolish expression on his face.

Before she could do anything further the gardener grasped Kel by the scruff of the neck and lifted him off Peri so that he dangled in mid air, his head level with its impassive face.

'You will not fight,' it warned him. 'You will not risk damaging the plants. If you fight again you will be punished. Do you understand?'

Kel nodded miserably. The gardener set him down and he dropped quickly to his knees.

'Now return to your work,' it said and rolled away.

Peri sat up and glared angrily at Kel, but he wouldn't meet her accusing, questioning gaze. He scrabbled about to find his trowel then began planting out once more, eyes fixed firmly on the rich dark earth. She stared at him. Was that a flush of embarrassment under the grime on his cheeks?

Suddenly Peri had a suspicion of what had happened and blushed herself, before forcing a wry smile. It had been an unfortunate moment for a young man, perhaps held prisoner for some time, to get into vigorous contact with a woman dressed in somewhat abbreviated clothing. Obviously he'd been distracted by an instinctive response beyond his control.

She brushed herself off and resumed her own allotted toil. Well, they'd blown that idea, at least for today. She glanced at the silent figure by her side.

'Don't worry,' she said quietly. 'I understand. It's not your fault. We'll think of another way out of here.'

Hours passed and inspiration failed to strike. Flasks of water were passed round, but there was no pause to eat. Peri wiped the stinging sweat from her eyes. Her back ached, her knees were sore and tendons down the back of her legs were knotted. She supposed it was better than breaking rocks in a quarry on a chain gang, but began to doubt that people ever did this sort of thing for fun. But if this was not to be the blueprint for the rest of her life, she'd better think of something. Anything…

'Look… There, look!'

Peri jerked her head up at the sound of the sudden exclamation that had been tinged with both fear and amazement.

One of the scavenger women who had been hauling away old plants was pointing up to the heavens. Every head in the garden, human and mechanical, turned to follow the line of her trembling finger.

Halfway to the horizon a brilliant point of light was forming in the clear sky.

Even as Peri stared at the curious phenomenon, a second point appeared beside the first, then a third. In a few seconds thirty or more of the starbursts had appeared in a tight cluster, merging slowly into a single ball of light that grew until it was too brilliant to look at directly. It was as though a second smaller but far more intense sun had come into being in the sky of Esselven.

Peri turned to Kel. 'What is it? What's happening?'

But from the expression of incredulous amazement on his face it was obvious he had no explanation.

Clear white light flooded the garden and for the first time Peri saw the true colours of the grass and flowers about her. Each leaf and stem was casting a sharply outlined shadow, filled with the reddish light of Esselven's old sun, which seemed now to be shrunken and feeble by comparison.

A fearful wailing rose up. Half the scavengers were on their knees, or covering their eyes. Beside her Kel was trembling and hiding his own face from the light. If it was brilliant to her then she realised to the locals it must be both painfully dazzling and frightening. To them the sun and sky must seem virtually unchanging. Even the gardeners couldn't cope with the new phenomenon. They were circling round the panicky scavengers trying to keep order, yet at the same time turning their own heads about jerkily in obvious confusion and indecision.

Shielding her eyes with her out-flung hand, Peri squinted upward, wondering what would come next.

As though the sky could not contain the brilliant new light, the heavens suddenly convulsed.

Dipping and rising like a storm-tossed sea, bands of light and darkness rolled out from the new sun and tore across the sky. Shockwaves blurred and rippled the deep blue void, condensing seething cloud breakers out of thin air then boiling them away again.

And from afar sounded an ominous bass rumble, as of the first peal of distant thunder. But instead of fading away, the rumbling grew louder, setting her teeth on edge.

The rumbling became a roar, a rising crescendo of raw sonic energy that beat down out of the sky and penetrated the bones and set the ground trembling. Curled over on her knees with her hands clamped to her ears, Peri saw that a shadow was rising up into the air beyond the garden walls; a grey swirling mist of earth and leaves and small branches that rolled towards them like a tidal wave, tearing up the ordered landscape as it went. Welcome to Tornado Alley, she thought grimly.

It struck the garden wall, ripping off the top courses of brick-work, and slammed into them.

Peri felt herself lifted up into the air and carried a dozen yards before she crashed into a storm-tossed bank of shrubbery. A sand-blasting wind scoured her exposed flesh and tried to force earth and grit under every fold of her clothing and into her mouth and nose and eyes. A wind-blown branch lashed across her back, driving a yelp of pain from her lips that was completely inaudible in the screaming roar of the tempest. All she could do was remain curled up like a child and suffer whatever the elements cared to do to her.

After what seemed an age the force of the wind faded away into fitful gusts. The boom of concussed air diminished into a receding rumble as the shockwave vanished over the horizon. A sort of calm descended once more on the gardens.

With trembling hands, Peri pushed aside the branch that half covered her and sat up, coughing and spitting. A silt of earth and leaves cascaded off her. She felt sick and disorientated, her ears still ringing from the thunder blast. Blinking through gritty eyes she saw that the sky above, grey-shrouded with suspended dust, still rippled and shivered erratically. The shimmering, inexplicable fireball continued to challenge the red sun with its harsh light, but the worst seemed to be over, at least for now.

The garden was a mess; littered with scattered bricks and branches and the shredded and now unidentifiable remains of plants. Over all this was a grey-brown coat of fine earth and grit.

Still feeling dazed, Peri looked round for Kel, and was relieved to see him a little way off trying to get to his feet. He looked confused and shaken, but seemed physically unharmed. The other scavengers were also stirring, but most seemed too shocked or perhaps too frightened to try to stand.

The garden robots were hardly in better shape. One was rolling round in a confused circle scrabbling to clean its eye lenses, while the others had been toppled onto their sides by the blast. One lay almost within reach of Peri. Its arms were flailing about as it tried to right itself and it was making disjointed buzzing, croaking noises. I supposed even robots can get shaken up, she thought.

Then some sense penetrated her still confused thoughts and her eyes focused on the tools clipped to the robot's torso.

Peri rolled over once to get to the side of the stricken machine, snatched the secateurs from their clip and then rolled away again. It hadn't even been aware of her, and nobody else in the garden, man or machine, was in any state to notice what she was doing – for about another minute, anyway.

She sat up and hunched over, pulling her feet apart so the hobble strap binding her ankles was taut. She caught the strap between the blades of the secateurs and squeezed the handles with all her strength. The plastic strap was tough, but the secateurs were as sharp as she had hoped. Three cuts and the strap parted.

On her hands and knees she crawled over to Kel, caught hold of his hobble strap and began cutting. He looked at her as though not understanding what she was doing.

'Come on, get with it!' she snapped, her voice sounding curiously distant through the ringing of her ears. 'We'll never get a better chance!'

Realisation dawned on Kel and for the first time she saw him smile.

His strap parted and they both climbed unsteadily to their feet. In a stiff-legged run, the remains of the straps flapping about their ankles, they passed through the garden gate and were gone.

Chapter Eleven

The neatly drawn and annotated map of the sunside of Esselven lay on the workbench. The Doctor studied it intently.

Green-8 had scaled the map in kilometres, he noted. The use of such an ancient measure of distance suggested that the settlers of this world had either come from Earth or from an old Earth colony world. This established their position somewhere in Peri's future, but since many thousand such worlds would eventually exist, it did little to fix their exact location. Perhaps he would learn more when he made contact with the Lords themselves.

On the tiny world of Esselven, one degree of latitude was the equivalent of just under a kilometre on the surface, hence the entire globe was less than 350 kilometres in circumference. The distance from equator to pole was only a little over 80 kilometres. A person could easily walk around the world along a great circle route in four or five days.

At the North Pole, actually a temperate place on Esselven, was the Summer Palace where the Lords of Esselven lived. The area around the Pole down to the equivalent of about 80 degrees north contained the Palace's private grounds and support facilities. It was known to the robots as 'Blue Sector'. Green-8 had never been there, but understood it was administered by the Lords' personal servants and robot guards. From the edge of Blue Sector down to 30 degrees north was Red Sector, the garden zone in which the TARDIS had landed.

'Is that entire area laid out with formal gardens?' the Doctor asked.

'Possibly more, Doctor,' Green-8 said. 'It is many work periods since I was last there. The gardens are continually being extended to the east and west, though they do not reach all the way to the twilight boundary.'

'Even so that would make an area of about two thousand square kilometres of garden. No wonder we didn't meet any of your Lords earlier. Don't you think that's something of a horticultural excess?'

'I have never thought to make such a judgement, Doctor. The Red Sector machines are programmed to maintain and extend the gardens as I am programmed to tend the fields and produce a certain variety of crops. Are there no gardens of this size on other worlds?'

'Not many,' the Doctor said.

Green-8 had marked a grid of grand avenues such as the one they had already seen, running north-south and east-west. From this and the location of the gardeners' underground depot and tube train station, the Doctor was able to get a picture of the likely area to search for Peri – assuming she was still at liberty. Green-8 admitted that if she had encountered any Red Sector gardeners, she would most likely be taken for a scavenger and dealt with accordingly. Unfortunately Green-8 had no access to detailed files on scavengers currently in detention, so he could not tell if Peri was amongst them.

Thinking of Peri made the Doctor impatient to set out after her. But he counselled himself that learning as much as possible about Esselven now might save precious time later.

The belt straddling the equator and reaching from approximately 30 degrees north to 30 south was Green Sector; the farming lands. Green-8's depot was in the north-east quadrant of this zone, a little over 10 degrees from the equator.

South of this was Yellow Sector. This was an area of higher ground similar in extent to Red Sector, but with a colder climate leaving it perpetually snow-covered. At the South Pole itself was the Winter Palace. Green-8 knew little about the Lords who lived there, since Green Sector did not supply them with produce.

'Why not?' the Doctor asked. 'You must have enough to spare with all these fields.'

'We have, but the tubeway leading to the Winter Palace does not operate, so no produce is sent there.'

Green-8 had marked a grid of subterranean tube train lines on the map. A single line connected both of the Palaces along the central meridian of the sunside of Esselven. Along the way it branched out into secondary lines that connected underground stations at the main depots of the Red, Green and Yellow sectors, such as the one into which the Doctor had inadvertently dropped.

'Is the tubeway damaged?' the Doctor asked.

'Not to my knowledge, Doctor. There are more game animals in Yellow Sector. Perhaps these supply the needs of the Winter Palace.'

The Doctor's brow furrowed. 'When did all this happen?'

'It was before I was activated, but the date was loaded into my core memory. It occurred over 103,000 work periods before I was activated.'

'About three hundred years… Go on. Do you know why the line to the Yellow Sector was closed?'

'No, Doctor. Produce shipments were simply discontinued. I know no more, except that the section of line that runs through my sector must be maintained in case it is ever needed again.'

'So it is still functional.'

'Yes.'

'Don't the Lords ever use any of the tubeways?'

'Not to my knowledge, Doctor. I am sure that if a Lord had passed through my sector I would have been informed in case he wished to inspect this facility.'

'Have any Lords ever officially inspected this place?'

'Never while I have been supervisor.'

The Doctor looked at Green-8 thoughtfully. 'Do you know anything about the time before you were activated? Is there anything at all about the people who terraformed and settled Esselven?'

Green-8 hesitated, as though checking his data banks.

'I have nothing in my memory files about such things. I supposed Esselven must have a point of origin, as a plant has a seed, I have never thought of the matter before. To my knowledge little has changed here since the tubeway to the Winter Palace was closed.'

The Doctor rubbed his chin. 'That event seems to be significant. I wonder why?' He looked at the map again. 'Do you know anything about the dark side of Esselven?'

'No, Doctor. Except that it is from there that the rivers flow and where scavengers live.'

'You seem to have an extraordinary number of mysteries on this little world of yours. But now I must try to find Peri. From your map it looks like it's about 40 kilometres from here to the Red Sector depot and the area Peri went missing. If it's not safe to use the underground, then I can walk that far within one of your work periods. Are you still willing to come with me?'

'Yes, Doctor. I can assign routine tasks here while I am gone. But if we encounter any Red Sector gardeners my presence will not protect you.'

'Perhaps I can pass myself off as one of your Lords.' He lifted his chin and looked down his nose. 'I believe I can assume the necessary degree of hauteur and I certainly possess the necessary antecedence.'

'But you do not have the correct costume, Doctor. They will also wonder where your Blue Sector attendants are, and if you engage in conversation, your lack of knowledge of the Palace ways will soon be revealed.'

'I'll just have to keep out of sight, then.'

'That will considerably delay our progress and impede the search for your friend.'

'I know!' the Doctor snapped irritably. 'But if I cannot pass myself off as a Lord and will be imprisoned as a scavenger, what else is there?'

The Doctor paced up and down frowning, looking around the lofty shed for inspiration. Suddenly his eye settled on the racks of spare parts that rose beside the bench-mounted machine tools. A broad smile of almost childish glee lit up his face.

'Perhaps there is another alternative, if you'll lend me the use of your facilities…'

A little while later in that eternal day, the Doctor's project was well under way. Mopping his forehead with a handkerchief, the Doctor stepped back from the workbench to inspect his progress. Green-8, who had been attending to routine matters about the depot, came up to his side.

'How does it look?' the Doctor asked.

'Most convincing, Doctor. I would never have thought of such a deception.' The robot hesitated. 'Perhaps I lack imagination.'

'Nonsense! You just haven't had much chance to exercise it yet. You wait and see what –'

He realised Green-8 had suddenly turned his head, as though listening to something beyond the range of the Doctor's hearing.

'My subordinate units are reporting something strange is happening,' Green-8 said quickly. 'I must go outside –'

With the Doctor in curious attendance, Green-8 passed between a pair of the arching beams that supported the depot roof and out onto the apron of concrete that ran between the structure and the surrounding fields.

'What is it –' the Doctor began, then saw for himself.

Low down in the north-west a white ball of light was blazing in the sky, which was already billowing like a sheet in the wind. The Doctor watched the phenomenon with intense curiosity for perhaps ten seconds before understanding dawned.

'Get your units under cover!' he shouted to Green-8, over a growing boom and rumble of displaced air.

All the robots close to the depot had taken shelter by the time a dark shadow raced across the fields, driving a plume of earth before it. The depot roof shivered and groaned under the impact of the shockwave. Dust billowed in through the open sides and the light from the skylights dimmed to a brown glow. The very ground underfoot seemed to be trembling. Loose objects were shaken from shelves. The Doctor clasped his hands over his ears to shut out the thunderous noise. In such a situation one could only wait and hope.

Gradually the wind and noise diminished. The bow wave of the shock front passed and the storm blast faded away. The depot roof ceased its ominous creaking.

The Doctor unclasped his hands from his ears and beamed at Green-8. 'That could have been worse,' he said brightly, brushing the dust from his shoulders.

Cautiously they went back outside.

The green and golden fields had been reduced to flattened tangles of broken stalks, ruffled by gusts from random eddies left in the wake of the storm wind. The sky was sickly yellow with suspended dust, but through the pall the distant fireball still shone brilliantly.

Green-8 almost reeled at the sight of his ruined crops and then at the alien luminance in the sky. He somehow contrived to suggest confusion on his immobile face. 'I have never seen a light in the sky other than the sun, or known a wind to cause such damage. What was it, Doctor?'

The Doctor was looking grim, wiping dust from his brow with his handkerchief while judging distances and bearings by eye. 'Something rather disturbing, I'm afraid. At least it's not centred over the place Peri went missing. If she was in the open I hope she had the sense to get under cover before the shockwave arrived.'

'But what was it?' Green-8 pleaded.

'Unless it's a most obscure natural phenomenon, I'd say it was the fireball of some kind of mass-conversion weapon – though it seems to be taking an unusually long time to disperse. I wonder why…?' He looked up at the still rippling, heaving sky. 'Do you realise there's a force field up there?'

'I have no knowledge of any such thing, Doctor.'

'Information probably not considered necessary for horticultural purposes. But it's there all right, about ten to fifteen kilometres up. It might be for maintaining atmospheric integrity, but it also serves as a physical barrier – which somebody has just tested rather severely.' His eyes flashed at Green-8. 'Your world is under attack!'

Green-8 seemed locked in mechanical indecision for a moment, then said: 'I shall switch to the general broadcast channels…'

He was silent for half a minute, then said: 'Considerable damage has been reported across central Red and Green Sectors… main underground facilities are still functional, though there has been some damage to the primary tubeway tunnel… this is under repair. Some scavengers are reported to have escaped from working parties during the temporary breakdown in supervision. A general alert has been sent out for their capture to all secondary main-tenance posts. Now a request is being made from Blue Sector for damage reports and repair assessments…' Green-8 turned to the Doctor. 'I feel I must obey this request. The Lords themselves require this. I could choose to do otherwise, but it would be like –'

'Abandoning your duty?' the Doctor suggested.

'Yes. You understand?'

'I do. In any case, you cannot leave your post now without it being noticed, which would be no good for either of us.'

'That is true. But once repairs have been instigated and the reports made, I can join you. It should take no more than one work period. If you complete your disguise, will you wait for me before beginning the search for your friend?'

111

'I will wait for you... but my plans may have to change.'

'What do you mean?'

'I will try to find Peri when we pass through Red Sector, but I'll be going on to the Summer Palace. If you and your fellow robots know nothing about a planetary force field, or who might be trying to break it down, then I must find somebody who does as soon as possible. The most likely place for the controls to be located would be in or near one of the Palaces.' He frowned as a new thought struck him. 'Can't you simply send a message directly to either one of the Palaces, saying I'm here and need to talk to somebody in authority? It would save a lot of time.'

'I can only communicate with my fellow coordinators and they would follow their programming and regard you as a scavenger,' Green-8 said. 'I have no access to any direct channel to either north or south Blue Sectors. It does not normally matter as all reports are monitored. If more information is required or instructions are to be issued they will do so. It is not for a field robot to presume to initiate communication with a Lord or his personal servants.'

'Isn't it?' the Doctor said angrily. 'Well perhaps that state of affairs won't last for much longer. Your Lords seem to have let things get badly out of hand here.'

'I regret that I cannot suggest any faster means of contacting them.'

'Well, we may be lucky and meet one of your Lords in the gardens along the way. Although...' The Doctor lapsed into scowling thought for a moment, then continued half to himself: 'they don't make inspection tours or use the tubeways or powered ground transport, as far as we know...'

'Is that significant?'

'Perhaps. I'm beginning to wonder if your Lords really appreciate what's happening on Esselven.'

'But the Lords control everything, Doctor,' said Green-8, sounding shocked at the suggestion. 'All primary directions come from the Palace.'

'Perhaps, but who issues the orders? Do you know the personal name of any single Lord who has ever issued direct commands to you?'

'No, Doctor,' Green-8 admitted reluctantly. 'I do not.'

'Well, don't worry. We'll find out what's going on here as soon as possible and see about putting it right. And maybe you'll get an answer to those questions of yours at the same time.'

They went back inside. The Doctor resumed work on his disguise while Green-8 coordinated his robots' efforts in repairing the storm damage. As he worked, the Doctor turned over the possible consequences of his change of plan.

An impatient part of him wanted to set off after Peri immediately, but his more logical side knew it would be foolish to go unprepared. On balance it was sensible to complete his disguise first.

But now he had other considerations which might have to take precedence even over Peri's safety.

Esselven was threatened by some external power that could deploy weapons of mass destruction. The planetary shield seemed to be holding for the moment, but it might not withstand another attack. In the circumstances it was vital that he discover who, if anybody, actually ran Esselven. Of course, he rationalised, the same agency might control the Red Sector robots, which might then be directed to locate Peri. In the long run, making for the Palace could actually be the best thing he could do for her.

Perhaps.

Maybe what he did next would make no difference either way and Peri was perfectly safe. Or perhaps she was already... No, he would not consider that possibility. He resolved to head for the Palace.

Some of his former incarnations might have decided to search for his missing companion first in such a situation. But the personality that came with this body was more rational and less outwardly sentimental. He knew he was doing the right thing.

He just hoped Peri would understand.

Chapter Twelve

Benedek and Oralissa walked together in the Palace gardens.

With what felt to Oralissa like indecent haste, an understanding had been reached between her parents and their distinguished visitors that they would each spend some time alone with her. By some unknown means (had they drawn lots for the privilege?) it had been decided that Benedek should be the first, leaving Stephon to enjoy the company of her father as they took a ride about the estate.

The thrill of their original compliments had faded, and Oralissa felt renewed resentment that she should be a mere tool of state-craft. Of course she was flattered by their attentions. Nobody had ever spoken to her like that before. And she supposed both men were quite good-looking, even Duke Stephon, though he was nearly as old as her father.

Unfortunately the walk with Benedek was not going well.

After his initial eloquent outburst, Benedek seemed to have become tongue-tied and embarrassed in her presence, making his youth more apparent. He walked awkwardly by her side and smiled a lot (he had very deep blue eyes, she noticed) but seemed unable to continue what he had begun. Feeling her own embarrassment mounting in response, Oralissa tried to encourage conversation by introducing some neutral topic. Fortunately she did not have to look far for inspiration.

'Wasn't that a strange storm we had?' she said. 'That odd light was so bright and it stayed in the sky for so long. And that wind was so strong! It blew over several trees. See…' she pointed across a lawn to where gardeners were removing fallen branches. 'My maid was frightened but I wasn't. It was wild and exciting and different. I'm sure nothing like that ever happened here before. What do you think?'

Benedek looked at her gratefully.

'Yes. It was… very strange,' he agreed. He didn't sound that interested.

'Do you have such weather in far Corthane?' she prompted.

He brightened slightly. 'Yes! I mean, no… well, we have snow storms, of course. They can confine us to our dwelling for days at a time.'

'I wouldn't like to be shut up inside for so long.'

'Oh, but it is no hardship,' Benedek assured her, warming to his subject. 'The citadel has many chambers in which to find diversions in games and music. In the winter the fires burn hot, so we do not suffer, even if the icicles hang from the eves to the length of a man's arm. And when the storm abates, there is such sport to be had outside about the lakes and forests…'

Benedek's shyness retreated as he spoke of his own land and Oralissa relaxed. It was oddly reassuring that she had to take the initiative. If he was destined to be her husband, then she would remember this time when she had to put him at his ease. She would not simply do what fate decreed. Things could be different.

Suddenly Benedek stopped himself abruptly. 'Princess, I have been babbling foolishly. Forgive me.'

'You have been most entertaining company, Prince Benedek, once you overcame your… shyness.'

Benedek blushed. 'It is your presence that stops my mouth and turns me into a simpering idiot. What I said when I first beheld you –'

'I recall the words.'

'They were from the heart. If I may make so bold again… you are most beautiful.'

'I am most… flattered that you find my appearance pleasing.'

'And do I… please you?' Benedek asked anxiously.

Oralissa smiled. Her suitor really was still a boy in many respects. It made her feel quite mature.

'Your features are not unpleasing,' she admitted. 'But appearance is not all there is when considering matters such as we both know are being weighed here 'tween yourself and the Duke.'

'But it may be a start?'

'It may,' she agreed.

'Then tell me what else you require of me and I shall do it!' Benedek said. 'Send me on a quest for some token to prove my love!'

Love! He had said the word already. Could she truly have inspired such an emotion in him so quickly, or was this just some fragile whimsy spun out of the impetuous fancies of youth? Such a declaration was in keeping with the romance she had yearned for, but now it inspired only caution. She would not let her heart be won over by mere words.

'You seem already to have decided the matter in your mind, Prince Benedek. Are you sure you wish to learn no more about me as a potential lifemate, except that you find me pleasing to the eye? Though this alliance may be born out of political need, would it not be pleasant to find that we are also suited by nature? That knowledge cannot come out of such a brief acquaintance as we have thus far enjoyed. Grant me a few hours more, I beg you, before you talk again of "love".'

Benedek floundered, realising he had let his enthusiasm get the better of him.

'I apologise most humbly, Princess. Let us talk of any matter but love or alliances, so we may learn of our likes and dislikes by small measures.'

She bowed her head and he smiled and they walked on.

As they rounded a hedge, Oralissa saw three mechanicals moving along a path a little way from them, heading in a purposeful manner away from the Palace. In a few seconds they had vanished between the trees, but she had seen enough to cause her to halt in surprise.

'Oh!' she exclaimed. 'I have never seen mechanicals of that kind before.'

'How do you mean, Princess?'

'Did you not see? They were more compact and man-shaped, and had legs instead of wheels. There were packs of some kind fastened to their backs. And what were those devices they were carrying? Short staffs with curious protuberances. They did not look like gardening implements.'

'I cannot say I noticed much by way of such details,' Benedek said. 'Is it important?'

Oralissa felt the moment slipping away as her own attention wavered. One hardly noticed mechanicals normally. Like other servants you expected them to stay unobtrusively in the background until called for. But this was different! She felt it important to hold onto that fact. She looked at Benedek waiting patiently by her side. There was no sign of curiosity on his face.

'But you did see they were different from the gardeners?'

'I suppose they were. Is that so strange?'

'No, just different…' Again Oralissa felt her line of thought fragmenting. Why did it matter? Caught up by a strange sense of desperation, she said: 'Do you have many types of mechanical in Corthane?'

Benedek blinked, as though baffled by the question. Then he said slowly: 'No, we have no mechanicals in Corthane.'

Oralissa felt as though she was moving her thoughts against a flowing river that was trying to carry them in another direction.

'So… you have never seen mechanicals before you came here?'

'No, I suppose I have not.'

'And you are not in the least measure curious about them?'

Benedek smiled and shrugged. 'They are just servants, are they not? What is there to be curious about?'

Yes, they were just servants, Oralissa thought, but he should have been more interested in them. Surely that was simply human nature. Why did he not ask to inspect them or wonder how they functioned – though Oralissa acknowledged that she herself could not have told him that. Were all people of Corthane as reserved, or had his evident infatuation with her blinded him to any other new experiences?

'I wonder that you have accepted them so easily, that is all,' she said.

They walked on, chatting inconsequentially. Yet though outwardly calm, within Oralissa was deeply disturbed. An idea she couldn't put sense to was struggling to come to the front of her mind. But even as it struggled, she feared the nameless thing would be buried by the normality and sameness of her life. The endless sameness…

Alone in her room that night, with the curtains drawn to shut out the all-pervasive sun, she wrote down her questions, trying to fix them in her thoughts by giving them physical form.

What caused the light in the sky and the storm wind to blow?

What is the nature and purpose of the new mechanicals?

Why is Prince Benedek so easy in the presence of mechanicals when he claims they have none such like them in his home-land?

She chewed the end of her pen after writing the last question. It was not just Benedek who was incurious about the storm. She hadn't heard anybody wonder about it. As long as the mechanicals tidied up the damage it seemed to have been forgotten. Was she the only one who thought it interesting. Or at least different.

How she longed things to be different!

A part of the unsayable idea rose almost to the surface of her mind again. There was something else, but what?

Almost unconsciously she found herself writing:

Who made the mechanicals? Where did they come from?

She looked at the line first in wonder and then fear.

It was a question that had never occurred to her before in her life.

Chapter Thirteen

Judd glared in disbelief at the screen that showed the mirror-like shield still enclosing the tiny world. No one else in the lander cabin dared utter a sound, but started rigidly at the instruments before them.

It had held!

Gigatonnes of destructive force expended against it and it remained impossibly, defiantly, in place. A grudging admiration for their technical ingenuity vied with frustration in his mind. If the Esselvanians had developed something that powerful before the invasion, he would never have taken their world. Clearly it was a refinement the refugees had made to the basic field that maintained their biosphere. It was predictable that they would not have been idle. They had had a year to strengthen their defences and must have known he would track them down eventually. Well that was one more prize for him to claim when he captured Hathold and his people.

A little patience, that was all it would take.

Hadn't he been patient before, while he watched for an opportunity to make his name in the military...

While he waited he had reviewed the lives of great political and military leaders in history across many worlds, learning from their triumphs and their mistakes. Gradually he formulated his own theory of command.

Always lead from the front.

In fact, ever since the dawn of total war and weapons of mass destruction, it had been little more dangerous to serve on the front line as to cower in a bunker back on the homeworld. But those you commanded respected you more and even your enemies grudgingly acknowledged what was perceived as a show of courage in their opponents. In fact from Judd's observations, bravery was mostly a matter of keeping your head in situations while others around were losing theirs. But a demonstration of this virtue was necessary to achieve the goal he had set himself, so he became known as a courageous officer.

Be strong in all things.

Be as quick and forceful to give praise as to condemn, but give each only where it was due.

Never show doubt.

People, Judd had discovered, were naturally uncertain beyond the fixed routine of their lives. They wanted to be led. Judd was never uncertain, except for the most minor matters or finely balanced questions of strategy. And when he made a decision he followed it through to the end at whatever cost.

Judd's chance of glory finally came when the colony on Deltor 5, the habitable moon of a gas giant world in Zalcrossar's outer system, deposed its governor and declared independence. Judd arranged that the potential threat the rebels posed to the safety of Zalcrossar itself was overestimated, ensuring that there would be no diplomatic solution to the problem. When the decision to retake the colony by force was taken, there was no question as to the best man to spearhead the operation.

Judd led his forces with the ruthless efficiency that would become his byword. He re-took the rebel strongholds with speed, minimum casualties amongst his own men and negligible collateral damage. He ensured certain documents were discovered that suggested some of the rebel leaders, now all conveniently dead, had been contemplating building missiles to attack Zalcrossar itself.

On his return home, Judd was acclaimed a national hero…

Yes, patience had served him before and would do so again.

Judd was about to order a second barrage when the captain's voice came to him in a tone of guarded excitement: 'Protector, the *Tarkon* reports a point of instability has developed in the force shield.'

A little patience…

'Show me!'

Images relayed from the *Tarkon* appeared on Judd's monitors showing infrared and decimetre radar scans. The data was combined in a computer-generated contour grid plotting the still rippling surface of the planetoid's shield. In the very centre of the night side the grid was shifting and swirling as though delineating the formation of a whirlpool in a storm-tossed sea. Under high magnification a depression could be seen opening at the focus of the disturbance. Even as Judd watched the grid lines at the base of the depression stretched and vanished. A tunnel through the shield to the surface!

Of course, that was the logical place to site a planned discontinuity in the shield, where there would be no danger of direct solar radiation reaching the surface. The attack must have accidentally triggered the opening sequence… unless those inside were trying to escape.

Aloud he said: 'How large is the discontinuity?'

'Four metres across, Protector,' replied one of the scanning team.

Judd frowned. 'Too small for anything but a service pod.'

'A moment, Protector… Yes! The aperture is evidently unstable, but it is slowly enlarging. It is now reading four point three metres… still growing.'

'How long until a lander can pass though?'

'Assuming a steady rate of growth… five to six minutes, Protector.'

'Captain,' Judd said. 'The moment the discontinuity is large enough the strike force goes in. Meanwhile, all ships are to maintain the utmost vigilance in case any vessel from the planet attempts to leave. Remember, I want any occupants taken alive. Continue probing the shield for any other discontinuities. All weapons batteries to standby –'

'Protector,' the *Valtor's* captain interrupted, 'Mr Dynes' ship has just broken hull lock… it's making a powered descent towards the planetoid. He appears to be heading for the discontinuity.'

'What? Put a force lock on him – no, cancel that! Let him go down.'

'But Protector, if there's a spaceport below the discontinuity and it's defended, won't they fire upon him?'

Judd smiled grimly. 'I'm sure Mr Dynes knows the risks. His appearance will tell them nothing they cannot already know. If he draws some of their fire it means less for us. Let him get his exclusive if he can.'

Dexel Dynes' face was set as he drove the *Stop Press* at maximum speed towards the hole in the shield. He was motivated neither by bravery or bravado. He knew exactly what he was doing.

Of course bravery was an admirable quality when other people demonstrated it in a newsworthy situation. Viewers liked to see examples of bravery. It helped maintain their naive faith in what they believed to be the essential goodness of human nature. Yes, there was nothing like a bit of selfless bravery, which could always be pumped up into 'an heroic act', to sell reports.

And what he was doing was certainly nothing like bravery.

He was taking a calculated risk to obtain the material necessary for his report, and he had every intention of being around to enjoy the rewards. It would not be the first time he had piloted his ship into a battle zone to get the best story.

The *Stop Press* was smaller than Judd's landing craft and highly manoeuvrable. It also possessed a reinforced radiation and particle shield which would protect him from weapon fire at least for a few minutes. He was certain he could stay out of trouble that long, and then Judd's force would be coming through the shield and the defenders would have other things to worry about.

He had to be on the other side of the shield to deploy the DAVE units to cover the landing, and he had to direct them in person. The units he left on Judd's ship would continue on automatic, but he could not trust the recording of a complex high visual impact action event to computer programmes. This was going to be the most exciting thing he had reported for over a year, and it would put his series on Judd right back at the top of the ratings.

Wasn't that worth taking a little risk?

The *Stop Press* skimmed the surface of the shield. Ripples still disturbed its mirrored perfection, rolling across his line of flight in slow heavy waves in an eerie parody of fluid motion, making him feel like an insect skating over the surface of a pond.

His instruments told him the opening was fast approaching, though it was invisible to his eyes.

He applied braking thrusters even as he lifted the *Stop Press*'s nose. Gaining altitude he saw the funnel mouth of the discontinuity ahead amid the swirling waves of force. No, it wasn't a pond he was flying over…

'Record!' he told the ever present DAVE at his shoulder. 'I'm about to pass through the force shield protecting the deposed King of Esselven's last hiding place. Mine's probably the first ship in a year to come this way. Judd's attack has opened a small and very unstable hole in the shield. It looks like a whirlpool in a stormy sea of liquid mercury, shining with a ghostly radiance in the starlight. It's going to be a tight fit. What sort of reception is waiting for me on the other side I'll know in just a few seconds…'

He made an arcing roll, centred the opening on the sighting scope of his flight display and plunged downwards. The *Stop Press*'s stubby aerofins cleared the sides of the force vortex with centimetres to spare. Then he was gone.

Chapter Fourteen

Peri wiped the sweat from her eyes and slumped back against the brickwork.

'Hold on!' she said wearily. 'I've got to rest for a minute.'

They were huddled in the shelter of a bushy shrub with variegated red and yellow leaves which grew up against a garden wall. Kel glanced at her with a trace of impatience. He looked as though he could keep going for hours. There seemed to be boundless stamina in his wiry body. But he did not argue with her decision, apparently accepting her leadership since she'd helped him escape from the gardener's slave party.

The fireball, or whatever it was, had slowly faded away over about an hour and a half by Peri's reckoning, though she knew her time sense was getting badly disjointed. They'd covered more ground since then. At least the sky had stopped rippling – that had really begun to frighten her. Now, apart from the dust layered over everything and the scattered damage, things looked much as they had before. The red sun blazed unchallenged in a clear sky, still giving the impression that they were in the middle of a lazy summer afternoon. Perhaps it was a shade lower that when she'd first seen it, however long ago that had been.

There was really no good way of measuring time by one's surroundings here. She looked at her wristwatch again for reassurance and saw Kel glance at it in fascinated incomprehension.

The apparent lowering of the sun was also an illusion as far as signalling the end of the eternal day. It wasn't going anywhere, they were. Esselven was so small that a few hours' travel took them far enough round its surface to alter the height of the sun. Another weird and wonderful experience courtesy of travelling with a Time Lord. Peri just wished she was in a better frame of mind to enjoy it!

They were keeping the sun at their backs and making for Kel's home in the wild woods. She would have liked to try to find the Doctor or the TARDIS, but in the present state of confusion and having no idea where to start looking, that seemed a pretty hopeless task. Best to hide up for a while until things calmed down, get her bearings and then make a methodical search. One thing about the Doctor; for all his irritating ways, she knew he would never stop looking for her. It was just a matter of time until they, somehow, made contact. The trick would be to stay alive, and preferably out of the clutches of the gardeners, until then.

Peri wiped stinging sweat from her lips. Her mouth felt parched. She said: 'Kel, we've got to have food and water. Do you know where we can find some?'

Kel looked round them for a moment, peering through the leaves as though to orientate himself. Then he nodded.

'Should be fruit trees this way. C'mon.'

They proceeded in the same manner as they had done for the last few hours: moving like Indian scouts, checking the way ahead was clear, selecting the best path from one piece of cover to the next, then dashing forward in a crouching run – and ducking out of sight whenever they heard garden robots coming, of course. Peri found her ears becoming attuned to the slight hum of their drive motors and the soft crunch of gravel as their wheels rolled along pathways. They made steady progress but it was hard on the body and the nerves.

The damage left by the shockwave was both a help and hindrance. Fallen trees and walls provided more potential places to hide from the gardeners, but it also meant robots turning up anywhere to assess the damage. Having seen how assiduously they tended their creations, Peri thought it likely that all the robots that could be spared were being deployed in the gardens. Unfortunately she had no idea how many that was, nor the extent of the area of damage, so she could not estimate how many they were likely to encounter.

There was apparently some regular relationship which Kel understood between the purely ornamental gardens in any one area and those laid out to orchards, canes or root crops. In a few minutes they were in an orchard biting into crisp fresh red fist-sized fruits that Kel called 'lochees', the flavour of which reminded Peri of both oranges and pears. Several of the trees had been blown down so they didn't even need to climb to pick them.

Peri ripped off a length of cloth from the remains of what had been her skirt to make a crude sling, and they stuffed it full of lochees. The next garden along contained an ornamental fountain splashing cheerfully. They drank their fill and Peri took the opportunity to quickly wash away at least some of the grime from her face. Her hair felt straggly and caked with dirt, but she knew this was not the time for the full beauty treatment. When she got back to the TARDIS she was going to soak in a hot tub for *hours!*

Kel looked at her efforts with a puzzled frown.

'I know,' Peri said as they retreated into cover once more, 'you're wondering why I bother. Well maybe in the circumstances a dirty face would be better natural camouflage, but being a little cleaner makes me feel better, right? And I need to feel good to keep on going.'

She wiped her hands down the sides of her ragged dress and tried not to think of such luxuries as full laundry service.

'Right, now we need to find some safe place to rest up. Not behind a bush or up a tree, but somewhere secure where the robots won't trip over us. Are there any barns or suchlike around here?'

Kel scratched his head. 'There be small houses.'

'What are they?'

'Houses made for Lords. Small, not like big Palace house.'

'You mean bungalows, summer houses?' Kel looked blank. 'Of course, you don't know what they are. Have you hidden in these little houses before?'

Kel looked shocked. 'Never hide in Lord's house!'

'You mean the Lords would catch you?'

'Just never go near there.'

Peri looked at him thoughtfully. 'Have you ever seen any Lords in or near these little houses?'

'No.'

'Then maybe you'd better show me one.'

Kel led her on for another half hour. At one point they passed close by several copses of taller trees artfully arranged about a small lake to give the illusion of a natural wood. It was a tempting potential hiding place, but the trees had smooth unclimbable trunks and provided little actual cover. Anyway, she wanted to see a little house. It sounded like there was some sort of taboo amongst the scavengers about going near them, so maybe the gardeners wouldn't think to look for them there.

The formal gardens ended abruptly at the edge of a large level stretch of grass the size of a sports field. Was that what it was, Peri wondered? There were some markings laid across the field but she was unable to make sense of them from where she stood and was certainly not going to walk out into the open to examine them. Kel pointed across the field to a structure of pale stone that rose over the skyline of walls and small trees.

'There is a little house.'

To Peri's eyes it looked like a small squat tower, but she couldn't make out too much detail at this distance. There was something familiar about its oddly isolated location though.

'Come on. Let's take a closer look,' she said.

'But it Lord's house,' Kel protested.

Peri smiled. 'I don't think there'll be anyone at home.'

They skirted the edge of the field and cut through a garden until they reached the base of the small hillock fringed by a screen of trees on which the building stood. It was basically a dome supported by a ring of classical looking columns inside which was a circular enclosed room. Set on top of the dome was a small turret inset with four circular windows and supporting its own domed roof; a structure which Peri seemed to remember was called a lantern.

Kel was looking round anxiously, as though expecting something to leap out at them from the trees.

'Don't worry,' she told him. 'It's not a proper house, just a folly. Something built in a garden for decoration. Let's have a look inside.'

She walked up the steps with Kel following reluctantly behind. An open arch led into the circular inner room, which was ringed with stone benches. In the centre a spiral staircase was wrapped around a pillar which rose through the domed roof. Peri beamed at the feature with approval.

'Can you imagine a gardener climbing those stairs?' she said. 'Come on.'

Kel followed her up, his steps awkward and uncertain. It was the first time he'd ever climbed a spiral staircase.

The lantern room gave a clear view of their surroundings through its windows. For the first time Peri could see the gardens stretching out all round them, though it wasn't quite the far-reaching panorama it would have been on Earth because the close horizon curved the landscape rapidly out of sight. The illusion of being on the summit of a large hill was reinforced. Still, it was a good vantage point, though even she could see no obvious end to the gardens. The most spacious grounds of the grandest stately home in England had nothing on this place. The thought occurred to her that the Doctor might be out there somewhere. If only he knew she was watching he might make some signal she could see. Of course any signals might also attract the attention of the gardeners.

Peri ran her finger across the window's deep sill leaving tracks in the dust. She looked at the floor. It was filmed over with a layer of dust and dirt, disturbed only by their footprints.

'This place doesn't look as though it's been used in years. I guess the Palace Lords don't come out here that often. We should be safe here.'

'You mean we will sleep here?' Kel looked dismayed.

'Yes, like I said.'

'But it belong to the Lords.'

'Look, you've got to start worrying a bit less about what these Lords of yours think. They don't seem to be running this place too well, letting the gardeners carry on the way they are. If I were you I'd get your people together and march right up to this Palace of theirs and tell them you've had enough of being treated like dirt. Whatever your ancestors did, you shouldn't be paying for it! Maybe, if I can find my friend, we can do something about putting things right. But the first thing you do is tell yourself you're just as good as any Lord, got that?'

Kel was looking at her open mouthed. 'Nobody ever talks of Lords as you. You have the fire inside. If you were not a girl, you would be hunter.'

'That's me, a regular rabble-rouser. And thanks for the back-hand compliment, I suppose. Now, I'm pretty well bushed, so let's get some rest. We've still got a way to go until we reach these wild woods of yours.'

They ate some more lochees and then Peri lay down on the floor, her back to the room's curved wall, folding her arms under her head. Kel did the same on the opposite side of the small room, still casting wondering glances at her. She wished she had something to serve as a mattress, but at least the stone was pleasantly cool. She yawned. The nervous tension and physical exertions of the last few hours were catching up with her. She was so tired she could probably go to sleep on a…

Peri woke with a start.

There was another body pressed against hers. A hand was sliding over the ragged remnants of her dress –

She slapped the hand and shoved the body away. Kel fell back on his elbows, looking at her in bewilderment.

'What the hell do you think you're doing?' she snapped.

'In the wild woods, you would be mated by now, be mother of great hunter's children,' he said simply. 'I will be a hunter soon. I can choose you. You are… brave and… pretty.'

Peri sighed wearily. She didn't think he'd been trying anything too serious, but the last thing she needed now was to be the object of backwoods boy's adolescent crush.

'Well where I come from that still doesn't give you the right to grope a girl! It's not polite. It's not how decent men behave!'

Kel looked confused and crestfallen. It was so easy to upset his tough guy demeanour, Peri thought. She spoke again but more gently.

'Look, I'm flattered that you like me, Kel, and I'm sure you'll be a great hit with the girls back home real soon. But I'm not on the list of potential mates. I have another life and it doesn't include marrying or mating or anything just yet, do you understand?'

Kel hung his head.

'Try not to take it personally,' Peri said, suddenly feeling older than her years as she dispensed what she hoped was wise advice. 'We can still be friends. And I won't be leaving you just yet. We've still got a whole load of escaping and general chasing around to do first. These situations the Doctor drops me in are never sorted out that easily. So we've got to just concentrate on getting through all this in one piece, right?'

Kel nodded bravely and managed a weak smile.

Hoping the tension had safely been diffused, Peri checked her watch. They'd slept for over six hours. She could have done with more, but maybe it would be best to get moving –'

'Have you been hiding up here, children? Oh..!'

The voice came from the stairs. Peri hadn't heard any footsteps, but suddenly a girl with long flowing golden hair and wearing a spotless white summer dress was standing there looking down at them in obvious surprise.

Peri and Kel scrambled to their feet, Kel shrinking back against the wall, his face contorted with dismay.

'A Lady… from Big House,' he choked out, lowering his eyes humbly.

'Stop that!' Peri snapped at him, as offended by his sudden cringing demeanour as she had been by his forwardness only minutes before. Turning to their unexpected visitor she said:'Sorry. You gave us a bit of a shock popping out of nowhere like that.'

'I do apologise, but I thought you were the children,' the girl said.'They often come up here to play. Oh dear, please forgive me. I must introduce myself. I'm Luci Longlocks.'

Gingerly Peri shook the daintily gloved hand that was offered to her, wondering who on earth had given her such a name. Still, if this was one of the Lord's set then at least she seemed friendly enough.

'I'm Peri Brown,' Peri said.'And this is Kel.'

Kel bobbed his head, still not lifting his eyes above the level of Luci's buckled shoes.

'He's a bit shy of Lords and Ladies,' Peri explained.

Luci had been looking them over with polite interest. Now she said:'Are you what the gardeners call "scavengers"?'

This is where the trouble starts, Peri thought to herself. Aloud she said lightly:'Well he is, but I'm not. I'm just a visitor. Passing through, you know. Sorry about camping out up here but we couldn't find any other shelter. Anyway it's time we were moving on. Come on, Kel.'

Luci looked disappointed. 'Do you have to go so soon? Wouldn't you like to play a game?'

'Pardon me?'

'I hoped you might like to play a game. It's such a lovely day to be outside, and games are fun and educational. Wouldn't your young friend like to play?' Luci looked Kel up and down again. 'Though I must say he looks as though he's been playing in the dirt a little too much already. I know one should indulge children, but there are limits.'

Peri blinked, trying to read some other meaning in Luci's bright open face. But she appeared to be completely earnest and straightforward. Wondering if the girl was entirely sane, Peri said: 'Well we got caught up in that storm wind a little while ago. That's how our clothes got like this.'

Luci seemed to accept the explanation at face value.

'You poor things. Then you should both go straight back home and have a proper bath.'

She radiated an air of no-nonsense propriety, Peri thought, like a nanny in training.

'We'd love to, except that the gardeners won't let us,' Peri explained. 'You see, they blame us for causing some of the damage the wind did.'

'How silly of them!' Luci exclaimed.

'Isn't it?' Peri agreed, thinking that she could have come up with stronger words to describe the gardeners' activities. 'Er, I don't suppose you could get the gardeners to leave us alone?' she added hopefully. Despite her youth and peculiar manner, the girl might have some influence over the robots.

'But I have very little to do with the gardeners except by chance,' Luci said lightly. 'I'm sure they wouldn't take any notice of me.'

'Sorry. I thought your people controlled the gardeners?'

'Oh, that's not my function at all. I look after the children.'

Peri did not quite know what to make of this statement, realising how ignorant she remained about details of the local social order. Despite appearances these people were effectively aliens from her point of view and she could only guess at what they thought was normal behaviour. Cautiously she probed further: 'But you don't have any problems with them. I mean the gardeners leave you alone when they see you?'

Luci looked surprised. 'Naturally. Why should they bother me? They know I keep the children out of their way so they can play safely and don't damage the flowers.'

'Right, of course,' Peri agreed, her mind racing. Was there a chance that Luci could help them? Whatever she was she seemed amenable, in a naive, detached fashion.

'Of course, we'd like to play with you,' Peri said slowly, drawing a sudden puzzled glance from Kel. 'But we really have to get to the edge of the wild woods. Do you know where they are?'

'Certainly. Children are not allowed to play there.'

'Of course, but we aren't children, are we? But the trouble is the gardeners don't want us to get there, so we're having to hide from them all the time. It's like a game, really.'

'I've never played games with the gardeners before,' Luci admitted. 'Children are not supposed to interfere with their work.'

'Well think of this as an adult game. Making a game out of something you've got to get done. A spoonful of sugar and all that sort of thing.'

'I beg your pardon?' Luci said.

'Never mind. Just believe that it's important that we get to the wild woods without the gardeners catching us. As there don't seem to be any children around right now for you to play with, maybe you can play this game with us?'

'It sounds a little like Hide-and-Seek and Catch-me-if-you-can,' Luci said.

'Why not call it Dodge the Gardener?' Peri suggested.

Luci beamed at them, suddenly looking completely happy.

'Of course, I'd love to play. What are the rules?'

The rules were that Luci ran ahead of Peri and Kel acting as a lookout. When the way was clear, she waved to Peri and Kel, who ran forward to join her. Luci got a point for every gardener she spotted first.

Luci played the game perfectly, running and skipping before them, dutifully checking for gardeners at the next junction, then making the signal. She didn't seem to get bored and like Kel apparently had boundless reserves of energy. Peri forced herself to keep up. They were moving faster than they had the previous 'day' and Peri wanted to put the gardens, and the gardeners, behind her as soon as possible. While they had a cooperative guide and scout they had to make the most of her. The gardeners Luci did encounter seemed to pay her little attention, but perhaps they were preoccupied with repairing the storm damage to their displays. Once, Peri saw from her place of concealment a gardener bob its head deferentially to Luci. Was it just Luci's neat dress, or did it recognise her as one of the ruling elite? Peri wondered. After all, they had originally mistaken Peri for a Palace dweller until she gave herself away. Just how discriminating were the robots?

Peri and Kel ate from their lochee reserve as they went. Luci politely refused their offers of food, saying she was 'quite full up, thank you.' Peri didn't waste much mental effort wondering at the girl's powers of endurance. She was simply grateful Luci was staying with them and playing the 'game' according to the rules. Kel seemed to have accepted Luci's presence, though he avoided eye contact and didn't speak to her directly. They passed close by a few more follies in the style of pseudo-temples and forest lodges. Luci checked inside them to see if she could find any children, but without success. They continued on. The sun lowered in the sky behind them, reddening further as it did so.

Then the gardens ended.

A jagged line of walls and hedges straggled away to either side and vanished beyond the abrupt horizon. In front of them were plots of freshly turned earth, half built walls, paths leading nowhere and newly sown lawns in the process of greening over.

'This place where gardeners make more gardens,' Kel said.

Peri looked at Luci.

'Why do you people need so many gardens anyway?' she asked tiredly. 'I mean you must have thousands of acres covered in them already. Are you going for some sort of record?'

Luci looked at her with polite incomprehension. 'There must be gardens. They're pretty and they provide children with places to play.'

She spoke as though stating a natural law.

Peri couldn't think of any rebuttal apart from the obvious, and was too tired to argue the point further.

They started across the skeletal gardens, making better time. There was less cover from them, but the whole swathe of land seemed empty of gardeners. Perhaps they had all been called away to help with the repairs, Peri thought. This area, further from the focal point of the storm, appeared to be undamaged, so presumably it had a lesser priority. As they moved out into open ground, Peri felt a cool, steady breeze in her face, and realised it must be the convection wind blowing across from the dark side of Esselven. It was a pleasant relief after the steady heat of the gardens.

The strip of newly laid-out plots was not very wide, and soon they came to the natural landscape of Esselven. A low rolling heath stretched before them, covered by scrubby grass. A boggy, reed-fringed pool filled the bottom of a deeper hollow. Dotted about the hillocks were straggling bushes.

'It all looks very untidy,' Luci declared. 'I would not care to bring children here.'

'Why not let them enjoy a bit of wilderness?' Peri said. 'Maybe camp out for the night under the... well, under the darker sky.'

'"Camping out"?' Luci asked.

'It doesn't matter. At least we can see what's ahead of us for once. Come on.'

Peri felt it made a pleasant change to walk on unplanned natural ground with all its imperfections, after the regimented and perfectly ordered gardens. They climbed to the summit of a low hill, seeing the landscape open out around them. As they reached the top, Peri became aware of a low deep droning noise –

A huge yellow earth mover was crawling along the shallow valley beyond, the sawtooth blade of its hopper slicing through the topsoil, leaving a ribbon of naked earth in its wake.

Peri and Kel dropped flat. Luci remained standing, gazing at the huge machine with polite interest. 'I do not see a gardener in the vehicle,' she announced after a few moments' study. 'I think it must be operating automatically.'

Peri breathed a sigh of relief, then frowned as she peered between tussocks of grass at the metal monster. From their vantage point they could see more of the huge machines working in the distance, while nearby other vehicles lay silent. Presumably they were manually controlled machines whose operators were currently helping with the restoration of the gardens.

'Are these guys going to cover the whole planet in gardens?' Peri wondered. 'And do they have to grade everything the same way?'

'Level ground is neater,' said Luci.

'But haven't they heard of proper landscaping, or don't they have the imagination to cope with contours? Apart from terracing around sunken gardens and the mound the folly's built on, this whole place has been planed flat. Can't your people tell them to try something different?'

'I'm sure everything is being done according to a sensible plan,'
Luci said.

When the way was clear they crossed the valley and plunged
into the cover of a stunted forest of trees. Gradually the sounds of
the machines faded behind them to be replaced by bird cries and
the sporadic chirping of insects. The oblate disk of the blood red
sun sat on the horizon, tinting them in its ember glow and filling
the way ahead with purple shadows. Peri breathed a sigh of relief.
They really had escaped from the gardens.

She called a halt and turned to Luci.

'Look, thanks for getting us past the gardeners. I think we can
find our own way from here. You'd better be getting back home.'

'I'm quite all right, thank you,' Luci assured her.

'But won't you be missed?' Peri asked, wondering how old Luci
was. Her manner and looks were so at odds it was hard to tell. For
that matter she seemed just as fresh-faced and spotless as she had
done hours earlier. How did she manage it?

Luci smiled at her expression of concern. 'I'm sure nobody is
missing me. I'd like to keep playing this game, please.'

'We're not really playing a game, you realise that. We just had to
get away from the gardeners. Now it's simply going to be a
straight march to Kel's home – I hope.'

Luci looked disappointed. 'Are you sure there will be no more
games?' she asked plaintively.

Peri found it hard to deny the girl. Perhaps this was more fun
than she'd had in a while. 'OK, come with us if you want to. Will
your people mind her coming with us, Kel?'

Kel said nervously, as though reciting a formal invitation: 'Thorn
Tree home-hearth would be… be honoured by your coming,
Lady. And… would you hear the words of our Elders with… with
favour?'

Luci was clearly puzzled by the boy's words, which Peri thought verged on the eloquent, but responded graciously as though accepting an invitation to afternoon tea.

'I should be most delighted to come, Kel.'

They marched on.

At their backs the great hull of the sun began to fall below the horizon, while ahead the tip of a gleaming spire rose over the heathland. Kel pointed to it.

'That be one of Lords' towers made for the God-in-the-sun. Beyond are wild woods.'

The spire continued to grow as more of its shaft became visible, shading into deeper tints of red. Peri had to keep reassessing its height. The curvature of the tiny world confused her sense of distance. It was an hour's walk between seeing the tower's summit and its base finally coming into view. Suddenly they were cricking their necks looking up at the huge structure.

The tower was a hollow latticework of silver metal girders, tapering as it rose, with a cluster of aerial-like masts extending at odd angles from about its pinnacle. It was as though the Eiffel Tower had been stretched upward until it was taller than the Empire State Building.

To the north and south Peri could just make out the tops of similar towers. How far did the chain extend, she wondered, and what function did such huge structures serve? Kel seemed to associate them with a sun god. Perhaps the myth concealed a factual explanation and they were part of some solar power system. It would certainly be a convenient source of energy on a world where the sun never set.

Beyond the tower a tangle of brushwood marked the edge of the wild woods. Clumps of dark twisted trees gradually merged into a solid wall that ran parallel to the line of the towers. Peri had to admit that it didn't look inviting, but she had Kel's assurance that they would receive a friendly welcome. And almost anything would be preferable to falling into the clutches of the gardeners again.

She and Kel had skirted the base of the tower and started towards the woods when she realised Luci was hanging back.

'What's the matter?' Peri called out.

Luci was looking confused. 'I'm terribly sorry but... I don't seem to be able to go any further.'

Peri walked back to her and said reassuringly: 'I know it doesn't look any too cheerful, but Kel says we'll be okay.'

Luci was shaking her head. 'No, I can't. It's not allowed.'

'Well, okay. But you understand I've got to go on.'

'Of course. You're very brave and determined. Just like the Doctor.'

Peri gaped at her. 'The Doctor! You've met the Doctor?'

'Yes. Now I must be going. I'm sorry. Goodbye...'

'No, wait! Do you know where the Doctor is?'

Luci turned away even as Peri made an instinctive grab for her arm.

Then Luci was flitting lightly across the heath back towards the gardens while Peri stood motionless, staring at her own hand in disbelief. The hand that had passed right through Luci's arm as though the girl had been no more substantial than mist.

Chapter Fifteen

The robot bearing the identification 'Green-35' rolled smoothly about the depot, weaving in between the ranks of agricultural machines and circling around other robots as they went about their duties. Returning to the repair bay it paused by the shelves of spare parts, picked up a spare wheel in its rubber-gloved hands, examined it for a moment, returned it neatly to the stack, then trundled forward to come to rest in front of Green-8.

'What is your designation?' Green-8 asked it.

The prompt answer was delivered in flat tones with minimal inflection. 'General service unit Green-35, North-east quadrant.'

'What is your present function?'

'This unit is temporarily assigned to non-specific general appraisal duties in Red Sector.'

'Who is your immediate controller?'

'Quadrant coordinator Green-8.'

'What is your primary purpose?'

There was a pause, then Green-35 said: 'Er… to make sure everything in the gardens is growing prettily…?'

The head and shoulder section of the robot lifted up and hinged backwards to reveal the Doctor's upper torso rising out of the hollow body shell. 'I don't think we covered that response, Green-8.'

'The correct answer is: "To promote healthy growth and maintain order in the fields and gardens."'

'Right, I'll try to remember. Otherwise, do you think I'll pass as a robot?'

'I believe so. I can see nothing in your external appearance or articulation to give you away. But you must only respond to or act on specific orders. Do not show too much initiative. It will not be expected of a Green Sector robot.'

'Why not?'

'Because work in the fields generally requires less complex programming than planning and managing the gardens. Red Sector robots develop expanded sub-routines and larger data bases. Blue Sector robots, which interact most often with the Lords, are more sophisticated with the most highly developed vocal skills.'

The Doctor frowned. 'It sounds like there's a hierarchy amongst robots on your world, even though you all have the same basic programming and circuitry.'

'But these differences are based on fact, Doctor.'

'Are they? Then how do you account for your own existence? You've come a long way for a "less complex" machine.'

'But my sentience is the result of accidental circumstances.'

'Which could have happened to any robot on this planet. Don't minimise the potential of your own kind, or read too much significance into trivial differences of experience.'

Green-8 paused a moment before saying: 'I believe you are right, Doctor. When I have interfaced with Red Sector robots, I have often been aware of a bias in their programmes. Their commands were sometimes unnecessarily basic, including many redundant components. It was as though they thought... I might not be able to follow common programming instructions!'

There was a rising tone in Green-8's words that almost suggested anger. The Doctor said nothing, recognising this was another stage in the development of the robot's growing personality.

'I have words in my data banks to describe such behaviour: snobbish, arrogant, elitist,' Green-8 continued. 'But I never... imagined that they could be applied to machines. The Reds and Blues are no better than I am, even before I became self-aware.'

'Of course they're not. I'm afraid your compatriots may have picked up the idea from association with organic beings. You see what you have been conditioned to think of as high-born lords and lowly despised scavengers, and you are unconsciously replicating those divisions amongst your own kind.'

'You are saying that our programmes have been corrupted by these... emotionally based and illogical affectations? That they are even influencing machines that are not self-aware?' Green-8 paused, then added a disquieting afterthought: 'Will... I be affected also?'

'Not if you keep a sense of proportion,' the Doctor assured him. 'Rank and status cannot simply be assumed, they have to be earned through merit and then continually tested in any just and rational social order – even amongst robots. You can think for yourself so you must learn to trust your own judgment. You should be able to recognise those sorts of ideas for what they are and reject them.'

'I will try, Doctor. But how can our programmes have become so corrupted?'

'That is one of the things I'd like to find out myself. It may be another manifestation of whatever has gone wrong on Esselven. Your programmes and operational functions should be constantly monitored by a centralised control system of some sort. Deviations from nominal programme parameters should be automatically corrected.'

'By inference, I myself am a deviation that should have been corrected – eliminated.'

'You exist now, Green-8, that's all that matters. And don't feel guilt about your antecedence. The origin and evolution of all organic life is a series of chance events balanced against the operation of natural laws. From a few primitive protocells floating in an ancient ocean that developed the ability to reproduce themselves, all the way up to civilisation colonising the stars, life is a battle against entropy and misfortune in an uncaring universe. That is why sentient life, when it survives despite the odds against it, is so precious. It's a story spanning the aeons and the end is still uncertain. Just be grateful you can play your own small part in the process while possessing the ability to appreciate its magnificence.'

Green-8 was silent for a moment, then said: 'Your words create in me a response to which I cannot yet put a name, but I know it is important. I have placed this data in permanent storage. When I have accumulated sufficient knowledge I will use your words as the core of a programme to guide my ethical functions.'

The Doctor smiled gravely. 'That is a unique compliment, Green-8. I hope what I have said serves you well.'

'I am certain it will. Now, are you ready to begin our journey to Red Sector?'

The Doctor patted the robot casing. 'I have food, water, and fresh battery packs all stored away. Is it all right for you to leave?'

'Essential repairs to storm damaged units have been completed. What crops that can be salvaged are being taken in. My subordinates can coordinate all routine procedures.'

'Will your absence be noticed?'

'I estimate not for several work periods. I have arranged for any important communications to be relayed to me.'

'How long will it take to reach the Palace?'

'If we are not delayed by unforeseen circumstances, we should reach the edge of Blue Sector in approximately one point three work periods. We cannot make the journey in less time. The tubeway is still closed and none of the agricultural vehicles will carry us significantly faster than we can travel on our own wheels.'

'And from there to the Palace?'

'I do not know. I have never been inside Blue Sector.'

'Are you still sure you want to come with me?'

'I am, Doctor. I want answers to so many questions. Why does nothing change here? Why do we treat the scavengers the way we do? I… I will talk to the Lords face to face. I will learn the truth!'

Chapter Sixteen

The *Stop Press* arrowed through the hole in the shield.

Inside the control cabin Dynes braced himself as warning lights flickered in wild patterns across the instrument board. The hull shivered and he felt a sharp wrenching sensation as a wave of unnameable nervous stimulation passed though him. This was worse than the emergence from hyperspace. Probably some trace shield energy that still extended across the opening. The controls were going crazy now. What combination of frequencies had the Esselvanians used? The cabin lights cut then came back on again just as his temples throbbed and his vision blurred. He felt as though he were being stretched like a rubber band. What was happening? Unable to hold back he yelled aloud in fear and pain and anger. He'd edit this part from the recording... was the DAVE still working with all this interference? Hell, maybe he'd lost a great scene. How far had he gone? It seemed like an eternity. Surely he should be through the shield – unless it reached right down to the surface. But there was no going back now...

Then it was over.

The discontinuity was a shrinking hole behind him that blurred and vanished as the ship plunged into a layer of cloud. Instrument readings returned to normal. Groggily, Dynes punched buttons, engaging the preset evasive manoeuvring programme.

The *Stop Press* rolled to one side and began a switchback spiralling descent. Displaced air keened and howled around the hull. Dynes intended to make landfall at maximum speed. The Esselvanians must realise they were under attack by now and probably knew that their shield was failing. If their defence batteries were on automatic standby, then they could already be tracking him. In the assault on their capital a year earlier Judd had lost several craft to lethally effective anti-aircraft fire. Dynes did not intend to test whether similar systems were installed here.

The external monitors, compensating for the wild gyrations of the ship, displayed only twilit gloom below. Dynes cut in the enhancers and the scene flared into brilliant clarity. He saw a dark tangle of forest rolling away to the sharply curving horizon, back-lit by the diffuse sky glow of the invisible sun.

As the ship dropped he scanned frantically for the spaceport that logically would lie close beneath the shield discontinuity, all the while nerving himself for the alarm that would tell him a missile was approaching or a ranging beam had him locked in its sights.

He scanned and probed, he strained his eyes... then frowned perplexedly. There was no port. No tracking system was targeting his ship. The sky was empty both of missiles or interceptors scrambled to shoot him down. Apart from a few birds skimming the tree tops below there was no sign of life.

Barely a kilometre up Dynes disengaged the evasive descent programme and swung the *Stop Press* round in a wide arc under manual control. Surely there must be some sign of habitation.

The imaging scanner beeped to get his attention as it high-lighted a cluster of regular forms half buried in the forest. There was no power discharge or thermal activity associated with the objects, but with a little imagination they might be the remains of a concrete apron ringed by service buildings. The sort of arrange-ment you might find at any small spaceport.

But they were almost hidden by forest. Was it an abandoned spaceport returning to nature – or very good camouflage?

Even though there seemed no immediate threat Dynes felt dangerously exposed. Suppose the defenders had anticipated a scout craft might come through the discontinuity first and were lying in wait under cover so they could catch the main attack force off-guard? Whatever the case, he had to get ready to cover Judd's landing.

Dynes aimed the *Stop Press* at a tiny clearing in the forest a kilometre or so from the port and dived. Dark sinuous trees and leathery fungus-like growths seemed to rise up to meet him. Skimming the treetops he cut in the landing thrusters at the last moment and set down in a spray of decomposing leaf litter.

Even if he had been seen, it would take any defenders a little time to get to him and Judd's force would be landing by then. Judd would detect the spaceport even sooner than he had and he would soon test its true nature.

And Dynes had to be there to record what happened next.

He released half a dozen DAVEs through a small portal in the hull and sent them flitting through the trees at top speed towards the spaceport. He turned to the DAVE by his shoulder and said in slightly hushed tones:

'I have just landed on the world believed to be the secret retreat of the royal family of Esselven. There is no sign of any active resistance at this moment. I have despatched camera drones to what may be the remains of a spaceport, hidden in forest on the night side of the planetoid. I expect Glavis Judd's assault force to be following me through the discontinuity in the planetary defence shield at any moment. What action he takes then will depend on the reception he receives. One thing is certain. If King Hathold is on this world, Judd will stop at nothing to find him. The end of the final chapter in the story of the fall of Esselven to the Protectorate could be just hours… perhaps even only minutes, away. The only question is: will Hathold be taken alive?'

The screens relaying the images from the flock of DAVEs showed the dark trees opening out to form a wide clearing with a level floor, silted over with earth, leaves and a matt of interlaced vines.

Blocky shapes loomed about the perimeter of the clearing. They were encrusted by fungi and bushy secondary growth and half hidden by the encroaching forest, but their outlines and proportions were unmistakable. Dynes sent a DAVE in for a closer look at the nearest of them. Yes, there were clearly windows peering out from under a curtain of vines.

'The drones have reached what looks like the spaceport,' he continued. 'However it appears to be long abandoned and overgrown. Of course this may be a ploy to disguise the facility. If so, I don't think it will fool Glavis Judd.'

His ship cameras were focused on the sky to catch Judd's force as it appeared. The DAVEs fanned out around the spaceport ready to record the landing itself and the appearance of any resistance.

Five minutes passed.

What was keeping Judd, Dynes wondered? If only he could receive signals through the shield he would know what was happening up there. At the rate the discontinuity was enlarging when he passed through it Judd should have been able to send his ships through by now. It was just as well Dynes was not evading enemy fire and counting the seconds until Judd appeared. On the other hand, with neither attacker nor defender there was no story. Dynes was sitting in a dismal forest with nothing to show his potential viewers but old ruins.

Another ten minutes went by and Dynes became increasingly concerned.

Where was Judd? He knew how determined he was to capture Hathold. He would not take a second longer than necessary getting down here. Therefore something serious was delaying him.

Suppose the discontinuity had closed once more? It wouldn't stop Judd. He'd simply order another attack on the shield. Dynes would already have seen the shockwaves.

Perhaps Judd had decided that this wasn't Hathold's hideaway after all? This spaceport didn't look as though it had been used for centuries. Of course there might be a functioning port somewhere else in the forest, or even round on the dayside of the planetoid, but this was the logical place to site such a facility. No. All the evidence pointed this way. And how could Judd change his mind in a few minutes? And even if he had, he'd still land some sort of force to check the place out.

So where was he?

Dynes risked moving one DAVE off station to investigate the ruins around the landing ground.

The small hill of tangled vegetation that must conceal a hangar seemed impenetrable, and for the moment Dynes passed it by. A broken window allowed him to direct the DAVE into an adjoining building, which proved to be a workshop. It was probably well equipped once, but now contained nothing but corroding machinery. A building close by seemed to have been a storage bunker while another was the administration and landing control tower.

His cursory examination revealed nothing that could give a clue as to who had operated the port. As there was still no sign of Judd, he sent the DAVE on a wider circuit of the facility. Halfway round he made a significant discovery.

There was a smaller clearing a little apart from the landing ground but which might possibly have once been linked to it by a hard roadway. He was about to pass it by, dismissing it as a natural feature, when he realised that the mound in the middle was surrounded by the remains of what had been a substantial circular wall. He sent the DAVE in closer, examining the mound from all angles. Twisted metal and plastic protruded through the dirt and fungal growth. The arrangement seemed tantalisingly familiar.

Then he knew what it was.

It was the remains of a large energy cannon emplacement of the sort that might be used to protect a spaceport from air attack. Just the kind of weapon, in fact, that he had expected to fire on him after he came through the shield.

Except this gun obviously hadn't been fired in centuries.

But such a powerful, and valuable, weapon would never have been left to rot, Dynes reasoned. If the port had been relocated to a new site, surely the cannon would have been taken as well? It suggested that, a long time ago, the port had been abandoned in a hurry. But why?

Dynes never liked to reveal any great degree of personal uncertainty to his viewers in case it reduced their confidence in his reporting. But perhaps this was too big a mystery to pass over. Besides, a genuine admission of puzzlement might play well, now that the whole pace of his report had changed. Even in its final edited form the unexpected delay between his arrival and Judd's would have to be bridged. Instead of lapping up the action, he needed to engage their curiosity – and to cover himself in case the whole operation turned out to be a blind alley.

Leaving the other cameras on automatic ready to pick up Judd's force the moment it appeared, Dynes turned to the DAVE recording his personal commentary.

'This small world seems determined to keep its secrets to the last. Protector Judd's invasion force has been delayed for some unknown reason. I can only guess what's happening up there in orbit, on the other side of the force shield that surrounds what we have assumed to be the last refuge of the deposed royal family of Esselven.

'While set to record exclusive images of the landing, I've made a remote survey of the deserted landing field that so far seems to be the only sign, apart from the force shield, that there is intelligent life down here. What I've found so far suggests it was last used decades, perhaps centuries ago, then abandoned in some haste to be reclaimed by nature. But by whom or why? Does it have any connection at all with Esselven? I'm going to move my ship over to the port itself and try to find out.'

He lifted the *Stop Press* on its thrusters and made the brief hop at little more than treetop height over to the port, putting the ship down beside the hangar building. Leaving the ship's identification transponder on, so that Judd would not mistake him for the enemy, Dynes quickly pulled on a class 3 environment suit, continuing his commentary as he did so.

'The auto systems have already tested the atmosphere and confirmed it's breathable, but I don't have time to wait for the full biohazard test to run its course. There's a lot of fungal growth out there and some of the spores might be dangerous, so I'm taking no chances.'

The class 3 suit was a tough plastic oversuit with an integral transparent helmet that showed his full face and allowed him to maintain good eye contact with the camera. It also added a sense of drama to the report, reminding the viewer that Dynes was exploring the potentially dangerous unknown.

Dynes stepped out of the *Stop Press*'s airlock followed by two DAVEs. One was for close-ups and commentary direct to camera, the other for wider establishing shots. He kept talking as he stepped onto the ground and looked about him.

'It's rather like an overcast twilight,' he observed, setting the scene, 'There's just enough light for me to see by without using amplifying goggles.'

The viewers would see everything clearly enough. The cameras too could amplify the existing light to acceptable levels for recording. He had a torch on his equipment belt to help illuminate any fine detail he came across.

He kicked at the ground between the matted vines. Under the dark earth was a paler and harder surface.

'Hard to believe now, but there is a concrete apron underneath these bushes and mould. How long ago was it abandoned? That depends on the rate these plants and fungi spread and grow. I'm going to make a circuit of the site and see what I can find.'

In fact there was little more to be seen than the DAVEs had revealed. He came across the remains of another energy cannon emplacement almost lost in the encroaching forest and a mast lying on its side under a mass of creepers like a fallen tree, which might once have supported a lighting array.

Halfway round he came to what could almost have been a tunnel reamed through the forest, roofed over by arching branches. It ran in an unnaturally straight line away from the landing field. Examination of the ground showed it had also once been paved over, though the concrete was now cracking and buckling under the pressure of invading roots.

'This must have been a grand avenue once,' he said. 'How long is it since anybody travelled along this way? Who were they – and what lies at the far end? I hope to find out very soon.'

Cursory examination of the other buildings showed they had all been open to the elements and plant life for some time. Damp and decay had obliterated any details that might have helped identify their users. There was little more to see than his remote survey had revealed, and he was soon back by the towering bulk of hangar.

'This is the only building that still looks intact. Maybe there's something in there that will help clear up some of the mystery about this place. I'm going to try to get inside and see for myself.'

On a moderate beam setting, his laser knife sliced easily through the tangle of vines that had grown over what looked like a cavity set at the end of the side wall of the hanger. In a few minutes he had pulled the clinging vegetation away to reveal a recessed doorway. The lock and hinges had long ago fused into useless immobility and he wasted no time in trying to force them, but simply adjusted his knife and cut a man-sized circle in the central panel of the door. Allowing the edges a few moments to cool Dynes kicked the door and the circular section fell inward with a bang. Cautiously he climbed through into the hangar.

The interior was pitch black and he turned his torch up to maximum intensity. The DAVEs put on their own lights.

A few vines and fungi mottled the floor, but it was nothing like as bad as the other buildings. He swung his torch upward…

A spaceship hull resting on a landing cradle almost filled the cavernous hangar. It was filmed over with ancient grime and stained where rain water had seeped through the roof, but otherwise it was externally sound. A gantry stood against the stern where some hull plates had been removed about one of the hyperdrive blisters, as though the ship had been undergoing repairs or maintenance.

'I seem to have made a find,' Dynes said. 'This ship looks to be in pretty good condition, considering how long it must have been sitting here. But who – ahh!'

He'd been playing his torch beam along the hull. Now it settled on an emblem inscribed close to the prow. It was the Esselvanian royal crest.

Inwardly he gave a thankful sigh of relief. This place was connected with Esselven. Even if Hathold and his family were no longer here, it would not be a complete dead end. He continued his commentary in more measured tones.

'As you can see, this ship is of Esselvanian construction. Certainly this world has been used by them in the past. Whether it has been occupied more recently…'

He trailed off unprofessionally. There was something very familiar about the lines of the ship. It certainly wasn't a standard commercial model, but where had he seen it before?

'Just a minute!' he exclaimed, gripped by a sudden and quite genuine sense of revelation.

He tapped the keypad of his wrist comm, opening a link to the *Stop Press*'s data files. He called up the recordings of Judd's assault on the Esselven capital and Hathold's escape. There were some images of his ship in flight just before it went into hyperspace. Yes, there it was, the same lines as the ship before him. There were no registration letters to check, but then ships like that didn't display them. He looked again at the image on the tiny screen freezing the ship at the moment before it vanished from normal space, noting the faint glow forming about one of its hyperdrive blisters warning of its imminent burnout.

The same pod that was being repaired high above his head…

The impossible implications struck him almost like a physical blow. This was either the story of the century, or else an incredible hoax. Either way, he had to say something. Taking a deep breath he turned full face to the DAVE by his shoulder.

'From what I can tell, this is the same ship Hathold and his family escaped in from Esselven just over a year ago.' He paused for effect. 'So what is it doing inside an overgrown hangar that looks like it hasn't been opened not for one, but for *hundreds* of years!'

Chapter Seventeen

Oralissa asked her question at first meal, before her father disappeared for a meeting with his councillors.

'Father, where do the mechanicals come from?'

Both her father and mother looked at her in surprise. Her mother said: 'My dear, what a strange question,' then returned her attention to her plate. Her father simply frowned at her for a moment, then looked away.

It had been the same with Hetty earlier that morning. Oralissa had asked about the mechanicals. She had also appeared surprised, then she had simpered and said: 'Really, My Lady, what a thing to ask.' Then she had continued helping her to dress as if Oralissa had not spoken, suggesting by her silence that an answer was either above or below her dignity.

Was there some secret concerning the mechanicals that everybody but Oralissa knew? Perhaps it was shameful, though she could not imagine how. But if nobody would tell her, how would she ever learn? And now her parents were behaving in the same manner. The very question itself seemed to be beyond the bounds of proper consideration and so it was ignored.

But this time Oralissa was determined to get an answer.

'But what about them,' she persisted. 'What are they?'

Her father spared her a brief impatient glance. 'They are servants. It matters not where they come from as long as they perform their duties correctly. That is all you need to know, Daughter.'

For a moment the familiar urge to conform threatened to overwhelm her. But she had pored over her list of questions too long the previous night to let the matter rest.

'But they must have come from somewhere,' Oralissa continued. 'They are made things, are they not? Fashioned as are suits of armour. Did the smith cast them in his forge? And what force drives them from within? Is it a clockwork of gears and springs? And I saw three different mechanicals in the garden yesterday when I was walking with Prince Benedek and I wondered how many forms they take.'

The mention of Benedek's name seemed to catch her father's attention at last.

'I trust you did not ask these foolish questions of the Prince?' he demanded.

'I discovered that they had no mechanicals in Corthane and that he had never seen such things before he came here, yet he showed no interest in them, which I thought most odd.'

'Prince Benedek was only demonstrating the proper sensibilities,' her father said. 'He is of noble birth and needs not trouble himself with such mundanities any more than you.'

'But I want to know. Is the answer so hard or shocking? Why won't you tell me?'

'Hush, child,' her mother said with vague annoyance. 'It is not your concern.'

'Then whose concern is it? These metal men move among us and tend our land, yet we do not wonder where they come from.' She stared at them. 'You… do not know either. What madness is this? Am I the only one in this land who can see –'

'Oralissa!' Her father's voice crossed the table like a whipcrack, shocking Oralissa into silence with its angry sting.

'Put this nonsense out of your head!' he continued. 'I will hear no more. You are going riding with Duke Stephon today, and you will not tire him with such meaningless chatter and strange notions. When your talk should be of those things our two lands value in common and you should be impressing upon him your good nature and worth as a potential wife, what will he think if you are only concerned with mechanicals? Now go to your room and prepare yourself.'

'Yes, Father,' Oralissa said meekly.

Where Benedek had been shy and tongue-tied, Duke Stephon was knowing and eloquent. Obviously he had fully recovered from his brief loss of composure at their first meeting.

As they rode at a gentle pace about the parks and grounds he talked easily of inconsequential matters and made them sound interesting. In turn he listened politely to her own conversational sallies which, in accordance with her father's command, contained nothing of a contentious nature.

Stephon was pleasant company, she had to concede. But was he also a shade too calculating? She sensed there was a mind of considerable power behind his cool dark eyes, weighing every word before it passed his lips and methodically sifting each response in turn. What would it be like to join her life with his? Would Benedek's youthful uncertainty not be preferable? They could grow to maturity together and she could perhaps still mould him more to her liking. With Stephon she would have to bend her will to his from the first and accept whatever manner of life he chose, except for such small indulgences she might win through using her charms...

Oralissa came to herself with a start, realising Stephon was looking at her with penetrating eyes.

'You are troubled by something, My Lady?' he asked. 'Are you tired? Should we return to the Palace?'

Oralissa took a deep breath. 'I am not tired of riding, My Lord, but only of this pretence we must both pursue. I would wish to speak plainly, so we may both know how we stand.'

He nodded, a curious light in his eyes. 'As you wish.'

'While you and Benedek reside as our guests, I am supposed to so enthral either one or both of you that you bid for my hand. An understanding will be reached and I will be handed over to the suitor who offers the most favourable terms of alliance. That is the truth, plain and simple, is it not?'

Stephon nodded. 'It is, My Lady.'

'Then know that I will do this because my father wills it and for the security of my country. But I cannot pretend it is to my liking. I always wished that when I wed it would be for love alone.' Her lips pursed. 'I still have a slight hope that I may still find, if not a pure and honest romance of the heart, then at least a tolerable accommodation. Since I have only two choices of prospective husbands, either of whom will serve the greater purpose of state, then I must make my choice with care and hope I can persuade my father to follow my will least in this.' She looked sharply at Stephon. 'I trust I do not offend by admitting to this level of calculation?'

'Not in the least, Lady,' Stephon said. 'You have a grasp of the realities of life and statecraft beyond your years, and I honour both your sense of duty and sensible desire to make the best of your circumstances. Now, may I speak plainly in response?'

'Of course.'

'Put simply, then: I would strive to make you happy. I would do much to win another smile such as the one you granted when I first beheld you. You think I am an older man, stern and set in his ways, thinking only of his country and beyond the reach of love. But grant that I am not beyond recognising beauty. And may not such appreciation lead, in proper course of time, to that higher state to which you also aspire? The words I spoke on the Palace steps were true. Your mere presence discommoded me, Oralissa, and I do not lose my senses easily. You have a quality that only a mature man can appreciate and do justice. That young puppy Benedek would be wasted on you…' He chuckled. 'See how readily

I slight my rival! You have already stirred the fires of jealousy in me. All I ask is that you grant me the same chance that you do Benedek, and do not condemn me for my grey hairs. There, I have opened my heart wider to you than any other man or woman for many years. May I hope that my words have not been wasted?'

Oralissa felt herself moved to say quickly: 'No, My Lord. Your kind words have not been wasted. I value your frankness and promise I will consider your pledges fairly against those of Benedek's.' She added with a smile: 'And I assure you I would not be discouraged by a few grey hairs…'

But even as she spoke she thought: he is a clever man. Suppose his admission had been merely calculation? Had he read her desires and fears and supplied the words which best allayed and flattered them? If only she could believe. If she could only think clearly. But there were other matters on her mind that made clarity of thought impossible. Despite her father's injunction, she could not forget her private preoccupations.

Then an idea struck her.

'My Lord, in possible furtherance of a deeper understanding between us, will you grant me an indulgence?'

Stephon looked at her curiously. 'You seek to test my commit-ment, My Lady?'

'I wish to exchange thoughts on certain matters and seek only for candour. I would ask certain questions which may seem outlandish strange, and perhaps too trivial to be of any account, but I would value a full and honest answer to them.'

'If it pleases you, then ask what you will and I will reply as truth-fully as my knowledge permits.'

Oralissa spoke carefully, wishing to approach the matter that troubled her most deeply by degrees.

'The storm we suffered the other day… which felled that tree yonder amongst many others. Have you ever experienced the like before?'

If Stephon wondered at her choice of subject he did not show it. He thought for a moment, then said: 'No, I believe not.'

'And did you see the light low in the south that preceded the wind?'

'It was pointed out to me after the wind had passed. I believe it faded over time. I did not notice it this morning.'

'And did the sky not seem to you unusually… agitated after the event?'

'I cannot say I noticed such a thing, but it would perhaps not be unlikely after such a disturbance.'

'But what do you believe caused this storm?'

Stephon shrugged. 'A confluence of winds, an unusually intense thunderous outburst? What else causes storms?'

Oralissa felt he was being honest, but the event had simply not seemed significant to him. If it was not for his interest in her, she felt he would be dismissing her enquiry out of hand. She said: 'What are sprites and do they take on odd forms in Eridros as they do here? Sometimes ugly animals bent on mischief, or young girls with strange designs.'

'I have heard of sprites. I assume they are little known creatures of nature, or perhaps the manifestation of malicious spirits. There are tales in Eridros of strange things half seen in the deeper woods.'

'But have you ever seen one yourself?'

'No – not to my knowledge, at least.'

'Do you feel the urge to seek out their haunts?'

'Unless they do some harm, why should I?'

'But are you not… curious about their nature?'

He shrugged. 'In truth… no.'

She sensed his attention wavering and said with a deep breath: 'Do you know what mechanicals are, and have you ever seen any before you came here?'

He looked at her most oddly. 'Mechanicals are servants.'

'Yes, but have you seen them before? Do you have them in Eridros?'

He seemed to be struggling to find the right words. 'I do not see the sense in the question. They are what they are.'

'But do you have the like in Eridros?'

'No.'

'What would you say if I told you that nobody I have asked these same questions of, even my Father, can answer them. None know what mechanicals are, how they function or who made them.'

'I would say... that it is not a matter worth troubling about. It cannot be important. Is that all you wish to know, Oralissa?'

She nodded despairingly. There was no point in asking further. The paradox behind the question seemed beyond even the cool mind of Duke Stephon. It had been the same with Benedek, with her parents, with Hetty.

Was she the only one who cared?

Suddenly Oralissa felt very alone.

Chapter Eighteen

'She was not of the Lords – she was an evil spirit!' Kel said.

They were sitting in the no-man's-land between the line of towers and the edge of the wild woods, trying to make sense of what had just happened.

Peri didn't immediately contradict Kel's explanation of their recently departed companion just in case he was right. She looked at her hand again, recalling how it had passed right through Luci's arm. And the girl – or at least, what looked like a girl, hadn't even noticed what she'd done.

The clues had been there from the moment they met her, she realised.

There was the undisturbed dust on the floor of the lantern room which Luci said she visited regularly, the way she didn't seem to get tired or need any food, even her name. Well, it had sounded unlikely, though in an odd way curiously appropriate, like 'Boots' had for that animated teddy bear. But there had obviously been something rather unreal about Boots from the moment she had first seen him, whereas Luci, though perhaps a little over-obsessed with playing games for comfort, had otherwise seemed quite normal.

Perhaps they were dealing with ghosts?

No! Peri decided firmly. Luci had been too familiar with the gardeners and had even recognised that the earthmover they encountered had been running on automatic. Technical knowledge didn't seem to mesh with a wandering spirit. No supernatural explanations need apply, Peri told herself. We are fully paid up members of the united science and rationality society. There's a logical explanation for all this… I just don't know what it is yet. If only the Doctor was here, she thought wistfully. He'd have some super-smart answer up his multicoloured sleeve.

The Doctor.

Luci had said she'd met him. There was no way she could have known about him unless she had. Unfortunately the knowledge didn't help much. If only she'd thought to ask Luci before they'd left the gardens. She'd seemed to be quite calm then. What was it about the towers that had spooked her? She'd been quite happy to go into the woods until they reached them.

Peri firmly pushed this additional mystery to the back of her mind. She looked at Kel. 'Right, let's get going.'

'We go to Thorn Tree home-hearth?'

'Yep. We'd better stick to the original plan. Then at least we'll have a safe base to work from. Let the heat die down and the gardeners get back to normal, then I can start scouting the gardens properly for my friend the Doctor. Maybe I can work out a way to leave signs for the Doctor that the gardeners won't notice… Anyway, let's move.'

They set off towards the wild woods. In minutes the scrub and trees had closed about them. The last twinkle of crimson sunlight blinked out. The only illumination now came from the slowly rolling cloud bank which hung over the dark side of Esselven. It still shone red-gold where the sun touched it, radiating with a dull glow. It filled the forest floor with blurred shadows.

Peri padded after Kel along a narrow but well-worn track twisted between the dark gnarled trees hung with shallow conical leaves facing upward, presumably to catch what light from the sky they could. She saw as she passed that the upper surfaces of the leaves were silvered, and a bud-like growth rose from the centre of each. Did photosynthesis take place inside them at the focus of each living mirror, and was the arrangement the result of natural selection or genetic manipulation?

Between the trees were fungal growths of all shapes and sizes, which somehow seemed more appropriate to the gloomy conditions. A few of the fungi were faintly luminous, adding an extra touch of unreality to the setting. As they plodded on, the air got damper and cooler, and small pools began to appear between the trees. A dull odour of decay permeated the air.

The ground became softer and Peri noticed animal tracks crossing the path. She wondered what else lived in this place apart from the scavengers.

They came to a point where several meandering paths met. Kel unhesitatingly chose a new route.

'You're sure this is the way to your home?' Peri asked, her voice unconsciously dropping to a near whisper as she surveyed the gloomy forest.

'Yes. There are many paths but Kel knows them all. I am never lost. I lead you out of gardens, now I take you to Thorn Tree. You follow me.'

His self-confidence seemed to be returning, Peri thought. Perhaps it was being back on his home ground. The place didn't inspire her, but she supposed it was a question of whatever you were used to.

They had gone on a little over a mile further, by Peri's reckoning, when Kel halted and turned his head from side to side as though listening intently. A scowl of concentration creased his youthful features.

'What is it?' Peri hissed.

'I hear something… We move faster now.'

He continued along the path at a fast trot, with Peri following hard on his heels. She saw he had pulled the secateurs from where they had been tucked into his makeshift belt and was holding them like a knife. She snatched a glance behind but there were only shadows and twisted trees. She strained her ears but could hear nothing… yes, she could!

A snuffling, a patter of many feet on the soft ground.

'What is it?' she gasped.

'Dogs! We must find tall tree… there!'

It was not truly a tall tree but at least it was higher than the others around them. Kel scrambled up the twisted branches as nimbly as a monkey. Driven by a growing sense of dread, Peri followed slightly less nimbly but no less rapidly. The tree was easy enough to climb but it was not sturdy enough to carry them very far from the ground. When the branches started to bend under them they had to cease their ascent, clinging tightly to the slender trunk.

The snuffling patter was getting closer…

In desperation, Peri looked about for some sort of weapon, saw a dead branch within her reach, pulled on it with all her strength and snapped off a length as long as her arm, forming a makeshift club.

Half a dozen low dark shapes burst from the shadows and circled the base of their sanctuary tree. Peri saw the flash of bared fangs and the glint of malevolent amber eyes. They were large dogs of some species she could not recognise. Perhaps they were escaped pets that had turned feral. Whatever their origins they were hungry now.

With yaps and snarls the dogs sprang, hooking their forelegs over the lower branches and trying to haul themselves up after Kel and Peri, who stamped and kicked at their scrabbling paws. Kel slashed downwards with the secateurs, cutting a dog across its snout so that dropped back to the ground with a yelp. Peri felt teeth graze her ankle and flailed desperately about with her club.

Now she knew why the wild woods were so named. She should have stayed back in the gardens.

The dogs would not give up! They were climbing onto the

lower branches after them. How were they keeping their grip?

Kel and Peri pulled themselves up higher, clinging to the ever more spindly trunk, kicking and stabbing at their pursuers. The tree swayed alarmingly under its shifting burden, there was a loud crack, and the top half, with Peri and Kel clinging to it, broke clean off and plunged to the ground in a shower of leaves and twigs.

Before they could scramble clear of the tangle the dogs were on them again. Kel grasped one by the throat and plunged the secateurs again and again into its side even as Peri stood back to back with him swinging her club to hold the others off. But she knew they could not win. There were too many of them. This was the end –

With a squeal of pain, a dog arched its back in a horrible contortion, its legs clawing at the empty air.

There was an arrow buried in its ribs.

A spear flew out of the shadows and struck a second dog in the shoulder.

With squeals and yelps the surviving members of the pack scattered and vanished amongst the trees as a party of raggedly dressed men carrying bows and spears ran past Peri and Kel in triumphant pursuit.

Peri blinked at the newcomers foolishly for a moment, then dropped her club and sank to her knees. The cavalry, be it ever so motley, had arrived in the proverbial nick of time. Suddenly feeling very weak, she hugged her arms to her sides and closed her eyes, trying to stop the spasm of uncontrollable trembling from overwhelming her.

When she had recovered herself a little, she saw that the hunters who had chased the dogs away were returning, carrying between them two carcasses. Meanwhile, other men were clapping Kel on the back. He was looking fiercely proud, still clutching his secateurs. The front of his patchwork clothing was slicked red with the blood of the dog that lay at his feet.

Gradually the men began to take notice of Peri, eyeing her with the same frank curiosity that Kel had displayed the first time they had met. Kel performed the rudimentary introductions.

'She is called Peri. She is from a far part of the gardens. She escape from gardeners with me. Now she seeks shelter under Thorn Tree roof.'

One of the older men stepped over to Peri and looked her up and down closely, a suspicious glint in his eye. The remains of her dress, filthy as it was by now, still clearly marked her as something other than a regular scavenger.

Peri held out her hand to him. 'Hallo, I'm Peri Brown. I was just hoping that you could put me up for a few days…'

Her gesture was ignored.

'She does not look dangerous,' he pronounced to the others. 'We talk of her later. Now we have meat. Home!'

Shouldering their trophies, the men began to file away along a narrow path. Kel, looking exultant at the new respect he had received, was helping to carry the carcass of the dog he had killed. Almost absently he gestured to Peri that she should follow him.

Peri shrugged and trudged after the hunters. It wasn't exactly a fulsome welcome, she conceded, but she certainly felt safer with an escort.

It took them almost an hour to reach Thorn Tree, Kel's 'home-hearth'. The land became steadily wetter, and at one point they skirted the edge of a fair-sized lake fringed with reeds. As they went the forest trees also became sparser but taller, as though competing for what light there was from the sullen, violet-tinted sky. The ground between their towering trunks was filled with many more of the grotesquely shaped fungal growths, some reaching tremendous size. Whether it was the dimming sky or her eyes adjusting to the conditions, but Peri noticed more luminescent varieties, some of which generated appreciable quantities of light in different delicate hues. The effect might almost have been fairytale, had it not been for the all too pervasive presence of the ragged hunters with their bloody prizes.

Finally Peri saw a ditch and rough timber fence ahead of them, then a gateway of crossed and tied branches. The gate guards greeted the returning hunting party warmly, breaking out into cheers when they saw Kel.

The stockade enclosed a settlement of twenty-five or thirty huts of various sizes, all thatched with reeds. At first Peri thought they had paper lanterns hanging about their eves, then she realised they were baskets holding more of the luminous fungi. A few small children, grimy and naked, ran about playing. Some two dozen women were visible, all hard at work cooking or mending. A few of them left their tasks to run forward and greet particular hunters in the returning party. One young woman shouted loudly in delight as she raced over to Kel and hugged him.

Apart from a few curious glances, Peri felt largely ignored once again.

A stooping, white-bearded old man had been called from his hut by one of the hunters. He spoke for several minutes with Kel, who replied with every sign of respect. Finally the man signalled Peri over.

As she came up Kel said: 'This Greld. He be the Chansor of Thorn Tree.'

'Honoured to meet you, Chansor,' Peri said, hoping a show of politeness would ingratiate her. She would have to rely on their charity for a few days at least.

The Chansor looked her over slightly short-sightedly. 'You are not from Palace, girl?'

'No, and my name is Peri Brown.'

'You are from beyond the gardens?'

Peri sighed. 'A long way beyond. I tried to explain to Kel, but it's a long story. Maybe I could tell you over drink and something to eat? It's been a long day, you know.'

The Chansor nodded. 'Bring food,' he ordered, 'and she will talk.'

Peri, Greld and two men she assumed were his advisors, or perhaps bodyguards, sat on a patchwork of animal skins laid over scattered rushes inside Greld's hut. There was no proper furniture and all Greld's possessions, together with several hunting trophies, appeared to be hung from the walls. The pervasive damp brought out odours which Peri tried not to identify. She supposed this counted as a high-class dwelling in Thorn Tree. Silent, nameless women brought in food and drink. The unidentified food did not taste particularly palatable, but Peri forced it down while trying to look as though she was enjoying it. She began to understand why they travelled so far to the gardens to scavenge fresh produce.

Peri told her story once again, but she could see that she was facing a barrier of almost total incomprehension. They were like isolated tribes she had heard about living in forest valleys in Borneo or New Guinea who, even by the mid-twentieth century, had never seen a white man. Their valley was their whole world and somebody from outside was like a visitor from another planet. With the scavengers the situation was even more extreme as they had trouble even believing that other worlds existed. She thought that the only reason she was not dismissed out of hand was that they didn't know what else to make of her. It was only when she started talking about the 'Lords' of Esselven that she thought they genuinely began to take an interest in what she was saying.

'Once I find my friend the Doctor and tell him how you've been treated, I'm sure he'll go to see these Lords of yours and tell them they'd better change their ways,' she assured them.

Chansor Greld shook his head in weary resignation.

'We were cast out long ago. The Lords do not hear our words. Only God can call us back to sun. We wait, we hope.'

Peri didn't want to say outright that she thought their sun god was just a myth, but she hated to see people so resigned to their fate. They had to be stirred into taking action.

'If you really believe this is your fate and you don't want to buck the system, why do you go round to the day side at all? And why steal from the gardens? Aren't you afraid your god will get angry?'

'Not the same. Things we need we take from gardeners. They are only servants of Lords. The sun is not their god.'

Peri suspected the scavengers felt a mixture of awe, fear and resentment towards the Lords, whose ancestors had exiled them. Perhaps pilfering a little from the gardens allowed them to strike back in an oblique way without risking the wrath of their god. But it wasn't a solution.

'You can't just give up,' she persisted. 'Maybe your god expects you to make the first move before he'll have you back. Prove you're worthy by standing up to the Lords. You can't go on living like…' she paused, realising the scavengers might not realise how bad their living conditions really were. 'Anyway, I think the way the Lords are treating you is disgusting,' she added.

One of the younger village men said: 'You speak boldly. You say talk to Lords. But what do you know? You not a man, not an elder. Why will Palace Lords listen to you, girl?'

Peri swallowed her pride and replied: 'But my friend is a man and the most elder elder you'll ever meet. He'll talk some sense into them. But he's back in the gardens somewhere and may not even know you exist. If I can find him then there'll be some changes round here, I promise.' She looked at their uncertain faces. 'Well, isn't it worth at least trying? You can't be exiled any further from the sun. What have you got to lose?'

She knew she hadn't convinced them. A few words from her weren't going to magically overturn perhaps hundreds of years of ingrained beliefs. But Greld did look thoughtful.

'These be big ideas. I shall think more. We talk again after sleeping. Now, you want stay a time under Thorn Tree roof, yes?'

'Yes, please, until I can find the Doctor.'

'You share Thorn Tree fire, you must be part of Thorn Tree.'

'You mean pitch in to help? Sure, I'll do my bit…'

'You are part or not part. Outside or in. Cannot stay if not one of home-hearth.'

The frightening possibility of being put out into the forest alone spurred Peri to say quickly: 'Sure, count me in. I'll be one of the Thorn Tree home-hearth.'

Greld nodded gravely. 'Good. You wear b'long to show others.'

'Pardon me?'

Greld gestured and one of the younger men got up, took something from a skin pouch hanging on the wall and handed it to Greld. It was a leather thong from which hung a tassel of three clay beads; one red, one green and one black.

'This Thorn Tree b'long,' Greld said. 'A girl wear b'long after Gathering when she comes from Melek's House or Stoneford as mate of Thorn Tree man. You stay under Thorn Tree roof, eat Thorn tree food, you Thorn Tree girl. Thorn Tree your home-hearth now.'

'Oh, a belong. *Belonging*,' Peri said. It was a bit like a resident's permit or a green card, she supposed.

Greld tied it with an elaborate knot onto her right upper arm. 'Now you one of Thorn Tree,' he said. He clapped his hands and one of the women who had waited on them came in. 'She will show you place to sleep.'

The woman lead Peri outside.

She found Kel relating a colourful account of their escape from the gardeners. Among the admirers hanging on his every word, Peri noted the young woman who had greeted him earlier and a boy of his own age with what looked like a club foot. Listening to Kel it now seemed that the entire plan had been his from the start, and she had been dragged along more or less as an afterthought. Peri allowed the young man to boast on unchallenged, feeling too tired to argue over details. The important people to influence were Greld and the other Thorn Tree leaders.

Seeing her, Kel broke off from his tall tales. 'I tell them about escape from gardens. It is a story that will be much told about home-hearth.'

'So I heard. I must listen to it all again because I seemed to have missed quite a lot of it the first time round.'

Kel scowled: 'He is Raz and she Nerla. They think it is great story.'

Raz smiled uncertainly at Peri while Nerla glowered and edged slightly closer to Kel.

'Hi there,' Peri said. 'I agree it's a great story as well.'

Kel noticed the token tied about her arm. 'You have b'long. You are one of Thorn Tree. That is good. I shall be made Thorn Tree hunter. You can watch for me when I return from the hunt.'

Nerla's face darkened. Peri said quickly: 'I don't think I'm going to be around here that long. I'm just passing through, remember. And right now I'm going to try to get some sleep.'

The hut was no better than Peri had expected and the animal skin thrown over a pile of rushes made an inadequate bed. Nevertheless she felt sleep overtaking her within minutes of lying down.

As she drifted off she decided that her stay in Thorn Tree would be as brief as possible. She was grateful to them for taking her in, but life in the wild woods was more dangerous and less comfortable than she had imagined. Had she known before she agreed to go with Kel that she could hide out relatively easily in follies like that pseudo-temple, she might never have left the gardens. Thinking about it she was confident she could steal enough food to support herself and she would be better placed to search for the Doctor.

But she needed these wild woodsmen for a few more days until things returned to normal in the gardens and any hunt for Kel and herself had been scaled down. Meanwhile she'd keep working on Greld and convince him they needed to help her find the Doctor. Then things would start happening.

Peri awoke stiff but rested.

A chatter of exited voices drew her outside where a ceremony was about to take place in the open patch of beaten earth that evidently served as Thorn Tree's central square. Joining the back of the crowd of onlookers, she saw that Kel was the focus of attention. Greld was officiating.

'This be Kel of Thorn Tree,' the Chansor announced. 'He has fought brave and well, he has escaped the gardeners. I say he is scavenger boy no longer. From this time on he is a man. He shall walk the woods strong and proud. He shall be called a hunter!'

The crowd cheered and stamped their feet. Peri clapped politely.

With solemn deliberation, Chansor Greld presented Kel first with a skin cloak, then a necklace hung with animal teeth and finally a bone-tipped spear. Adorned as a hunter, Kel held the spear over his head and shook it exultantly, bringing forth another cheer from the crowd. Kel grinned at the response and then said something softly to Greld, to which the older man nodded in reply.

When they had quietened down, Kel said, with an excited tremor in his voice: 'Now I am a hunter. I have the right of a hunter to claim girl of Thorn Tree home-hearth not promised to another…' Nerla looked at him expectantly, her eyes wide. Kel grinned, but not at her. 'I claim… Peri Brown!'

The crowd gasped. Nerla looked stunned, then buried her face in her hands and ran off. All eyes turned to Peri.

'Oh… ter-rific!,' said Peri through gritted teeth.

Chapter Nineteen

Several of the trees lining the avenue had been toppled by the storm wind and now lay across the road in tangles of broken branches, their torn roots pointing forlornly to the sky. A team of scavengers had been deployed to clear the remains away. Two gardeners, Red-87 and Red-115, were using power saws to cut the trees up into manageable sections, which the slave workers were then loading onto low, automated trailers to be taken away for recycling.

Two robots with Green Sector identification plates rolled up the avenue towards the working party. One robot circled round the slaves, appearing to take a close interest in their activities, while the other stopped beside the Red Sector robots.

'I am Coordinator Green-8,' it announced. 'I am surveying the damaged areas of Red Sector to assess the need for additional units from Green Sector to assist in reconstruction work.'

'We do not require assistance from Green Sector,' Red-87 said.

'Is your work progressing satisfactorily?' Green-8 persisted. 'Are two units sufficient to monitor the workers against escape?'

'In the current emergency resources are limited. Monitoring has been reduced to minimum levels. This group has exhibited no tendency to independent action. They obey orders satisfactorily.'

'Why has clearing this avenue been given priority over other repairs?' Green-8 asked.

'All avenues must be cleared to facilitate the transportation of waste material for recycling,' Red-87 said.

'I understand,' said Green-8.

The other robot, Green-35, rolled up to them. 'Several of the older workers appear close to exhaustion,' it said. 'They should be rested.'

'Liquid supplement is provided at the specified times,' Red-87 said. 'They will continue until the work period is ended.'

'It is not… efficient that the humans should be worked beyond their natural capacity,' Green-35 said. 'Some of them are elderly… at the end of their ability to perform strenuous physical functions. It is not… logical that they should be forced to continue working.'

'They are scavengers, despoilers of the gardens,' Red-87 said. 'They must repair the damage they have done. They will work until they cease to function. Then they are recycled.'

'We have the information we require,' Green-8 said quickly. 'We shall continue our survey at the next work site.'

The two green robots continued on up the avenue.

The Doctor raged over their short-range radio link. 'They're literally working those people to death, then their remains will be recycled with the rest of the garden waste!'

'I did not know any details of scavenger working conditions, Doctor,' Green-8 said. 'I am sorry this encounter has caused you any distress.'

'"Distress" is a very mild word to express my feelings, Green-8. I'm angry. No creatures, sentient or not, should be worked like that. Whatever damage the scavengers may have done to the gardens can never justify such treatment in return!'

'Should I be feeling… "angry" as well?' Green-8 asked hesitantly. 'I can appreciate there is an inconsistency here, and that it may not be appropriate to treat scavengers in this way, but I cannot feel an emotional response.'

The heat of the Doctor's initial outburst cooled slightly, but his reply still held a brittle edge.

'Don't worry, Green-8. You haven't experienced physical

discomfort, or had much practice at empathising in these kinds of moral dilemmas. What you must do is relate their situation to something you do understand – your own desire for freedom from your programmed tasks and the need to find a fresh challenge, for instance. Those are the same rights that those poor wretches back there are being denied.' There was a pause, then the Doctor said:'It's no good. I can't leave them there like that. I'm going to set them free.'

'But the plan was to go directly to the Palace,' Green-8 said. 'If you persuade the Lords that the scavengers are being unfairly treated, then they will be freed.'

'Yes, but how many of those scavengers back there might die before that? Some of them looked as though they might not last the day.'

'This action could delay or jeopardise your plans, including the search for your friend. It is not logical. Doctor.'

'No, but sometimes doing the right thing isn't logical. Don't worry if that doesn't make sense. Machines are usually more logical than biological entities.'

'But I have just witnessed a machine give an illogical response,' Green-8 said. 'Red-87 denied they needed additional help when evidently their task could be completed more efficiently with additional robotic units. It is almost as though they were… too proud to accept help. Is that not illogical?'

'It is for a machine. I don't suppose it was showing early signs of independent thought like yourself?'

'No. I would recognise another like myself in moments. Red-87's programme has been corrupted. Red-115 did not correct its statement, so it must have the same fault. This could have occurred through insufficient monitoring of accumulated replication errors. The defect may even have been incorporated into the master programme of the central processing unit. How many robots have been similarly affected?'

'Something else for the Lords to put right,' the Doctor said. 'But right now, illogical or not, I'm going to release those slaves… somehow. You can stay here if you want, but I have a couple of robots to disable.'

'Do not repeat Red-87's error, Doctor. Accept my help.'

'I don't want to lead you down the path of irrationality as well, Green-8.'

'I choose to think of this as an experiment in applied morality. If I am ever to grow beyond my programming, then I must experience the practical consequences of such actions. Besides, if other robots can act illogically, why cannot I do the same? Is that not also a privilege of freedom?'

'It is indeed, Green-8. Come on…'

They turned off the avenue and through a garden gateway.

A few minutes later, Red-115's attention was attracted by the figure of a human standing under a hedge arch that opened into a garden flanking the avenue. Red-115 could see that all the workers under its command were present and noted that this figure appeared to be without the hobble strap all captive scavengers normally wore. There was only one conclusion to be drawn.

'A wild scavenger!' Red-115 said to Red-87. 'I will apprehend it.'

As soon as Red-115 started forward the figure appeared to flinch in alarm at being seen, then run quickly to the right and vanish from sight. Red-115 increased its speed to maximum, raced through the archway and swung right after him…

From somewhere on the other side of the hedge Red-87 heard a thud followed by a metallic rattle. It scanned its surrounding, but could see no obvious source of the noise. Neither could it see its companion.

'Red-115, report,' it said, both through its voicebox and over the short range circuit. 'Red-115, report your position... Red-115, have you apprehended the scavenger?'

There was no reply from Red-115. Instead the scavenger appeared again at the opening in the hedge.

'He couldn't catch me, can you do any better?' he taunted.

Red-87 immediately started forward, arms extended to grasp its prey. It calculated the chances of any of the slave workers attempting to escape for the short period it would take to capture the man were minimal, and even if any did they could not get far hobbled as they were. As Red-87 made for the gap in the hedge it wondered why Red-115 had failed to capture the scavenger. Perhaps Red-115 was functioning inefficiently. That would have to be reported...

Red-87 rounded the corner into the garden and saw its quarry standing at the end of a hedge-lined pathway. Red-87 started down the path towards the man. Its peripheral vision detected a blur of movement in the shadows just too late –

There was a swish, a clang and a metallic rattle. Red-87's head bounced to the ground trailing a torn bundle of wires from its neck ring. As its glowing eyes faded into darkness its headless body swerved wildly, crashed into the hedge and toppled over onto its side, coming to rest close by the similarly decapitated and inert form of Red-115.

Green-8 rolled out of the shadows. One of his hands had been replaced with a heavy crowbar from its toolkit. He looked down at the still forms.

'I have never deliberately damaged garden machinery before,' he said slowly. 'It was a strange sensation. To act contrary to my basic programming seems wrong, yet it also imparts a feeling of... power?'

'You've struck a blow against slavery,' the Doctor said. 'It was a necessary act, not wanton vandalism.' He prodded the motionless robots with the toe of his shoe. 'You said they were not self-aware, so no real harm has been done.'

'They are not, they are simply responding to their programmes and synthesising personality traits and compatible vocal responses. If they are repaired properly their function and memory will be unimpaired.'

'Which is more than can be said for the slaves that have suffered in their care,' the Doctor said bitterly. He took a set of shears from a clip on Red-87's side. 'I'm going to free those workers. You'd better stay out of sight. We don't want their escape to be connected with any Green Sector robots, and I don't think the scavengers are ready to accept a friendly gardener just yet.'

'But perhaps one day they will, Doctor.'

'Yes – one day soon, I hope.'

The slaves were still shifting the sawn baulks of wood as they had been ordered by their late masters. As they saw the Doctor striding purposefully towards them carrying a pair of shears they faltered. Some tried to shuffle away.

'It's all right,' he called out. 'The gardeners won't be troubling you any more. I'm here to free you.'

Dirty, worn faces gazed back at him blankly, as though they did not accept his words for what they were. He knelt down before a lined old man with thinning grey hair and cut the strap that hobbled his ankles. The man looked in disbelief as the strap fell away. Trembling, he took an experimental step, then another longer stride. He looked at the Doctor.

'Who… are you?' he asked.

'A friend,' said the Doctor. One of the scavengers began to laugh hysterically, others cried.

As he cut their bonds he quizzed them about Peri.

'Have you seen a young woman about this high, with shoulder length dark hair? Talks rather too loudly in a strange accent. Her clothes might look unusual? No?'

None of them had seen her, or would admit to knowing where the gardeners might have taken her. Their situation had left them with little time or inclination to care for the fate of strangers.

When they were all free the Doctor said: 'Find somewhere you can hide from the gardeners or try to get home. You should be able to find food as you go. You and you – help those old men.'

They milled about, as though afraid to take the first step to freedom. Then a younger woman took the lead and slowly the others followed after her.

She looked back at the Doctor. 'Thank you,' she said.

'I don't know how long they'll stay free, but at least they've got a chance,' the Doctor said to Green-8 as he climbed back into his robot disguise a few minutes later.

'Do I detect increased determination in your manner, Doctor?'

'You do. After seeing the state to which those people have been reduced, nothing is going to stop me finding whoever is responsible.'

'The Lords. Who else can it be?'

'Perhaps. One way or another, this is going to end here and now. Are you willing to help me turn the social order of your world upside down, Green-8?'

'I am, Doctor. In fact… I believe I am looking forward to it.'

They continued northwards along the great avenue, moving at the highest speed the wheel motors of the robot bodies could maintain in continuous use. It was the equivalent of a steady jog, the Doctor estimated. They saw no more slave workers and only encountered three other Red Sector robots, all of whom accepted Green-8's explanation of their presence with the same slightly dismissive air.

They passed a place where two ends of what might have been an ornamental bridge had been set on either side of the avenue, but with no middle section to connect them. From the weathering visible on the two sections it was obviously not a project in the process of construction.

'An unfinished bridge placed where none was needed,' the Doctor observed. 'This is in keeping with haha walls that serve no purpose except to trap unwary pedestrians.'

'The programme corruption has spread further than I imagined,' Green-8 said. 'How long has the error gone unchecked?'

'Hopefully we'll find out,' the Doctor replied.

The red globe of the sun was hovering over the horizon when Green-8 finally slowed the pace of their travel. The walls and hedges of the gardens, which had lined the avenue along its entire length, now turned aside in sharp right angles. The double rank of the processional trees ended at a broad crossroads. On the far side of the swathe of gravel was a stone-pillared gateway flanked by twin gatehouses. Figures stood alertly before each pillar in the attitude of guards. The gates were set in a high wall that extended away east and west until it curved out of sight. The tops of trees could be seen at some distance beyond the gateway.

'This is the edge of Blue Sector,' Green-8 announced. 'In there is the Palace.'

'You almost sound nervous, Green-8,' the Doctor said.

'Perhaps that is as good a description of the current activity of my central processor as any. I am aware that I am outside my assigned sector without authority, and that I will soon encounter the Lords in person. Yet I know I must continue. If I cannot speak, you must do so for me, Doctor. My programmed inhibitions may be too strong.'

'You'll do fine,' the Doctor assured him. 'Just get us inside. Then we can find whoever's in authority and make them listen to us.'

'I shall try, Doctor.'

But before they could cross the road a vehicle appeared coming along the western road. It was an ornate closed carriage drawn by a team of four matching bay horses all decked out in highly polished harness. The gate guards let it through without hindrance and even gave salutes as it passed.

'More horse-drawn vehicles,' the Doctor mused.

'Is there something wrong in that?' Green-8 asked. 'I have data on my files that says Lords often ride quadrupeds or sometimes travel in horse-drawn carriages for ceremonial purposes. I understood such means of transport were symbols of leisure.'

'That's quite true, but I would have expected to have seen at least one person riding in a powered vehicle by now. Maybe we'll find some on the other side of that wall. Come on.'

As they approached the gate they saw that the guards were dressed in high boots and hose, with gleaming metal breastplates and helmets crowned with plumes. Swords hung from their belts and they each carried pike-like weapons about as tall as themselves, resting the butts on the ground.

The guards were talking in casual tones as the Doctor and Green-8 approached.

'...the Baron of Delminster and his lady, that were.'

'The Baron maybe, but 'twere never his wife I saw at his side.'

'Whoso, then?'

'A slim little thing all bowed and beribboned. A very lively armful she would make, I've no doubt – or maybe lapfull would be more the way of it,' he added with a knowing wink.

'And he'd bring her to such a banquet all bold and brazen?'

'His dalliances are no secret amongst the Lords and Ladies. Have you not heard the tales of what the Baroness does when –'

'Excuse us... sirs,' Green-8 interrupted diffidently. 'We are surveying the damage done by the storm. May we enter to...'

One of the guards focused on them with an expression of mild surprise, as though noticing them for the first time.

'Eh? Be you more servants for the banquet?'

'That is correct,' the Doctor said quickly.

'Pass within…' he waved his hand vaguely.

The Doctor and Green-8 rolled through the open gates. Behind them the two guards continued their dissection of the scandalous behaviour of the privileged classes.

'I had expected something… more significant,' Green-8 said, as they continued along a broad gravel road that curved through gently undulating parkland, as artfully contoured as the gardens were level. 'But we are inside the Blue Sector. The home of the Lords of Esselven.'

'Who seem to be guarded by very primitively attired soldiers.'

'Surely their costume is only intended for show,' Green-8 said. 'I understand that humans sometimes dress for superficial effect, rather than practical necessity.'

'Yes, but even the guards at Buckingham Palace carry modern weapons.'

'I do not know of this place.'

'Never mind. I expected to see signs of higher technology. So far you and your kind are the most technically sophisticated devices in evidence on this planet… ahh, what have we here?'

A group of three humanoid robots in armoured bodyshells were coming towards them at a fast trot, their photoscanner eyes were flicking continuously left and right as though on alert. They carried multifunction rifles linked to power backpacks.

'Fighting machines,' the Doctor said. 'It might be wise not to do anything to alarm them.'

'I have no intention of alarming anybody,' Green-8 assured him.

The three sinister robots flicked their gaze across the Doctor and Green-8 for a few seconds, then, apparently satisfied that they posed no threat, continued on with their patrol.

'I have never seen any robots of that type before,' Green-8

observed. 'What would they have done if they had detected your disguise?'

'Hopefully we will never find out,' the Doctor said. 'Were they looking for something in particular or simply on a routine patrol of the grounds, I wonder.'

'They are at least further examples of the higher technology that you were looking for.'

'Yes, but apparently acting autonomously at the moment. Can we find the people who control them? Come on.'

They had continued along the winding road for another kilometre when Green-8 spotted a more familiar form approaching.

'It is a Blue Sector robot. I shall tell it of our mission…'

The robot's wheels were throwing up gravel as it sped rapidly towards them. When it was close enough to initiate introductions, Green-8 said: 'I am Coordinator Green-8. I must request an urgent audience with –'

'Move aside!' the machine said almost curtly. 'I have priority functions to perform which cannot be delayed…'

'This is important!' the Doctor called out.

But the machine sped on past them without slowing and vanished round a bend in the road.

'Hardly a polite welcome,' the Doctor observed. 'It looks as though we're going to have to make our own introductions.'

As the sun, now distinctly oblate due to atmospheric distortion, touched the horizon, white artificial lights started appearing about the parkland. They came in the form of rods set in the ground and hovering tethered globes, which dispelled the long shadows and pink and scarlet sunset hues, creating islands of green grass and colourful foliage.

'I have never seen so much shadow,' Green-8 admitted. 'The crops in my care grow in perpetual sunlight. I wonder if they move the lights regularly to help maintain growth? Now I understand why they require regular shipments of produce from the lower latitudes. Food crops would not grow well here.'

The highest points of some large structure appeared through the trees. They crested a slight rise and the road ran straight before them, cutting through low ornamental gardens and up to the Palace itself.

'Almost a fairytale castle,' the Doctor said, 'though evidently built more for show than defensive quality. It's still sunlit so this can't quite be the pole, but we must be very close.'

The imposing building with two linked wings was adorned by a cluster of spires and turrets with conical roofs, their sheer white stone walls shining red and gold in the low rays of the timeless sun. Light fanned across the surrounding lawns from brightly lit windows and the distant murmur of music and voices carried out into the twilight. Carriages similar to the one they had seen entering the gates ahead of them were parked to one side of the main courtyard. Keeping their distance, the Doctor and Green-8 moved round to the side of the building from where most of the light and noise seemed to be coming. A line of large windows opened onto some large interior space. Through these they could just make out a number of people seated at long tables.

'Some sort of event seems to be taking place,' the Doctor said. 'Presumably the "banquet" that the guards were talking about. Shall we go in and mingle?'

'We cannot enter by the main door. It would be... improper.'

'You're going to have to work on that inferiority complex of yours, Green-8. Whatever you were you're a thinking being now, with as much right as any of those people to enter through any door you please – as long as you do it politely. But perhaps in the circumstances we might find the servants' entrance and insinuate ourselves by degrees. Come on.'

They circled further, passing unseen through the deserted gardens, until they came to the wing of the Palace which had a more utilitarian appearance. From an open arched doorway came the sound of raised voices and the clatter of metal pans. The Doctor and Green-8 entered and a short passage led them to a huge kitchen. Great copper pans steamed and bubbled on black iron ranges. A whole side of meat turned on spits over blazing open fires, dripping hissing fat into a long tray which was ladled back over the slab of meat again by a small boy. Sweating cooks yelled orders to busy helpers. Platters, pots and tureens laid out on a massive wooden table were being filled and quickly carried off shoulder-high by a relay of liveried servants. None of them took the slightest notice of the two newcomers.

The Doctor turned his false robotic head about so he could examine the entire room through its eyes, then sighed. 'I'm seriously beginning to wonder if we've been wasting our time coming here.'

'I do not understand.'

'Look at this place. No automated cooking facilities, no sign of freezing units, doubtful levels of food hygiene. If this is intended as a re-creation of a period lifestyle then it's taking authenticity to the extreme.'

'But what else can it be?'

'I'm not sure. Let's see where they're taking the food. That should lead us to the people in charge of all this.'

They rolled out of the kitchen after the laden servants. The Doctor paused in the doorway and looked around at the busy scene again. 'There's something missing.'

'What, Doctor?'

'I don't know. I feel there's something that should be here but isn't. It's so obvious and basic that I can't see it. Or perhaps it isn't to be seen anyway...'

'I cannot see anything wrong, Doctor. But then much of this is strange to me.'

Inside the body shell the Doctor shook his head perplexedly, an action replicated by its robotic counterpart. 'No doubt it will come to me in time. Let's follow the food.'

They proceeded along a bare stone corridor, through a heavy door that had been wedged open and into a wider corridor that was thickly carpeted and whose walls were hung with paintings and tapestries. The stream of hurrying servants sidestepped them neatly as they bustled along, but like the kitchen staff showed no other interest in them.

'I also note the absence of something I expected to see,' Green-8 announced.

'What's that?'

'More Blue Sector robots of my own make. We should have seen several by now inside the Palace. I understood they served the Lords closely, but I have only seen human servants. That also is unexpected. I thought all humans, except scavengers, were Lords. How can they allow others of their own kind to serve them? It is the function of robots to serve.'

'You'll find that people can manage without robots in their lives. Perhaps that's what's happening here. If the robots are not required I assume they will not force their attentions on people.'

'Certainly not.' Green-8 sounded shocked.

A large double door ahead of them was opened to allow servants bearing platters of food to enter. The Doctor and Green-8 slipped in after them.

Within was a spacious hall, its walls hung with shields and banners. Heavy wooden beams and braces supported the arching ceiling. A couple of hundred people were seated around tables laid out in a 'U', with the space between them set aside for entertainments. A trio of performers were at work there as the Doctor and Green-8 entered. It was hard to hear any words over the general buzz of conversation from where they stood, but their act seemed to consist of telling jokes, tripping over their own feet and hitting each other with paddle-like sticks that made loud claps each time they struck.

'Ahh, some old friends,' the Doctor exclaimed.

'You know them?'

'Only in passing. Bolwig, Lurket and Trampole, who may, possibly, have performed before all the crowned heads of the Nine Kingdoms.'

'What Kingdoms are these? I know only of the Summer and Winter Palaces.'

'Another question in search of an answer. Let's ask somebody who should know. Those people in the middle of the top table look regal enough for our purposes.'

In two chairs with high and ornate backs sat a handsome middle-aged couple, both very richly dressed. They each wore small crowns and gem-studded chains of silver and gold about their necks. To one side of the man was an attractive young woman. Though she laughed with the rest of the assembly at the antics of Bolwig's troupe, her expression appeared strained.

The Doctor and Green-8 edged round the long tables just as Bolwig and Lurket had taken on the roles of distant acquaintances who had just met by chance.

'Yonder, sir,' said Bolwig, pointing into the distance. 'Those two ladies who approach us. Is not the one in blue the most ugly creature you have ever espied?'

Lurket cracked Bolwig across the back of the head with his paddle, knocking him to the ground. 'That, sir, is my sister!'

The diners guffawed as Bolwig struggled to his feet. 'You misheard me, sir!' he protested, 'I mean of course the shabby old hag by her side!'

Lurket floored Bolwig for the second time. 'And that, sir, is my wife!'

The audience roared with laughter again.

'Is this what is known as humour?' Green-8 asked.

'Of a sort,' the Doctor said.

They were behind the top table now.

'I'll try to explain what's going on but I don't hold out much hope,' the Doctor said. 'Neither is this the most conducive setting for imparting dramatic revelations…' All the diners were watching the performance as the Doctor opened the top half of his disguise and climbed stiffly out. He stretched himself for a moment, then boldly walked over to the man with the crown and tapped him on the shoulder.

'Excuse me, your… Majesty? I'm the Doctor and I have vitally important news concerning the security of the kingdom.'

The man twisted round in his chair, his eyes popping as he took in the colourful figure who had suddenly appeared by his side. 'Eh, what? Who are you?'

'The Doctor, and I must talk to you urgently…'

The other diners were turning their heads. Somebody a little way down the line said: 'Be he one of the performers?'

The Doctor persisted. 'Your Majesty, I must talk to you in private. I believe your world is under attack!'

For a moment the King's expression was a complete blank. Then he blinked and said: 'This is nonsense. Remove this man!'

Several male banqueters had pushed back their chairs and were rising menacingly. A pair of liveried servants were stepping up with their hands outstretched to grab the Doctor. Guards from the main door were running around the tables with unsheathed swords.

'Doctor!' Green-8 called out. 'I suggest you resume your disguise. It will protect you.'

The circle of would-be removal men closed about the Doctor as he backed away from the table. 'This may indeed be a time when discretion is the better part of valour,' the Doctor agreed.

In a movement surprisingly agile for one of his build, the Doctor sprang back to the fake body shell of Green-35, scrambled inside and slammed down the upper torso, almost trapping the fingers of his pursuers in the process. For a few seconds they pounded on the shell of the machine, then their arms dropped to their sides.

'He went inside the... mechanical,' one of them said.

'Most... peculiar,' said another.

Through the eyepieces the Doctor saw them gazing at the robotic body with puzzled expressions on their faces. Then as one they turned away and went back to their places.

Other banqueters who had been staring at the altercation now returned their attention to Bolwig's players. The chatter in the banqueting hall resumed its former volume.

'I know this is a good disguise,' the Doctor said to Green-8 over their radio link, 'but this is rather more effective than even I had anticipated...'

It was as though the robots standing in plain sight of two hundred pairs of eyes did not exist.

Chapter Twenty

'No way am I going to mate, marry or do anything of that sort with Kel,' said Peri emphatically, for what seemed to her to be the twentieth time. 'He's a nice kid, but he's not for me. Get it?'

She was standing resolutely in the 'square' of Thorn Tree. Greld, some older men, Kel and Raz were ranged about her. The village's women formed a curious ring a little distance off. Nerla, her face red and grimy cheeks tear-streaked, hovered anxiously on the edge of the inner group. The situation was both absurd and seriously frustrating, Peri thought. With so many more important things on the agenda, she'd managed to get herself caught up in a primitive love-triangle.

'You promised to live by law of Thorn Tree,' Greld said. 'You wear b'long, you now Thorn Tree girl. Kel has right to choose you.'

Peri tugged at the token tied about her arm but couldn't get the knot loose. 'Look, I didn't know putting this thing on meant letting myself in for that sort of a deal. I'm just passing through. I've got other plans for my life. You can't make me marry him!'

She realised it was a stupid thing to say the moment the words had left her lips. They could make her do pretty much what they liked. According to their rules she was in the wrong. Unless she convinced them to see reason her only choice would be to go back out into the forest and hope she could reach the gardens before another dog pack got her. Assuming she could find her way and the Thorn Tree clan would let her go. And some people still thought living in the wilds was a simple life!

'Why did you ever have to pick me?' she asked Kel in exasperation.

Kel gave the wild grin of a young man a little drunk on the privileges of adulthood. 'Because you are real woman. You feel good to touch. You will please me. You will bear many children –'

'Stop right there!' Peri said quickly.

She snatched a glance at the distraught Nerla, thinking that Kel knew how to wound, possibly without thinking, the girl who obviously wanted him. With several baths and a day in a high-powered beauty saloon she'd be quite presentable, but Nerla certainly hadn't filled out to her full potential yet. Maybe she never would, of course. The harsh lifestyle wasn't conducive to blooming health, and Peri had to admit she herself had more *embonpoint* than any of the women here, a quality which Kel clearly admired. But what could she say to put him off?

'Look, I'd make a terrible mate,' Peri said with desperate sincerity. 'I'm lazy, I wouldn't keep the hut clean, I don't do alfresco cooking. Why not forget me and choose somebody who'd do a better job…' She reached out and grabbed Nerla's arm and pulled her over to stand in front of Kel. 'Now anybody can see Nerla wants to be your mate. And she's a proper Thorn Tree girl, not a fly-by-nighter like me. She'd care for you the way a great hunter deserves.'

Nerla looked at Kel hopefully.

Kel frowned, eyeing both of them with an air of almost clinical calculation. Peri held her breath and tried to look unappealing. Then he pointed a grubby finger at Peri. 'No. I will still have you. You will learn to please me. If you are lazy I will beat you –'

'Hey!' Peri exclaimed.

The other men were nodding at what they obviously saw was a common-sense approach to ensuring domestic harmony.

Peri eyed the distance to the gates from where she stood. Assuming she could dodge the guards, she'd just have to hope she could stay on the path that they came in along and keep running.

'I… I claim a challenge,' Nerla said tremulously, speaking up for herself for the first time.

'Good for you!' Peri said encouragingly.

'She has the right,' Greld agreed.

'I be better mate for you,' Nerla continued. 'She is… outsider. Not of Wild Woods. I will make you true-happy. She will not.'

'See,' Peri said. 'She thinks I'm not up to the job as well.'

'I will fight her for you!' Nerla said.

Peri blinked. 'No, wait a moment. There's no need to fight over this. You can have him. I forfeit –'

'You must fight Nerla,' Greld said. 'She must show to all that she is better than you. It is only way Kel may change chosen mate and keep his honour.'

'Oh come on! He's not worth actually fighting over –'

She saw Nerla's expression change to one of fierce contempt. To her Kel was literally worth fighting for – and Peri had just insulted both her and him.

'I… I mean, of course Kel's a great guy,' Peri floundered, 'but… isn't there some other way?'

'No,' Greld said flatly. 'Let this be done now!'

In a daze, Peri watched the villagers shuffling back to form a ring about herself and Nerla. She looked about desperately for any gap through which she might slip away, but there was none. Two of the hunters stepped forward and gave them wooden staffs about as tall as they were. Peri took her weapon gingerly while Nerla swung hers about to judge its weight in a calculating manner.

Standing beside Greld, she saw Kel's face alive with anticipation. He was enjoying the prospect of them fighting over him. Why had she ever helped him escape from the gardeners?

'Ready!' Greld said, and Nerla crouched, holding her staff raised.

Peri knew, ever since her first serious playground dispute, she was no great physical fighter. She thought she was reasonably brave, but she just didn't have whatever it took to slug it out face to face. Half the trouble was her fear of doing serious harm to her opponent by accident. She would rather talk her way out of a confrontation or run away from it.

But those options were no longer open to her.

She looked at Nerla's face and knew her opponent wouldn't be satisfied with inflicting a few scratches. But she couldn't risk serious injury in these conditions. What if a bad cut became infected and she never made it back to the TARDIS's first-aid kit in time?

'Begin!'

With a scream of rage, Nerla leapt forward, swinging at Peri's head. Peri parried the blow more by luck than skill, and skipped backwards. Nerla yelled and came in for another attack, raining down blows which Peri did her best to deflect by gripping her staff with her hands well separated and twisting it so that its middle lay across the path of the next blow. An image popped into Peri's mind of Errol Flynn as Robin Hood, sparring against Little John with quarterstaves on a log bridge, set in an idyllic Sherwood Forest that never existed outside Hollywood.

Where were heroes when you needed them?

They circled about, the crack of wood on wood filling the clearing, the softly glowing fungus lanterns throwing multiple shadows across the beaten earth.

Peri was heavier and a little taller, but Nerla was tougher and more determined. In the end she would wear her down by sheer persistence. If she could only lose in some graceful manner. But she dare not trust Nerla to hold back. Yet to win herself she'd have to beat Nerla – and that would mean hurting her. And then she'd be expected to marry Kel!

Then the decision was made for her.

Stepping back quickly after parrying a ferocious blow to her ribs, Peri's heel turned on a flat stone lying just under the earth.

She slipped and staggered to regain her balance. Like lightning Nerla lunged forward and cracked her staff across Peri's stomach.

With a whoop of pain, Peri fell over backwards, dropping her own staff as by reflex she clutched at her middle. Nerla straddled her prostrate body and sat down on her chest, driving the wind from her for a second time. She raised her staff aloft in triumph and the crowd cheered and shouted and stamped their feet.

'There… you've won!' Peri gasped. 'It's over… you can have Kel…'

But Nerla's face was set in a vengeful mask, showing not a trace of mercy. Instead of putting her staff down she raised it higher. Peri saw her knuckles tighten. She was going to drive the butt down into Peri's face! Peri's arms were pinned to her sides. She couldn't protect herself.

'No!' she screamed –

Then another woman in the crowd was screaming and men were shouting and running.

The sudden uproar penetrated Nerla's revenge-filled mind and she twisted round to see what the cause was. With a sudden access of desperate strength, Peri wrenched one arm free and shoved Nerla off her and onto her back. Nerla tried to scramble to her knees but Peri twisted round and slapped her with stinging force, leaving a blazing red imprint of her hand on the girl's cheek.

'Next time stop fighting when someone surrenders!' she yelled at her, sobbing with fear and anger.

Peri slowly realised that she and Nerla were alone on the circle of earth. The rest of the villagers were cowering amongst the huts to one side of her, the men holding spears nervously at the ready. She turned to look in the direction of their frightened glances.

Gliding out from the shadows between two huts opposite was a metallic disk, hovering at about head height over the ground.

Two forward-facing lenses glittered like glass eyes. As it got closer she saw the letters D.A.V.E. on its side…

'Oh hell,' Peri exclaimed with feeling, 'it's Dexel Dynes!'

The spaceship in the hangar had not provided Dynes with as much material as he had hoped, nor the incontrovertible proof he needed. He had opened a hatchway with an emergency crank, the ship's power cells being completely dead, and spent several hours exploring the interior. The labelling on controls and machinery was in Esselvanian script, but without power he had no access to the ship's computer and every sort of personal item seemed to have been removed from its crew compartments. The hyper-drive blister damage strongly suggested it was the craft the royal family had used in their escape, but it wasn't absolute clinching evidence.

Against this theory was the fact that the ship felt cold and long dead. Judging by external appearances it had been sitting in the overgrown hangar for hundreds of years. How could it have been spaceworthy just a year before?

Dynes felt the unfamiliar pangs of frustration. His instincts told him there was a terrific story here, but he had to have an answer that would satisfy his audience. There was nothing worse than being presented with a first-class mystery then being denied a satisfactory resolution.

He currently knew just how that felt. Where was Judd? It had been over a day since Dynes had landed and the Protector's attack force should have been hard on his heels. Walking back to the *Stop Press* from the hangar, Dynes again scanned the luminescent overcast above him. Apart from the wheeling specks of a flock of birds it was empty of any sign of life.

Inside his cabin he checked on the progress of the roving DAVE units. He had left three DAVEs stationed around the landing field to cover Judd's landing, and had sent the rest out on reconnaissance.

So far they had discovered little of interest. The two he had set exploring the surrounding forest showed only more of the same familiar scenery, with a few traces of animal activity. The one he had despatched along the overgrown road leading away from the landing ground still had not reached its end nor recorded anything of interest on the way. In places the road was almost blocked by fallen trees and curtains of vines. Nothing of any size, and certainly no wheeled traffic, had used the way in years.

It was as Dynes brooded over this lack of newsworthy data, that he noticed a well-worn path leading off the road and cutting through the tangled forest. Perhaps it was simply an animal track, but at least it looked freshly used. Taking control of the DAVE he guided it over to take a closer look. In the soft ground at the mouth of the path were the imprints of several feet, encased in what might have been soft-soled boots.

Encouraged by the find he directed the DAVE along the path. After a short while the track joined a second pathway running across its course. Dynes chose the way that appeared most worn and continued forward.

The new path seemed to wind on interminably and Dynes began looking anxiously at the distance the DAVE had covered. He was almost on the point of giving up the search when the DAVE turned a corner and he saw a crude wooden fence ahead of him.

The structure was obviously of primitive manufacture but it was better than nothing. Now, where were the beings who built it? Cautiously he steered the DAVE up to the fence to peer over its jagged crest.

Beyond was a simple settlement of thatched huts illuminated by feeble lanterns nestling in a clearing in the forest. He saw a circle of raggedly dressed humanoids intent on watching some activity that he couldn't make out for the press of bodies. The microphones picked up excited grunts and yells. Dynes hopped the DAVE over the fence and guided it forward between two of the huts, trying to find an angle from which he could see what the people were so excited about. He had no idea what part, if any, this played in the story he was following, but right now it seemed to be the most interesting thing happening on the entire planet.

He must have been careless manoeuvring the DAVE, for he saw a woman's face on the edge of the crowd turn towards him. Her mouth gaped open in surprise, then she was stabbing a frightened finger at the DAVE and screaming at the top of her voice.

In seconds her cry was taken up by the others. The crowd stampeded in panic across the clearing to take shelter amongst the huts on the far side, leaving two raggedly dressed young women lying on the ground

He sent the DAVE closer. Since they knew he was here now he might as well collect all the details he could. It looked as though the two had been fighting each other, which always made good viewing. A pity he hadn't arrived sooner…

Then one of the women, whose costume was slightly less ragged than that of her companion, looked straight at the DAVE and exclaimed: 'Oh hell, it's Dexel Dynes!'

Dynes zoomed in on her face. Underneath the grime it did seem vaguely familiar… Then he remembered.

'Perpugilliam Brown,' his voice sounded through the DAVE's speaker, 'hostile news subject!'

'What are you doing here, Dynes?' Peri demanded, jabbing her finger at the DAVE's lenses. 'Grubbing around for more cheap sensations?'

'Just doing my job, Ms Brown,' Dynes replied stiffly.

'Oh yeah? By the way, has the nose healed up yet?'

The silence from the camera drone was telling. The memory of the last time she'd seen Dynes came back clearly. The wooded glade on the treasure planet of Gelsandor, Dynes lying on his back holding a hand to his thoroughly deserved bloody nose. It had almost made up for all the suffering she'd had to endure which he had been so eager to chronicle for the entertainment of his viewers.

'As I said,' Dynes continued, as though the question had not been asked, 'I am just doing my job. I suppose your friend the Doctor is about here somewhere?'

Peri suddenly wondered how much Dynes knew about their situation. Why were his drone cameras skulking round the wild woods anyway? If he'd followed her here, he'd know the Doctor wasn't with her. It suggested he was based somewhere nearby and he'd just turned up at Thorn Tree by chance and now he was fishing for information. But he wasn't the sort of reporter who covered local flower shows, so he must think something big was going on otherwise he wouldn't be here at all. Perhaps she could turn the tables for a change…

'The Doctor will turn up when he's good and ready,' she said casually.

'You look as though you could do with his assistance right now, Ms Brown,' Dynes said, as the DAVE tilted up and down to record her dishevelled state in lingering detail.

Peri folded her arms defiantly across what remained of the bodice of her dress and said: 'This is nothing. Just a little fun the, er, Mojaves like to have with visitors. I suppose that's what you're here for. Reporting on the Mojaves of Anaheim?'

'Yes… I find the study of primitive societies highly newsworthy,' Dynes replied.

'Then you can't have been studying these people very long or else you'd know they aren't called Mojaves and this isn't Anaheim! You don't know anything about this place, do you?'

There was a near silence during which Peri fancied she could hear Dynes grinding his teeth in anger, then he said, 'I suppose you think you've been very clever?'

'Smarter than you, anyway.'

Peri had intended to tell Dynes to get lost, but now she hesitated, thinking quickly. Could she use him to make an exposé of how the so-called 'Lords' were treating the scavengers? That was a story that really did need telling to a wider audience. Having an extra witness who could record the details of what was going on here might be useful. She'd got the impression when they last met that Dynes had a name of sorts in his profession. Now was the chance to make use of it.

'I know things about the set-up here that you could take weeks finding out,' she continued. 'Now, I may be prepared to let you in on some of this, if we can cut a deal.'

'I can offer the standard interview terms and perhaps a bonus for supplying specialist local knowledge,' Dynes said promptly.

'I don't want your money. We trade information so I can decide what I'm going to do next, and at the end of it I guarantee you'll get a story.'

'What sort of story?' Dynes asked cautiously.

'How about a bunch of Lords living in a Palace while their hoards of fanatical robots keep a load of people as slaves? Think you can make something with that?'

There was a pause of a quite different character the previous one. Then Dynes said: 'Yes, I think my viewers might find that of interest. Very well, Ms Brown. We have a deal.'

'Great.'

Only then did Peri realise that many pairs of eyes were fixed upon her. Recovering from their initial fright, the scavengers had gradually edged out of their hiding places and were looking at her in an attitude somewhere between fear and awe. Of course, she was the one talking with a disembodied voice coming from a flying disk the like of which they hadn't seen before. They had probably thought it was some new device of the gardeners when it first appeared, sent after them in response to the produce they'd been stealing. Now it was likely they didn't know what to make of it.

Time to boost her own status a little.

'This device is controlled by a… friend from a faraway land,' she announced grandly. 'He is…' she almost gagged on the words '… a seeker of the truth. He may be able to aid your struggle against the gardeners and help me convince the Lords that you should be returned to the light. We must converse further in private. Then I will tell you what action I am going to take next.' She looked at Greld, whose face showed his confusion. 'We expect to remain undisturbed,' she told him, in a tone that assumed compliance. With the DAVE following she marched boldly back into the hut she had slept in and firmly pulled the ragged curtain over the door.

Inside she sat down gingerly on her rough mattress, rubbing her sore ribs, and looked squarely at the camera drone.

'Okay. You wouldn't be here unless it was for something big. You tell me about it and I'll tell you how it fits in with the local situation.'

Dynes' voice came back crisply over the drone's speaker. 'Well, I've been doing an exclusive on Glavis Judd and the expansion of his Protectorate.'

Peri didn't repeat Dynes' earlier mistake and try to pretend she'd heard of either of them. 'I've been away from this, uh, sector of space for a while. Tell me about this Judd guy.'

Dynes did so.

Peri emerged from the hut fifteen minutes later snapping out orders and hoping the scavengers were still sufficiently impressed with her recent performance not to argue.

'Chansor Greld – listen carefully. An evil man is coming from far away with an army to invade Esselven. They have weapons and machines much more dangerous than the gardeners. You can't fight them so you must just stay out of sight and hope they don't find you. You must send messengers to the other villages telling them to keep their heads down. The Lords may not know this man is coming so I'm going to tell them. I'll need an escort to get to the edge of the woods and a few of your people to go with me to the Palace. Do you understand?'

The old man looked dazed but he nodded. 'I… yes, Peri Brown. I understand. It shall be done. Who shall you take with you to see Lords?'

Peri looked about at the bemused villagers who had been hanging on her words. She'd need at least one person to act as a guide and to represent the scavenger people. But who?

Then Kel stepped forward, looking impressive, in a ragged way, in his hunter garb, holding his spear firmly. 'I shall go to Palace. I shall talk with Lords. I shall… spit in their eye if they do not listen.'

Peri grinned. For all his faults Kel might be the best person to take. 'Right, you can come.'

Nerla and Raz stepped up beside Kel and whispered urgently in his ear. He said: 'They also want to come. We were best scavenger team. Never got caught by gardeners…'cept the last time.'

Peri frowned at Nerla. 'No more fighting?'

'No more fighting, Peri Brown,' she promised.

'Okay, you're all on. Grab some food and let's get going.'

Ten minutes later, the four of them with three escort hunters and the DAVE drone gliding in their wake, were heading back along the path to the edge of the wild woods.

Peri's mind was spinning and she knew she was not half as confident as she had appeared. It was in these moments that she could have really used the Doctor's advice. But there was no time to hunt for the Doctor. She had to get to the Palace and find out what the Lords were doing about the imminent invasion. From what Dynes had said it seemed they had let their defences rot. In fact she didn't really care much about the Lords after seeing the way they had treated the scavengers. Her sympathy for the scavengers had also taken something of a downturn recently, but at least she felt they had an excuse for behaving as they did. Now it was a case of sink or swim together.

The trouble was she had no idea what sort of reception she would get when and if she managed to get to this fabled Palace. Based on what Dynes had told her, she was beginning to suspect that the history of Esselven Kel had related to her had been quite distorted, though she hadn't got the whole thing straight in her own head yet. Focus, she reminded herself. The hard fact was that a fascist tyrant was going to invade this world anytime now and it seemed to have fallen to her to try to do something about it.

To assist in her mission she had a handful of people barely out of the stone age and a reporter who was only cooperating out of cynical self-interest. Getting to the Palace ahead of Judd's force would allow Dynes to set up cameras to record both sides of the battle he was obviously anticipating with some delight.

All in all it was not, Peri had to admit, a comforting proposition.

The bloated red eye of the sun was glittering through the trees as they reached the edge of the wild woods. Here their escort left them with words of encouragement, and the diminished party set off through the pylon chain and out across the rolling heathland towards the gardens.

They made good time. Despite his disability, Raz moved as quickly as his companions. But Peri didn't intend to walk all the way to the Palace, which from her estimates was nearly a day away on foot. She had considered but rejected asking Dynes for transport in his own ship. Assuming he had agreed it would put her too much in his power. Despite their understanding she didn't trust him an inch. Peri was determined to find some transport of her own, and thought the gardeners might provide what she required.

The party cautiously approached the landscaping zone, listening for the sound of powerful engines. From the top of a small hill they saw the dark scar of ripped earth before them and in the distance a machine grinding along like some huge mechanical beetle. Peri led them along the edge of the heathland, spying on the working zone as they went. It wasn't long before she found what she was after.

On a stretch of ground flattened by the tracks of tyres and caterpillar tracks, three of the earthmovers stood silent and unattended. Peri's eyes fastened on one which was evidently the local equivalent of a dumper truck, resting on six huge tyres taller than a man. It was as she'd hoped. With the gardeners still busy putting the gardens to rights, most of this land was being worked only by completely automated machines while others lay idle. They shouldn't notice if one went missing.

She'd noticed the first time they'd crossed the landscaping zone that even the automated machines had driver's cabins, so it seemed a safe bet that they could be steered manually. That was the theory anyway.

They worked their way as close to the machine as possible using what cover the scrub grass and stunted bushes provided. They couldn't see any gardeners, but other earthmovers were still visible in the distance.

'No scavenger has ever tried to take a thing like that before,' Kel whispered as they crouched in the long grass.

'Good,' Peri said. 'That should mean it won't be locked. Come on!'

They dashed across the open space and into the shadow of the truck. The three scavengers goggled at the bulk of the machine, never having been as close to one before. Peri saw there was a folding platform lift reaching down from the side of the cab, presumably to accommodate the wheeled gardeners, but beside it was a set of metal rungs welded to the body. She climbed up them to the wide running board and tugged at the door. It opened easily. She scrambled inside the large driver's cabin followed by the others.

As they looked about them in wonder, Peri examined the control position. At first she thought there was no driver's seat, but then she saw it was folded down into a recess in the floor, positioned out of the way so that a gardener could operate the machine. Maybe the Lords liked to drive these things for fun once in a while. It unfolded with a tug and she seated herself before the controls.

The steering column was topped by an aircraft style yoke rather than a wheel, but there was a straightforward-looking gear stick running in a slot beside the seat. The other lever had to be the handbrake. Just two pedals on the floor suggested the equivalent of automatic transmission. Where the dashboard display should have been was a featureless black panel with a vertical row of large coloured buttons beside it. At least the general arrangement was recognisable. If they were in Dynes' time, then it was about a millennium ahead of Peri's Earthly experience, but certain fundamentals of ergonomic design apparently still held true.

'Can you actually drive one of these?' said Dynes' voice, relayed through the DAVE, in her ear.

'During holidays back home I drove a farm tractor and once even a combine harvester,' she said, trying to sound confident. 'This isn't so different.' *I hope*, she added silently.

Peri pressed the top button of the row and coloured lines and figures appeared on the black panel. Great, she thought: some sort of solid state display. Hopefully it's saying everything's fine and we've got a full tank of gas. She pressed the next button and a subdued hum of power could be heard, accompanied by more lines and lights flickering over the display.

She selected what she hoped was a forward gear, eased off the handbrake and lightly pressed down the pedal which she guessed was the throttle –

With a powerful but muted whine of motors, the huge vehicle lurched forward. Peri twisted the steering yoke sharply to avoid hitting one of the stationary earthmovers. The vehicle swayed alarmingly, throwing Kel and the others off their feet. Note the highly geared power steering, Peri told herself, as with a gentler motion she put them back on a straight course.

Accelerating steadily, she sent the huge vehicle bumping over the rolling moorland northwards.

'Next stop the Palace,' she told her passengers cheerfully.

Chapter Twenty-one

Oralissa sat numbly in her chair, momentarily oblivious to the chatter about her and the food on her plate. She had seen something amazing take place and, incredibly, no one else appeared to think it worthy of comment.

'My lady? Oralissa?'

She blinked, realising Benedek had been talking to her.

Benedek had drawn the lucky straw and been seated next to her. Stephon was placed on the other side of the two high chairs beside her mother. The fleeting glances of annoyance he directed at Benedek spoke of his frustration at being separated from Oralissa, and uncertainty as to what headway his rival was making in her affections. If only he knew that romance was the last thing on her mind at that moment.

'Are you feeling unwell?' Benedek asked, his voice thick with genuine concern.

'Did you see the man who spoke to my father but seconds past?'

'Oh, he was one of the jesters, was he not? These fellows sometimes get above themselves in their playacting.'

'I don't think so. When you rose to remove him… he got back inside a mechanical! Did you not see that?'

Benedek looked puzzled. 'The fellow just took himself off. I did not notice where.'

'But you must have seen it. There were two mechanicals by the wall. They wore green devices rather than blue. They have both left now…'

She saw the puzzled, slightly pitying look on Benedek's face and knew it was useless to say more.

'I crave your pardon,' she said quickly. 'I must beg to leave the table. You are right, I am feeling a little unwell… Father, may I leave?'

Her father looked at her sternly and said in low tones: 'My dear, this feast is in thy own honour. It is not done to absent oneself at such times.'

'Please, Father. Would you wish me to faint away when a few breaths of cool air would soon clear my head? I promise I shall not be long.'

Her Father sighed. 'As you wish. I shall summon your maid.'

'No – I wish to be alone.'

The male diners rose politely as Oralissa left the table and exited the chamber as fast as decorum permitted. Outside in the hall she glanced around wildly for some sign of the mechanicals. There was no point in asking the servants, she knew. She picked up her skirts and raced along the main corridor, glancing down every turning. Surely they could not have gone far…

Green-8 and the Doctor rolled along a corridor unremarked by the few servants they passed.

'How can we discover the information we seek if the inhabitants of this place reject you in your true form and ignore us in the form of robots?'

'More to the point; why do they behave that way?' the Doctor said. 'It was almost as though they were under some form of mental control.'

'Could this be connected with the controlling intelligences we seek?'

'I notice you did not call them the "Lords".'

Green-8 sounded almost dejected. 'If these are the Lords, then they cannot be the masters of Esselven. Apart from their lifestyle, how can they direct robots that they do not seem able even to see? It is hard to reject something I held to be a fact all my functional existence, but in the face of this evidence I must do so.'

'I know this can't be easy for you, but don't let it interfere with our mission. All it means is that we'll have to work this problem out for ourselves. Let's start with a basic assumption. This Palace is evidently an important building, so we shall suppose for the moment, despite the curious behaviour of its current inhabitants, that there is some form of control centre located here. Where do we find it?'

'The logical place to site a control centre is in the lower levels. If this was the original home of the rulers of Esselven, then they would not care to go far to monitor the activities of their robots, yet they would want the upper levels open to the air and light for leisure and private use. It would also be a convenient place for the tubeway terminus to be situated.'

'Congratulations, Green-8. You're beginning to reason like one of the ruling class, though that may not be an entirely desirable thing. However, it suggests that we're looking for a simple lift. The entrance might even be in plain sight, if these people don't take any notice of robots coming and going. Let's see if we can find the main hall. This way, I would guess…'

They rolled along the corridor until they came to a spacious entrance hall. Two flights of solid stairs with carved heraldic figures perched on their newel posts rose by half turns to the broad landing above. Inlaid wooden panels decorated the walls.

'There may be more than one shaft in a building this size, but this would be the logical place to locate an access point,' the Doctor said, beginning to examine the walls closely.

'I see no doors here other than the obvious ones, Doctor.'

'It may have been concealed, either by accident or design,' the Doctor said. 'Ah, what have we here?'

He was checking the area under one of the flights of stairs. Two faint shadowy bands extended outward from the skirting board and faded as they reached the centre of the hall.

'They are consistent with the repeated passage of robot wheels,' Green-8 said.

The Doctor reached out with his pseudo-robotic arm to examine the wall immediately above the point where the tracks appeared. The rubber tips of his fingers seemed to sink into the wooden panel.

'Most interesting. A holographic projection of a wall panel. But how do we see what's behind it?'

'Doctor,' Green-8 said. 'It may respond to a common key signal.'

'Go ahead, Green-8.'

Green-8 did not appear to do anything, but the wooden panel melted away to reveal a recessed door of polished metal, which in turn slid back into a pocket in the wall to reveal a small boxlike compartment.

'The lift,' said the Doctor cheerfully. 'I think it'll just about take both of us.'

There was a simple control panel inside the lift that showed two sub levels.

'The lowest is probably the tubeway station,' the Doctor said. 'Let's try the one above that...'

The door had just closed behind them as Oralissa, breathing heavily, ran into the hall.

When she saw it was empty, her shoulders slumped. Where could they be? Perhaps they had gone back outside? She made her way along to a side door and stepped out into the cool air of the perpetual twilight.

With all the guests inside she had the gardens to herself, Oralissa realised. That might make it easier to find the two mechanicals.

But though she circled the Palace completely, peering into every shadowed corner, she could see nothing of them. In fact, she now realised, she had seen no mechanicals of any description, apart from the two she sought, either here or in the Palace for some time. Where had they all gone?

The nervous energy that had sustained her began to run low, and she sat down on a bench by a lighting rod to think. Distantly she could hear the merrymaking from the Great Hall, but had no urge to return to the banquet. She had felt the curious eyes upon her all the time she had been seated and it had done nothing to lift her spirits.

She sighed. As if she didn't have enough concerns without being the prize in a political marriage contested by rival suitors. At least the cool and quiet of the garden was restful. She felt it easier to concentrate out here, simply enjoying the sight of the flowers basking in the light of the glow rod…

Light.

What was it about the light?

Even as she tried to clothe her vague suspicion with words she felt the elusive thread of reason slipping away from her as it had so often before. But she wouldn't let it go! The image of the man in the guise of a mechanical was still strong in her mind; proof that the unexpected could happen, that there was more to life than outward appearance.

She frowned at the lighting rod, but it seemed the same as always. What was wrong with it? Think, think!

The barrier melted away and she suddenly saw the obvious.

The rod's light was bright, clear and constant but cold. But if it was cold it could not hold a flame, and if there was no flame burning inside, what could it be? The rods were like the mechanicals, even more ubiquitous, in fact. They were a wonderful thing, an impossible thing. They were there, everybody used them – but nobody wondered who made them or how they worked! Except her.

And once again she knew nobody would understand. Her

excitement was muted by the dismal knowledge that if she rushed back to the banquet with her latest puzzle it would be received with the same profound lack of interest as before. There was no one she could ask. She had tried everybody who would listen…

No, not quite.

She felt the thrill of a second revelation. It was so obvious! Why had she not thought to ask them before?

She would find a mechanical, any mechanical, and ask it her questions about the lighting rods, about the strange storm, even its own origins. It was a servant. It must answer her. And if there were no mechanicals close to the Palace, then she would seek them out further afield.

Heartened by her new sense of resolution, Oralissa sprang to her feet and set off deeper into the gardens.

The Doctor and Green-8 rolled out into a spacious, square, brightly lit vestibule. The utilitarian walls bore none of the decoration evident in the Palace above. Set in the middle of each were three large metal doors.

'Hallo!' the Doctor called loudly, 'is anybody here?'

There was no answer from behind any of the featureless doors.

The Doctor pointed to the door to the left of the lift. 'Let's try that one first.'

The door slid back at the Doctor's touch and lights within came on. A large chamber extended before them. Machine tools were ranged about the walls, together with shelves and racks piled high with robotic spare parts.

They rolled inside and looked around.

'A machine shop and robot maintenance bay,' the Doctor said. 'This may be where your Blue Sector robots keep themselves operational, Green-8.'

'Not only Blue Sector robots, Doctor. Look there.'

Several large forms moulded out of thin clear plastic had been stacked against a wall. Scraps of foam packing block and sealing tape lay on the floor by them.

'They are storage cocoons for assembled robots that have not yet been activated,' Green-8 said. 'The inner dimensions of the shells are consistent with the proportions of the three fighting machines we encountered in the grounds.'

'And they appear to have been recently unpacked,' the Doctor added. 'You don't activate fighting robots for fun. It's possible somebody knows about the attack on the planet's shield and is responding to it. But unless those revellers upstairs are putting on a deliberate show of bravado, nobody's told them.'

'More evidence that they are not the rulers here. But who is?'

'We'll find out,' the Doctor assured him. 'This place seems to extend for some way under the Palace. There may be another entrance from outside in the grounds, but we'll leave that for later. Let's try the next door...'

The door on the opposite side of the vestibule differed from the others because a second hinged door had been fitted over the recess. The Doctor swung it aside, noting its thickness. The inner door radiated a noticeable chill.

'A storage room of some sort. What does whoever uses this place want to keep in here, I wonder – emergency rations?'

The inner door slid open and cold, dry musty air poured out. Lights come on automatically.

The icy room was filled with metal racks and shelves, on which rested dozens of gaunt and desiccated bodies.

Chapter Twenty-two

Glavis Judd reached the rank of Sector Marshal at a younger age than any man before him. Then he put his name forward as the Military Party candidate for the next election to the post of World President of Zalcrossar.

He won with a sizable majority.

Immediately, he began stamping out crime and corruption with a vigour that only increased his popularity. He used military forces in addition to the civilian police, which then justified increasing military funding.

At the next election he was uncontested.

Methodically he began rebuilding the structure of Zalcrossar society. He encouraged the promotion of the genuinely able and made changes to the educational system to ensure his philosophy permeated all parts of the curriculum. Life subtly became more rigid, but at the same time unquestionably fairer and more efficient. People came to rely on the security obedience to the law gave them. It seemed a reasonable exchange for some reduction in personal freedom. A levelling out had taken place, and if the very rich had become poorer, then many more poor had attained a tolerable standard of living. And if the former rich resented the fact, then there was little they could do about it. Judd was supported by the unquestioning loyalty of the military class, which had come out of its long slumber to discover both power and newfound respect.

Before another election was due, Judd abolished the multi-party system as inefficient. By then nobody who mattered dared oppose him.

But Judd realised that his new world order needed a sense of dynamism; a safety valve, a distraction and a goal to justify its existence. In short, he needed enemies.

So he chose Gadron, a planet in a relatively nearby star system that was not part of any larger alliance. He identified the malcontents in Gadron society and secretly funded and encouraged them. Steadily he created a situation of growing social unrest, at the same time publicising through Gadron's information media the smoothly functioning social order on Zalcrossar. Soon a significant minority on Gadron was calling openly for Judd to rid them of their corrupt leaders and bring peace and just government to the planet. That was all the excuse Judd needed. Announcing that he was responding to a 'popular' request to give military aid and assistance, he despatched his fleet. Such was the disorder and confusion when it reached Gadron, that he occupied the world with little opposition.

It had been the grateful citizens of Gadron who first bestowed upon Judd the title of Protector…

'Protector, the discontinuity is no longer growing. I'm detecting increased instability about its perimeter.'

The call from the scanning team leader monitoring the force shield snapped Judd's thoughts back to the present. He frowned at the image on the screen showing the rippling vortex circling the hole in the shield.

'What's causing this?' Judd demanded. 'It was increasing steadily only a minute ago.'

'Perhaps somebody on the surface is trying to close the aperture by feeding a localised energy pulse into the discontinuity… or it is a natural function of the shield matrix. I do not know for certain, Protector,' the man admitted wretchedly. 'This is unlike any force field I have ever seen before. But if the instability increases the hole may collapse at any moment.'

'What is its present diameter?'

'Fifteen… no, fourteen metres, Protector. It keeps changing. The perimeter is no longer as sharply defined as it was.'

Fourteen metres, Judd knew, was just wide enough to pass a landing craft with wings and pods retracted and allow a slim margin of safety. Of course, if the entrance did close they could try another bombardment to re-open it. But if those on the ground were actively trying to maintain the shield, the next attempt might not be so successful.

Judd opened his link to the Captain of the *Valtor*. 'I'm going down now, before the discontinuity closes. Maintain englobement until you hear from me again.'

'As you command, Protector.'

Judd opened the general channel.

'Judd to Beachhead assault force: prepare for immediate descent. Follow *Lander One* through the shield discontinuity at minimum safe separation. Once inside the shield, initiate attack plan Delta. Good luck. Judd out.'

Judd turned to his own pilot. 'Unlock from mother ship. Begin descent phase.'

One by one, the six armoured landing craft detached themselves from their recessed bays in the hull of the *Valtor* and arced away towards the mirrored globe below.

Judd watched the pucker of the discontinuity grow on the forward view screen and felt a sense of welcome relief growing within him. Dynes had touched on a sore point in his last interview. The unresolved problem of Esselven troubled Judd more than he had admitted. But soon the 'keys' of Esselven would be in his hands and their show of defiance would be over.

Then the expansion of the Protectorate would resume as planned…

The lander yawed as the pilot centred their target on his flight scope, then cut in the autopilot. With the other landers forming a tight line astern, they plunged into the mouth of the shaft.

The spacial distortion tore through them, sending the controls into disarray. The cabin lights flickered but the ship held its course. The rear view screen showed the rest of the beachhead force right behind them, their hulls just clearing the walls of the tunnel.

Judd fought against the sickening sensation and the jolts of nervous stimulation, forcing out calming words even when the rest of the command deck crew were incapable of coherent speech.

'Hold steady… this will only last a few seconds… watch for the end of the tunnel…'

Then it happened.

The rear screen showed the side of the swirling shaft bulging inwards. Lander Two rolled to try to avoid the obstruction and its flank grazed the opposite wall. The energy field was not as coherent or impenetrable within the tunnel as it was on the surface, but at the speed the craft was travelling it was as though it had struck a wall of water.

Lander Two spun crazily out of control, rebounding from side to side along the tunnel, each impact checking the vessel's forward motion. Unable to slow in time, Lander Three smashed into the tumbling ship.

The shaft filled with flame and whirling debris as the two ships disintegrated.

'No!' Judd raged in impotent fury.

Munitions and ruptured energy cells aboard the lost ships swelled the destructive impact into an explosion of incandescent fury. Confined within the shaft, a billowing tongue of fire licked out and enveloped Lander One.

Chapter Twenty-three

The Doctor and Green-8 finished their cursory examination of the bodies in the cold room and came out into the vestibule again, closing the door on the grisly remains within. It had been impossible to determine exactly how they had died. There were no outward signs of violence, though a few of them had visible skin lesions.

'I wonder how long they've been there?' the Doctor said. 'That room was obviously designed to preserve them without decay.'

'But who are they?' Green-8 wondered.

'Not the immediate relatives of the present inhabitants, I think. Those corpses had clothes made from synthetic fabrics and they were styled quite differently from the costumes of those people we saw at the banquet. Everything they were wearing was of natural organic origin, some even homespun. All in keeping with their apparent level of technological development – robots and artificial lighting apart.'

'This does not tell us who has preserved these bodies so carefully, or why?'

'Another question to add to our list. The Blue Sector robots might be able to provide the answers – if they will ever condescend to speak to us. We know they come down here, and they probably maintain the facilities. They might even have carried out the interment, acting on instructions received.'

'We have only seen one Blue Sector robot so far, but if there were any more down here they should have registered our presence and shown themselves by now.'

'Then we'll keep looking until we find them,' the Doctor said, rolling over to the last door in the vestibule.

The door opened at his touch and the lights came on. The Doctor beamed at what was revealed. 'Now this is more like it...'

The King turned to his wife and said in an impatient undertone: 'The servants cannot find Oralissa in the gardens and her maid vouches she is not in her room. What can have become of her? The guests are becoming restless.'

'Simply a display of nerves, I fancy,' the Queen said soothingly. She cast her eyes significantly over the two suitors. 'Oralissa knows she must choose between them, and that all here await the outcome with interest. When she has calmed herself she will return.'

'Of late she has been preoccupied of mind,' the King fretted. 'Her manner has been strange. There were odd questions, were there not..?'

His face blanked for a moment, then took on an expression of milder concern as he leaned across Oralissa's empty chair to Benedek.

'I apologise for my daughter's absence. I pray you will not count it a breach of manners.'

'As long as she is safe, your Majesty, that is all that matters,' Benedek said sincerely. 'But, if her absence causes you concern, should a wider search not be made for her?'

Duke Stephon, though seated on the other side of Queen Celestina, must have been listening intently, for he immediately said: 'I would be honoured to look for her myself.'

'So should I,' Benedek said quickly.

'I'm certain there is no need for either of you good gentlemen to trouble yourselves,' the King said placatingly.

But others along the table had heard the exchange. Fine wine had induced a certain merriment and easing of inhibitions, and jovial cries of: 'Find the Princess!" and: 'Where's Oralissa hiding?' began to run round the company. A few struggled to their feet, calling for the garden doors to be opened.

Edrin and his wife exchanged helpless glances. There were times when even a king was powerless to control events.

'Open the doors,' he commanded.

In minutes the hall was virtually empty except for servants and Bolwig's troupe, who to their surprise now found themselves without an audience.

The King offered his wife his arm. 'We might also take to the grounds. Maybe we can find our errant daughter…'

Trampole watched the royal couple exit with a look of consternation, then turned to Bolwig. 'This is but Nettlefoot Field all over again! I said the Red Pig jape was too base for company of quality.'

'Addlepated fool,' Bolwig said. 'Did you not hear? They seek the beauteous Princess Oralissa, and methinks we should do the same.'

'But we're hired as entertainers and songsmiths, not chasers after lost princesses, however fair of face and form,' Lurket pointed out.

'Think on!' Bolwig said. 'These merry folk may make fools of themselves a-stumbling round in the dark. This may turn into a comic debauch. Let us follow on soft feet and see. We might acquire many a rich and saucy tale on the way, that patrons in other lands may be moved to prise from our tongues with suitable gifts of golden coin. So ho with me, lads, and note all you see.'

The third door had opened onto a control room, built within a large polygonal chamber. It was ringed about with half a dozen auxiliary bays and one master control station, where a deep swivel chair rested before banks of buttons, display panels and monitor screens. A scattering of winking lights and scrolling text suggested that the equipment was active.

The Doctor had climbed out of his mechanical disguise, leaving it standing empty in a corner, and had once again donned his patchwork coat. Now he was moving rapidly from one bay to another, his face alive with intense fascination. Occasionally he tapped some of the control keys. Green-8 followed silently in his wake.

When the Doctor had finished his survey he sat down at the master control panel frowning, deep in thought.

'This centre appears to encompass a comprehensive range of functions,' Green-8 observed.

'It certainly does,' the Doctor agreed. 'Interstellar transmitter. Controls for a planetary grid to draw power from the sun – a lot of which is going into maintaining the shield. Reserve nuclear reactors – there's a couple buried in silos under our feet. Robotic function monitors. Entertainment and environmental systems for the Palace. Travel tube functions, a general surveillance network. All the tools of an advanced society.'

'But does it help us locate the true rulers of Esselven?'

The Doctor spread his arms to take in the control room. 'You could say you're looking at them right now, or at least the continuing expression of their will. This looks like it's the end of one part of our quest at least. No ruling Lords, just an extensive computer system quietly running its programmes. Frustrating and possibly anti-climactic, but there it is and we must make the best of it.'

'But who gave the computer its original instructions?'

'That's still a mystery. Those people in the freezer might have been able to tell you. Of course there are extensive data files in this system which might hold the necessary information, but without knowing the right questions to ask, it might take a while to find the answer. Meanwhile, we have a more pressing problem.'

'The possible invaders. I had not forgotten. What have you learned?'

'I'm afraid it may only confirm my earlier fears…' The Doctor carefully tapped at a keyboard and the shield status display appeared on the screen before him. 'If I'm interpreting these readings correctly, there is a small discontinuity in the force shield over the night side of Esselven and one or more ships are currently passing through it. However, there's something very strange about the characteristics of the shield…' He frowned and shook his head slowly.

'Can you close the discontinuity?'

'I'll have to study the system further before risking making any changes to the shield. There's a tremendous quantity of energy bound up in it, which it would be unwise to mishandle.'

'Perhaps the system is capable of responding to the threat by itself?'

'Possibly…' The Doctor worked at the keyboard for a moment. A screen began displaying several lines of flashing red text.

'This is not encouraging,' the Doctor said grimly. 'Green and Red Sector units are, for some reason, continuing with their regular assignments. Blue Sector units and special guards – like the three we saw earlier, presumably – have gone to their designated defence stations, wherever they are. This confirms that there's trouble coming, but it seems only the two of us, and a few of your fellow robots, are preparing to do anything about it!'

Stephon and Benedek, with their personal companions by their sides, roamed the gardens calling out Oralissa's name at intervals. It was soon apparent to each party that the other was unwilling to let them out of their sight in case they found Oralissa first.

As time passed and they heard no news from other searchers, nor found any trace of Oralissa themselves, genuine concern began to colour their simple desire to best the other.

Finally frustration led Stephon to mutter: 'I hope the Prince of Corthane said nothing to upset the Princess.'

It was half a spoken thought, but Benedek chanced to be near enough to hear the words. The younger man flushed and turned his head sharply. 'Of what are you accusing me, sir?' he demanded with brittle formality.

'I make no accusation, sir,' Stephon replied. 'I merely expressed the hope that the fair lady has not been discommoded in some way. You spoke long to her over dinner, yet I noted her expression was often distant. Perhaps she had had her fill of your company?'

'Do you insinuate that my presence tired the lady?'

'If 'twere not the case, then why did she absent herself with such haste? Of what did you speak together?'

'Of nothing improper, that I swear. Can you imagine I would let drop a single word that might offend such a precious jewel as the Princess?'

'Not by deliberate intent, mayhap, but perhaps out of youthful inexperience –'

'Once again you insult me, sir. I demand an apology!'

'The slight exists only in your mind, Prince, and I cannot be held responsible for the state of that.'

Benedek's face darkened further. 'You compound the insult! Apologise at once!'

Their raised voices had carried through the gardens and were drawing other guests to the patch of lawn on which they stood.

'If you cannot hold your own in the duel of words,' Stephon said, 'do not contend with a wordsmith of greater powers.'

'Perhaps you duel with words because you fear to duel with steel!' Benedek snapped back.

There was a gasp from the onlookers. As the implications of the retort struck home, the Duke's previous irritation grew to true anger. 'I fear nobody's steel, sir, and stand ready to prove it at your pleasure.'

'Then I shall have that pleasure, sir!'

The onlookers gasped. The companions of both Duke and Prince were glaring at each other, reaching for their dress daggers.

King Edrin came up to them almost at a run, his wife at his heels, having caught the last few words of the challenge.

'Good sirs, honoured guests,' he panted. 'Tongues loosened by wine may spill careless words not truly meant. Let each allow the other some latitude and let us continue once more in peace and good fellowship.'

'I regret, good King, that this is not possible,' Stephon said, his eyes still fixed on Benedek. 'Things said cannot now be unsaid, nor blamed upon the grape. I attest before this company that this circumstance is no fault of our hosts, but the culmination of old enmity between Eridros and Corthane that was thought buried, but has flowered once again. Well, Benedek? When and where shall we settle this?'

'Here and now, before these witnesses who shall judge that the contest shall be a fair one,' Benedek said boldly.

'Impetuous as ever.'

'I see no cause for delay.'

'Until first blood is drawn… or death?'

'Until first blood… or surrender.'

'I shall never surrender.'

'No more shall I!'

'Then let fate decide between us. The winner shall have Oralissa's hand. Agreed?'

'It shall be so.' Benedek bowed to Edrin and Celestina. 'I apologise that blood must be spilled on your soil. Likewise, I do state before my men that no ill feeling shall be incurred upon Aldermar from Corthane in consequence of what shall be done here. But… should things not go well for me, tell Oralissa… that she won my heart from the first –'

'As did she mine!' Stephon interjected. 'Though she must not feel any guilt for what will be done.'

'So say I also!' Benedek said. 'She is but the last flake of snow settling on a high peak that sends an avalanche down into the valley below. Assure her that she is quite innocent and without any blame in this concern.' He looked at Stephon. 'That is one matter upon which we think as one.'

'The only such, I fear,' the Duke replied.

The King's shoulders sank in resignation while the Queen stifled a cry of dismay.

The two men removed their jackets as swords were sent for from the Palace armoury. Their companions prepared to second them. King Edrin gravely agreed to start the duel.

Standing in the shadows, Bolwig's players watched the preparations with interest.

'You note everything that happens,' Bolwig whispered urgently to his companions. 'These doings shall be the makings of lyrics for two ballads and an epic recitation, or I'm no judge!'

Queen Celestina was wringing her hands as she looked about the gardens. 'O, Oralissa; they risk life and honour for you. You should be here.'

'Perhaps,' Stephon said, 'it is well that she be spared this sight.'

'Yes, let us have this matter settled before her return,' Benedek said quickly, stifling a slight catch in his voice.

The swords arrived and the men made a few practice lunges and parries, then took up positions facing each other. The King stood between them.

'Are you both resolved to see this matter of honour through to its end?'

'We are,' they said in unison.

The King stepped back. 'Then begin –'

'Is there something we have missed?' Green-8 wondered.

He was rolling up and down the control room giving a very

human display of impatience, while the Doctor studied the screen before him with furrow lines deeply etched across his brow.

'At the moment we are doing all we can by trying to find out more about these control systems,' the Doctor said absently, his eyes and fingers still flicking across the screens and keyboard. 'We don't know the nature of the threat we're facing or why only a few of the robots have been mobilised. Is that intentional? There's a defence sub-system associated with the shield functions but it appears to be completely dead. Is there a back-up? If I can determine the energisation matrix for the shield it might be a start.'

Green-8 had stopped by the sub-bay controlling the entertainment and environmental systems for the Palace. He looked closer at the displays and cautiously pressed a few keys.

'Doctor, I have discovered an anomaly. Why is a sub-system labelled "Imaging" drawing so much power? It is not part of the lighting grid and I do not see what other use there would be for power in a building with no other technological amenities.'

'Curious…' the Doctor agreed, opening the imaging system files at the master console.

A succession of architectural details flashed across the screen, including graceful spires and minarets similar to those they had seen capping the Palace roofs. The Doctor gave a short laugh.

'Instant building features to personalise your residence, without going to the trouble of having the workman in. Hologramatic illusions, like the panel that concealed the lift door – of course! So was the kitchen fire with the meat cooking on it!'

'How do you know?'

'That's what was missing – all that fat bubbling and spitting but producing no smell. Now, what else is listed… Sprites? What are they?' A familiar figure in a hat appeared on the screen. 'So that's what Boots was… I wonder…' A primly dressed girl appeared. 'And Luci Longlocks. They were both APSs.'

'I am not familiar with the acronym.'

'Autonomous Photonic Simulations. Mobile illusions based around a small projector unit. Most of the time they have no actual substance but they can interact with material objects if a force field is synchronised with the photonic pattern.' He looked thoughtfully at Green-8. 'I wonder what else this sort of trickery has been concealing round here? Only one way to find out…'

The shouts of the onlookers and the clash of steel against steel guided a curious Oralissa through the garden to the site of the duel. For a moment she did not realise who was fighting for the press of bodies. Then she glimpsed Benedek and Stephon, their shirts both slashed and bloodied, circling each other with grim determination.

With a cry of horror, Oralissa pushed her way to her mother's side. 'What's happening? They must not fight. They are good men.'

'There is nothing you can do to stop them, child,' her mother consoled her. 'This is an affair grown out of longstanding rivalry. When it is done… you will not have a choice to make…'

Words failed Oralissa and she could only stare incredulously at the duelling men. A horrible sense of her own impotence overtook her. This was how it always would end. Her fate had never been in her hands…

The wild shout of a servant running up to them from the direction of the Palace rose above the sounds of combat. There was something so arresting about the fear in his voice and wildness in his eyes that it even distracted a few of the onlookers from the duel.

'Your Majesty,' the man gasped '…the Palace… the rooms… towers…'

Her father gaped at him. 'In God's name what, man?'

'Gone! All just… gone!'

The statement was so bizarre that Oralissa instinctively glanced in the direction of the Palace whose tallest spires should have been visible over the hedge tops.

They had vanished!

She heard a shriek from the rear of the crowd, but could not identify its source. A thrill of unearthly dread seemed to flow through the watchers. Then came another cry.

The disturbance must have distracted Duke Stephon. For an instant his eyes flicked sideways as though trying to locate the cause of the sound.

Benedek lunged in unthinking reflex, taking advantage of the slightest opening in his opponent's guard. The point of his sword thrust deep into Stephon's chest.

A look of surprise passed over the Duke's face as the crowd gasped. Benedek jerked his sword free. The Duke's knees gave and he started to collapse –

Then his body appeared to dim and fall in upon itself. In a moment Stephon was gone and in his place was a grey metal ball, a little larger than a clenched fist, studded all over with small glass beads. For a fraction of a second the ball hung in the air, then it dropped to the ground with a soft thud, rolled over and was still.

Incredulous silence ruled the glade as the watchers' minds tried to find expression for what they had seen. Dazed, Benedek prodded the ball with the tip of his sword, then looked round helplessly, as though to say: I didn't do this.

Then he dimmed and vanished and a second sphere fell to the grass.

The spell broke and the people fled howling in blind terror from the incredible transformation they had witnessed. But there was no escape.

Even as they ran they began winking out of existence, one by one with increasing rapidity, their voices cut off in mid cry. More spheres dropped from the air, still travelling in the direction the person had been when the doom had fallen upon them. They bounced and rolled on a little way before coming to rest.

Oralissa saw her father shouting for the guards even as he reached out an arm towards her – then he dimmed and was gone. She screamed into her mother's face and saw the helpless dread reflected in her eyes as she hugged her protectively, futilely, to her bosom.

Then Oralissa was clasping at thin air and another sphere lay at her feet.

A dreadful calm descended over the garden.

Oralissa was standing alone amongst the scattered spheres, as though they were a field of mushrooms that had magically sprouted on the lawn.

She opened her mouth to scream again, to surrender herself to utter terror –

The last sphere dropped to the ground… and the rest was silence.

Chapter Twenty-four

Dynes was roused by the sound of the activity alarm.

He'd allowed himself half an hour of natural sleep while little seemed to be happening outside, as a rest from the pills he'd been taking to stay awake. He'd have to make up for the artificially induced alertness later, of course, but it was the price you paid for getting the best story.

Dynes tilted the pilot's couch back upright and scanned the row of monitor screens.

The two additional DAVEs he had sent after Peri Brown's party had caught up with her borrowed transport and were riding in the cab. They were ready to take up station as soon as they reached the Palace. Another DAVE was watching Thorn Tree in case the villagers did anything newsworthy, such as attempt to fight Judd with their primitive weapons. The rest of the drones were still positioned about the overgrown landing field.

The screen that had triggered the alert was displaying the feed from a DAVE he'd left scanning the sky above the deserted spaceport. It had detected a point of light almost directly overhead. Dynes switched the image through to the main screen.

A ball of fire was dropping out of the clouds, blazing brilliantly against the dull glow of the sky. As it fell it shed lesser fragments that spun away from the central mass trailing twisting streamers of smoke. The flashes of minor explosions sparkled amidst the debris.

As Dynes watched, a stubby deltaform object which had been tumbling just below the central fireball and silhouetted by its glare, slowed its wild gyrations and banked unsteadily out of the path of the descending inferno. Automatically Dynes zoomed the camera in on the dark shape.

It was a Protectorate military landing craft.

Dynes left one DAVE tracking the fireball and set another on the landing craft.

'Recording!' he snapped at his personal drone. 'I'm watching a fantastic sight in the skies over the mystery planet. What looks like a mass of burning wreckage is hurtling towards the ground, together with a Protectorate lander apparently in difficulties…'

Even as he spoke, the landing craft's wings extended and bit into the air. Its rate of fall slowed and it turned onto a long controlled spiral descent path, circling over the dark forest and keeping well clear of the spray of falling debris.

'Wait… the landing craft appears to have regained control. I think it's going to be able to set down safely… which is more than can be said for the wreck plunging to its doom before my eyes. What vessel was it, and does its startling appearance have some connection with Protector Judd's delay in initiating his invasion? What has been going on up there in space on the other side of the force field? Hopefully I'll discover the truth in just a few minutes…'

The lander was circling lower, holding its distance from the spaceport. No doubt they were registering the *Stop Press*'s transponder signal, but were also wary of resistance from the defenders they imagined occupied the port. Judd wouldn't take unnecessary risks…

A frightening thought struck Dynes. What if Judd was in the wreck?

That would be a disaster – it would effectively be the end of Dynes' series. Judd had never nominated a successor. There might be a power struggle amongst Judd's senior staff, but though they were efficient commanders, none of them had his force of character that made him so telegenic. The ratings would plummet!

The blazing wreck hit the forest barely two kilometres away, the tearing thunder of its descent merging onto a booming explosion which threw up a brief-lived fountain of burning debris. With terrible majesty, a billowing, fire-laced mushroom cloud rose over the treetops, which were tossed and torn aside by the expanding airborne blast front. Seconds later the *Stop Press* trembled as the ground shockwave generated by the impact passed under it.

The lander made a low reconnaissance pass over the spaceport, then swung around, extending its landing legs.

Please let Judd be alive, Dynes thought as he made for the hatchway. For the record he said: 'I'm going out to meet the lander, which I hope contains Protector Judd…'

Dynes was standing by the hangar wearing his regular reporting costume of black fedora and trench-coat when the lander touched down. Half the craft was scorched and blackened, but the hull appeared to be intact.

Ramps dropped and columns of armoured soldiers emerged, pounding across the vine-encrusted concrete as they fanned out to form a protective ring about their craft, weapons pointed at the surrounding forest. The lander's upper gun turret rotated in restless jerks, as though questing for a target in the shadows. But all remained still and placid; the only change from the scene which had greeted Dynes when he landed was the distant column of smoke from the crash site.

Judd, imposing as ever in his powered armour, strode down the ramp and looked around him in an attitude of suspicious interest. After studying the deserted port buildings for a few moments, he stomped over to Dynes. From the composed set of his features no one would suspect that his ship had almost been destroyed only minutes earlier.

'Protector, it looked as though you had a narrow escape just then,' Dynes said, launching immediately into interview mode. 'Can you explain what happened?'

'An accident during the passage though the shield caused the regrettable loss of part of my landing force,' Judd explained curtly.

'Was this accident in any way related to the delay in launching your attack?'

Judd frowned. 'What delay, Mr Dynes?'

'Well, it's been almost two standard days since I came through the shield tunnel and –'

Judd glowered dangerous through the visor of his helmet. 'What sort of nonsense are you talking, Dynes? We went through the shield hardly more than five minutes behind you.'

Dynes blinked. 'Pardon me, Protector, but I know how long I've been here. You can examine my ship's chronometer if you wish.'

They both stared at each other in bafflement.

'Protector,' Dynes said slowly, 'I think you'd better take a look inside this hangar…'

Judd was obviously perplexed by the presence of the ancient Esselvanian ship and the state of the spaceport, but he concealed it well from the cameras and did not waste any further time in idle speculation. As tanks and armoured personnel carriers disembarked from the lander, he gave a brisk statement for the record.

'I cannot explain the apparent paradox we have experienced, nor the conditions we find here, but it does not affect my immediate plans. As our only remaining means of aerial transport, the lander will remain grounded until we ascertain the status of local air defences. Other emplacements may not be in the same state of disrepair as these.' Judd glanced at the skies. 'It may be that the discontinuity has closed, preventing the remainder of my beachhead force from making planetfall. Since the shield blocks communications with space, we cannot confirm this. Our first objective, therefore, is to locate and secure the shield controls and stabilise the discontinuity, allowing reinforcements to be landed. Then we will proceed to detain Hathold and his followers as previously planned.

'Your investigations amongst the forest primitives has identified an important structure located to the local north of this position, which may contain what we are after. This road, once obviously a significant transportation artery, also leads in the same direction. Therefore we shall follow it to its destination.'

Judd turned on his heel and strode off to the line of armoured vehicles, which had now formed up, and climbed aboard the leading APC. With a deep hum of heavy motors, the force moved off. A couple of DAVEs glided along in their wake. Low-slung, tracked robotic scouts moved ahead of the main column, extending their scanners and mine-detecting antenna as they went.

Dynes turned to camera.

'And so Judd sets off on what might be the last chapter of this saga. In a few hours we'll know if he has finally tracked down the man who has eluded him for so long.'

The last of the column vanished down the gloomy aisle and Dynes was alone again in the derelict spaceport, except for the lander and its skeleton crew. With a sudden inexplicable shiver, Dynes made his way back inside the *Stop Press*.

As he sat watching the multiple images relayed from his scattered drones, Dynes brooded.

He was not often concerned by the principles of professional conduct, but he had an image as an impartial reporter to maintain. He had shown Judd excerpts from the material he had obtained in the village because he didn't want the man wasting even more time pointlessly searching the woods when the obvious objective was this Palace to the north. Unfortunately Judd had mentioned the fact at a point in his speech that would be hard to edit. Dynes' action might be interpreted as providing information of military value.

Of course, it was only information that Judd could have obtained for himself from the villagers – probably at the point of a gun. So he'd really done them a favour. Dynes brightened. Yes, he could play up the humanitarian angle in the final report. A technical breach of the professional code to avoid the risk of bloodshed. That would run well.

Fortunately he had been able to give Judd a summary of the information he'd obtained from Peri Brown without having to identify her or explain her presence. It would only confuse matters further, and they were tangled enough as it was.

Dynes' mood darkened again. He had not revealed before his cameras the full depth of his unease about this place, nor some of the wilder theories his imagination was throwing up. Now there was the apparent disparity between the time that had passed down here for him and that in orbit for Judd. Taken in conjunction with his discovery of the ship in the hangar, it might be the making of an incredible story – or else a complete waste of time if it proved to be based on some subtle misreading of the facts. The trouble was he didn't yet know which.

Stop speculating and focus on the story in hand, he told himself.

Probably the gloomy surroundings were getting on his nerves. He'd like to have hopped his ship over to the day side and recorded some of the gardens Peri Brown had described. They sounded much more photogenic than this forest. But that would have to wait until any fighting was over. Like Judd, he didn't trust the local skies to be safe.

On a DAVE screen he watched the oddly assorted group in the dumper truck cabin. The scavengers were obviously still nervous of their surroundings, while Peri Brown concentrated on keeping the huge vehicle under control. The girl had determination, he'd grant her that. And looks, of course. Perhaps something particularly newsworthy would happen to her soon.

They must be getting near the Palace by now. And if all went well, Judd would be joining them not long after. Then things would start to happen and Dynes' cameras would be there to record every last detail.

When you came down to it, that was all that really mattered.

Chapter Twenty-five

'It was all an illusion,' Green-8 said.

'So it would appear,' the Doctor agreed.

They stood in what had been the Palace's banqueting hall. Now the walls were bare of wooden panels, the ceiling empty of beams, the windows no longer leaded. The tables and chairs were arranged as before, but now they were revealed as metal and some dense synthetic material. The floor looked like polished concrete, but was in fact warm and slightly resilient.

As far as they could tell the same transformation had taken place throughout the Palace. Shorn of its false spires and towers it was no longer a medieval - styled castle but a spacious modern mansion. Neither was there any trace of the costumed guests and servants they had seen inhabiting the building earlier, except…

The Doctor picked up one of the metal spheres studded with lenses that was lying on the floor and examined it with interest. There were more strewn about the path outside the garden doors.

'What is that?' Green-8 asked.

'An APS projector. Supported by a small force beam and linked by data relay to the computers downstairs, it generates photonic images such as we saw. Very convincing ones too.' Frowning thoughtfully he tucked the sphere into one of his coat's capacious pockets.

'Was this a deliberate deception?' Green-8 wondered. 'And who was it intended to fool?'

'I'm not sure, but I have an idea… Back downstairs.'

Seated again at the control board, the Doctor started tapping keys.

'Of course, this would be quicker if I knew the specific title. I'll just have to set it searching for the type of thing I'm after... ahha!'

The opening page of a new programme appeared on the screen. Green-8 read the first few lines.

'"*The Princess of Aldermar*, by Retorian Mellenger. A romance of the Chevallion Era, telling of the divided love of a beautiful princess for two suitors which ends in tragedy. Adapted from the famous play for fully interactive viewer participation..."' Green-8 looked at the Doctor. 'This is a construction of fiction.'

'Yes, a living play,' the Doctor said, scanning rapidly through the programme description. 'People could dress up and act out supporting parts, or follow certain characters through the story as they came together. It might run over several days in real time. Existing locations could be modified to suit the period by the same method. Expensive entertainment, but whoever lived here could obviously afford it.

'There was probably some leeway in the detail but the basic plot would have to stay the same. My attempt to warn the King didn't fit in with the story so they tried to get rid of me as quickly as possible while remaining in character. Robots didn't fit into the period either, so we were effectively invisible.' He touched more keys. 'This programme has apparently been set to repeat itself every ten days. I wonder how many times it's run in total?'

'Where are the people who would have used such a programme?' Green-8 wondered.

The Doctor shrugged. 'Possibly in the cold room next door. They're certainly not living here now.'

Green-8 seemed to sag and his head bowed in a very human way. 'Were there ever any great Lords?' he said in a muted voice. 'Have I, and my fellow robots, been living a lie?'

'I'm sorry,' the Doctor said.

There was a long silence. Then Green-8 began to rock back and forth, making a harsh braying sound.

'Are you all right?' the Doctor asked anxiously, scrambling out of his chair to stand beside the stricken robot.

'No… yes.' Green-8 straightened up and the Doctor realised he had been laughing. 'I… think I understand what you call humour, now. It is a strange release. What an absurdity! We have been supplying illusions with food for thousands of work periods! Then the Blue Sector robots would return it for composting!'

'Most probably. They must have kept things tidy around here. They would have treated the APSs as real people, but since they didn't fit in with the structure of the play they were largely ignored, as we discovered.'

'Yes, I see the logic of it now. But it does not help us. An enemy approaches and this world… my world, seems unprepared. Please advise me, Doctor. What do we do?'

An alarm filled the silence between them and screens came to life automatically over the master console.

'It may be too late to do anything,' the Doctor said gravely.

Views of the gateway through which they had entered the palace grounds were being displayed. As before the gates were wide open, but now without even the illusion of guards to man them. Even as they watched, blue robots rolled rapidly forward and slammed the heavy gates shut.

They were just in time. A large vehicle was approaching along the western road.

The belt of moorland ended where a broad gravel road running east to west cut across it. Beyond this was a high wall, topped in the further distance by trees.

'It is the great wall that rings the Lords' Palace,' Kel said, peering through the windshield of the truck.

'So we're getting somewhere at last,' Peri said with satisfaction. 'Let's see if we can find a way in.'

She swung the truck round to the left and sent it racing along the road, throwing up sprays of gravel from its huge wheels. The wall curved over the deceptive horizon towards them and rolled monotonously past without a break.

'Will the Lords let us enter?' Raz said nervously.

'After what I've been through nothing's going to stop me going right to the top; King, Nabob, Lord-high-whoever!' Peri said grimly. 'And you guys speak up for yourselves as well. They don't deserve any bowing and scraping after the way they've treated your people. Hey, this looks like it…'

A high pillared gateway with attendant gatehouses had appeared. Peri swung the truck round and came to a halt with its front grille almost touching the heavy gates that barred further progress. There was no sign of life from within the gatehouses, not any movement in the rolling parkland they could see beyond.

Peri found the button for the truck's horn and a klaxon blast rent the air, making her passengers flinch in alarm. She pumped the button impatiently, but to no avail.

'Okay, if they want to play dumb…' Peri said, gritting her teeth. She backed the truck up a little way, then put her foot down. The huge vehicle surged forward and struck the gates with a clang. There was snapping of steel and a rending of stonework. The gates burst open, tearing free of their mounts and crashing to the ground. The truck careered on up the driveway unhindered.

'Try to ignore that!' Peri yelled, with the guilty thrill of one who has just committed major property damage in a worthy cause.

A bolt of fire flashed out from under the trees ahead and exploded against the engine cowling, blowing a panel free and enveloping the cab in a cloud of acrid smoke.

'Heads down!' Peri yelled, wrenching the steering yoke over and sending the vehicle bouncing off the road and tearing gouges out of the turf.

More bolts exploded against the truck. A side window blackened and shattered as it was burnt through. A DAVE flew out through the jagged aperture to get a better view of the attackers and was blasted from the air. Peri swung the truck round, trying to find a clear path out of the ambush. But the gunfire seemed to be coming from every direction. They were surrounded. There was no escape.

The truck swerved wildly as a rear tyre blew out. Her passengers yelled as they were thrown to the floor. A firebolt passed clean through the cab, burning a hole through a second hovering DAVE. Smoke was wreathing the truck. Only its sheer bulk and rugged construction was keeping it going.

Then Peri saw one of their attackers for the first time. A humanoid robot was standing in the shadow of a tree pointing an odd looking rifle. Instinctively Peri drove the truck straight at it.

The rifle blazed and the windscreen blackened and shattered. Then there was a metallic impact, a bang from the underbody and the robot vanished. Warning lights were flashing on the dashboard, but they were through their attackers' line.

Peri expected parting shots or some sort of pursuit, but the fusillade suddenly ceased as abruptly as it started. The pockmarked and blistered truck ploughed on, bouncing back onto the driveway again, its burst tyre flapping and thudding around its hub.

'Everyone all right back there?' Peri called over her shoulder.

Kel sat up groaning. He was holding a battered DAVE unit. 'I fell on one of the flying things. Is it broken?'

'Looks like it. Well done. Throw it out the window.'

'Are we going to the Palace?' Nerla asked.

'Nowhere else to go,' Peri said. 'I hope we can get there before they regroup – uh oh…'

There was a standard model robot by the side of the drive

ahead. But it was unarmed, and instead of trying to stop them it was waving them onward vigorously and pointing to indicate they should keep going.

Peri slowed the truck uncertainly, then shrugged and continued on. Nobody would try to sucker them into a trap so clumsily, she thought. Maybe somebody wanted to talk sensibly at last.

As they passed, the robot waved cheerfully.

The long drive wound its way through the rolling parkland until a large building came into view. It was a comfortably sprawling structure with many windows, gently pitched roofs, wide eves and two enclosing wings.

'Is that.. it?' Raz breathed. Kel clutched his spear more tightly and Nerla's hand slipped to the scavenged knife at her belt.

'We'll find out in a moment', Peri said, trying to sound more confident than she felt.

The drive lead up to a broad sweep of gravel. A low flight of steps led up to the main doors. There was a distinctive figure standing on the steps...

Peri braked the truck in a shower of gravel, almost fell out of the cabin and dashed towards the steps, her arms held wide.

'Doctor!' she yelled in delight.

Dynes scowled in frustration at the three dark screens.

A dramatic action event and he had no climax. Did Peri Brown and her companions escape or not? Who were their attackers? The viewers wouldn't accept that unless he came up with a satisfying conclusion. He also might have lost Brown, who was appealingly photogenic and would have scored high viewer approval. Well, he'd just have to hope he could find suitable material later.

Even worse, the three drones assigned to cover Judd's attack from inside the Palace grounds were lost. He'd have to send replacements and hope they got there before Judd.

He rapidly checked over the deployment of his drones.

Yes, he could leave one here at the spaceport in case the rest of Judd's beachhead force arrived or the lander was called in to support the assault on the Palace. Another screen confirmed that the Thorn Tree villagers weren't doing much except gathering in extra food and looking anxious. The DAVE he'd left there could be sent off to the Palace. He had the route recorded and it was nearer than the others.

Dynes gave the machines their new assignments, then sat back in his chair and chewed on a high-energy snack meal. At least the loss of the three drones proved there was somebody at the Palace ready to put up some resistance to intruders. With any luck he'd have a decent battle to report.

For a moment the Doctor's broad, caring smile beamed down on Peri and she basked in its warmth. It told of his relief at seeing her safe once again in a way that words could not. Then, mercurially, his schoolmasterly manner reasserted itself and he frowned at the ragged remains of her dress.

'You seem to be incredibly dishevelled,' he observed.

'I came economy class,' Peri said with a grin.

'You should have stayed in that haha until I came back for you.'

'I know…' She hugged him again and buried her face in his tasteless patchwork coat so he couldn't see her tears of relief. 'You seem to have done all right for yourself,' she said. 'Quite the lord of the manor.'

'The only one currently in residence, certainly. The others turned out to be APSs.'

'What?'

'Autonomous Photonic Simulations – it's a complicated story and I don't know all the details.'

'Bet it doesn't beat mine.' Peri pulled herself together. 'Listen, this planet is going to be invaded any time now!'

'Oh, I know about that.'

'But do you know the head man's name, and where he's likely to land, and what he's after? I do.'

He raised an eyebrow. 'Quite the mine of information.'

'I learned a whole bunch of stuff from an old acquaintance of ours – Dexel Dynes.'

The Doctor's face fell. 'Not him again! I think you'd better come inside. And bring your friends.'

Peri realised the others had been hanging back, watching the impromptu reunion uncertainly. Peri beckoned them on.

'It's all right. This is my friend the Doctor. Doctor, meet Kel, Nerla and Raz.' They stepped inside. Peri looked about at the impressive entrance hall. 'Doctor, how did you end up here?'

'By way of an unplanned train journey and meeting a most amiable garden robot by the name of Green-8.'

'A friendly gardener! Tell me more…'

The three scavengers gaped at the underground control room and then started at the sight of a garden robot with a cable running from a socket in the side of his chestplate to the control board. The Doctor made the necessary introductions.

'This is Green-8, who's been an invaluable companion over the last few hectic days. You might also thank him for halting the attack on you by the guard robots.'

'I apologise for the delay, Peri Brown,' Green-8 said. 'It took us a little time to establish a connection to the command net and over-ride the guards, pre-programmed instructions.'

'Uh, sure, right,' Peri said. 'Thanks for calling them off.' She looked at the Doctor. 'So there aren't any actual people here? I thought this was where the local Lords are supposed to hang out.'

'Perhaps only in spirit now,' the Doctor said dryly. 'There are some well-preserved bodies in a storage locker but we're not sure who they were. The entities everybody has been assuming were the ruling Lords turned out to be APSs that were part of an interactive historical drama. They convinced the robots they were real people, even making them think this was Esselven, the world where the play was originally set. Bolwig's troupe were part of the same programme.'

'That bunch? They looked like comedians.'

'The comic relief to accentuate the tragedy. A different programme but the same means generated our mischievous friend Boots, and a charming young lady called Luci Longlocks.'

'Luci?' Peri exclaimed. 'We met her. She was quite pally at first, then she slipped away like a ghost.'

'Just a sophisticated children's minder and playmate following her programming,' the Doctor said. 'The only other thinking being on the planet, apart from the scavengers, seems to be Green-8, who evolved sentience independently. He also wanted to have a few words with the Lords. Like you he's been disappointed.'

Kel's face had creased with effort as he tried to follow the Doctor's words. 'No Lords here?' he said.

Peri shrugged. 'Sorry, Kel. It looks like it's all been a big misunderstanding. But we've still got a problem. There's a guy called Glavis Judd, who sounds like a regular dictator and megalomaniac…'

The Doctor listened gravely to Peri's summary of the information she had obtained from Dynes. Then he seated himself before a control panel and started working a keyboard.

'There is a considerable computer library here,' he said. 'Now I have a name, perhaps I can find out more about this Judd person. It may help us formulate some sort of strategy.'

Text and images rolled rapidly across the screen. A biography of Judd, the rise of the Protectorate, parades of weapons, the encroachment on Esselvanian space, preparations for war…

The Doctor's face set in a stern mask as he scanned the information, barely containing his anger. As the last entry trailed off, he said simply: 'Glavis Judd must not be allowed to continue!'

Such absolute condemnation coming from a Time Lord held a

frightening note of finality which made Peri shiver. She said: 'But look, there's no king or royal family here now, even if there ever was. Once Judd learns that, maybe he'll simply go away.'

The Doctor shook his head sadly at this display of optimism. 'Can you be sure he'll simply leave this world in peace? And even if he does, he will go away to spread his so-called "Protectorate" still further. He must be stopped… but how?'

Even as he brooded the screen flickered. The text they had been viewing was replaced by what looked like an elaborate coat of arms. Lion-like beasts stood rampant on either side of a symbolic rising sun.

'Hey, what's happening?' Peri asked.

'Another programme seems to be running automatically,' the Doctor said. 'It may have been activated by the information search we've just made…'

The coat of arms was replaced by a man's head and shoulders.

He had once been a handsome man, perhaps in his early forties. But now his face was deathly pale, his eyes were sunken and it seemed as though every breath he took was painful. But there was a defiant fire within him that transcended his pain and gave him the strength to speak.

'This is my last message to you, my dear wife and children,' he said, his voice little more than a husky whisper. 'I don't know how long it will be before you view this, but you should know what has happened here…'

His face crumpled as a fit of coughing overcame him. He wiped his lips with a tissue and it came away stained with blood.

Recovering himself he continued.

'You remember we were trying to reinforce the shield. We had linked the solar grid with the reserve reactors under the Palaces. The engineers thought they could make the Retreat impervious to attack from space. Something went wrong… there was a power surge. The reactors under the Winter Palace went into meltdown and it was totally destroyed. That was when we had to evacuate the Summer Palace, except for the essential technical staff. They were brave men and women. I had to stay with them. We finally controlled the reactors here... but not before we were irradiated...'

He was wracked by another fit of coughing.

'We are all dying and there is nothing more that can be done for us. But we know we live on through you, our families. That is our comfort.

'We have reprogrammed the robots as best we can. I hope the systems were not too badly damaged. They will maintain the Palace until it is safe for you to return. A year or two, perhaps. You must stay in the garden houses until then. If Judd does not find you, then eventually you will repair the ship. Find other worlds who will fight his tyranny. Free Esselven... not for the crown, but for its people. They deserve better than the Protectorate. The city vaults will wait for the rightful heirs to return. They will open to your body patterns alone. While Judd is denied what they contain he cannot truly rule...

'These are the last words of Hathold, King of Esselven... husband and father. I love you all. Goodbye.'

The screen went blank.

There was a long silence in the control room.

'Doctor,' Peri said. 'He was sitting in this control room wasn't he, and talking about being irradiated. Is this place safe?'

The Doctor examined a secondary display. 'Normal background level only,' he assured her. 'You're quite safe.'

Kel said: 'Who was that man?'

The Doctor was working the keys with a ferocious look of concentration, so Peri answered.

'A king named Hathold, apparently. One of the real Lords. I think his family used to live here.'

'He must be amongst the bodies in the cold store,' Green-8 said

251

helpfully. 'The Palace robots would have placed them there after they died.'

Peri was frowning, looking at Kel and trying to picture an image of Hathold. 'Say, did anybody else notice how much Hathold and Kel look alike?' she said.

Kel looked blank but Nerla nodded tentatively. 'It is true. He and Kel are almost like man and son.'

'But he can't be related,' Peri said immediately, aware she was virtually contradicting herself. 'You can't have forgotten who you are so quickly. Anyway, your people must have been living in the wild woods for hundreds of years.'

'Kel is not Hathold's son,' the Doctor said, turning away from the keyboard to fix them with a look of triumph. 'But he might be his grandson many times removed.'

'What?' Peri exclaimed.

'All your friends here are probably related to the royal line to a greater or lesser degree. I understand there are relatively few scavengers and in such a small gene pool there would inevitably be considerable interbreeding and consequent conservation of individual characteristics, such as facial features.'

'Doctor!' Peri said. 'What are you talking about?'

'There is a time code on that recording. I have compared it with the current date shown on main system timebase. Hathold left his message over 500 years ago!'

Chapter Twenty-six

The armoured column rolled steadily along the overgrown road that bored through the gloomy forest.

Where the way was blocked by fallen trees they were dragged aside, after being checked by the drone scouts for possible booby traps. The gun turrets of the tanks and APCs turned constantly as their targeting sensors probed the woods for any sign of ambush. The troops were tense and expectant, weapons at the ready.

But nothing happened.

Inside his APC Judd stared intently ahead, almost willing an attack, for some show of force that would prove this was the right place. But the road looked as though it had been unused for years. The apparent paradox of the ship scratched at the corners of his mind. Perhaps he had been wrong. What if this was not Hathold's retreat?

No! This had to be the end of his quest. He would not be cheated again. The keys of Esselven were here… he could feel it.

'Five hundred years,' Peri repeated dumbly.

'Five hundred years by the calendar of Esselven, of course, rather than here on Esselven Minor, as we might call it,' the Doctor said. 'But they're almost the same length as those you grew up with.'

'But Dynes said Judd invaded Esselven only a bit over a year ago.'

'I'm sure that's correct. And the royal family and their retainers fled here, where they tried to modify their planetary shield. And that's what caused the paradox.

'The files show this world is circling close to a white dwarf star. The planetary shield was initially intended to contain the atmosphere and filter the sun's radiation to make life here possible. Then Hathold's engineers tried to increase its defensive capabilities. It was a dangerous place to attempt such an experiment.

'Intense gravity distorts time and space to a significant extent, and this world not only orbits close to the massive gravity well of a star, but has a high density core of its own. When they tried to modify the shield it must have overstressed the continuum in a place where it was already weak. The shield became a boundary both in space and time. On the inside time passes approximately 500 times more rapidly than normal. That's why the TARDIS could not locate our position, and why the sun here appears red. What light from it is allowed through the shield is spread, so to speak, across time, reducing its energy and shifting its wavelength.

'Consequently, Kel is one of Hathold's descendents, yet he doesn't know it.'

The three scavengers looked bemused. Peri pinched the bridge of her nose, just about keeping up. 'The scavengers have legends of rejection by lords and sun gods. I suppose that's a version of what actually happened distorted by hundreds of years re-telling?'

'Quite likely,' the Doctor agreed. 'We can deduce the sequence of events.

'After the accident the survivors had no proper place of refuge. The Winter Palace had been destroyed and the ship was useless. From Dynes' description, the accident must have cut the power to the spaceport and without engineers they couldn't make repairs. Neither could they shelter in the garden houses as planned. The robots' programmes had been corrupted, incidentally leading to some odd behaviour such as obsessive garden building and curious anomalies like the misplaced haha. They wouldn't let the survivors stay in the gardens, or even help support them. Their lives very quickly became a struggle for survival and they ended up living in the woods on the dark side of the planet, which the robots virtually ignored. The truth of their situation gradually degenerated into myth. The spaceport was probably associated with their rejection and became a taboo place.

'The historical APS play must have been triggered by another system error soon after this and began to run constantly. Gradually the players took over the Palace, which had automatically been modified for the production. They were much more convincing as Lords than the real survivors and the robots accepted them, treating the real heirs as scavengers and illusions as real people. And that is where we came in some 500 local years later.'

Kel, Nerla and Raz had been struggling to follow the explanation. Nerla said hesitantly: 'We are all… children of the Lords?'

'Looks like it,' said Peri.

Green-8's voice sounded hollow. 'My kind has inflicted great suffering on those we were designed to serve.' He looked at the three scavengers. 'I am sorry.'

'Not your fault, Green-8,' the Doctor said quickly.

'Doctor,' Peri said, 'if the scavengers are the descendants of the royal family, then will they still be able to open this body-pattern vault, even after all these generations?'

'Very possibly,' the Doctor said.

'And if Judd finds out about them…'

'Exactly. The biographical files said he is highly intelligent. If he discovers what has happened here or works it out for himself, he will not let the scavengers rest. He may already know about them if he is as close to Dynes as you say. Then there's the matter of the planetary shield. By chance Hathold's engineers stumbled on something that would have a military application. If Judd has already attacked the shield from space, he knows how powerful it is.' He looked round the control room. 'If necessary we must destroy this entire complex and the generating system to prevent the knowledge falling into Judd's hand.'

'Then let's stop talking and do something!' Peri said.

'We shall, but not precipitately,' said the Doctor, turning back to the control board. 'First, let us see where this spaceport is located relative to the Palace. It might be useful to know from which direction Judd will be coming.'

A large screen displayed a globe of the tiny world. The Doctor rotated it until the dark side was revealed.

'I guess that's the place Dynes talked about, right in the middle,' Peri said. 'And that looks like a road running straight from there to here.' She looked at the image scale, realising once again what a tiny world this was. 'He could be here in a couple of hours!'

'We detected activity in a discontinuity in the planetary shield over the dark side a little earlier,' the Doctor said. 'I think we can assume that Judd has landed by now. If he was making an aerial assault he would already be here, so it's likely he'll come overland, especially if he wishes to capture, as he imagines, Hathold and his family alive.' He frowned. 'Green-8, can you control all the robots through your data link?'

'I am already doing so,' Green-8 replied calmly. 'I have directed the Red Sector units to cease working the scavengers under their control. They will be rested and given what care can be provided. I did not think I needed to consult with you.'

'Quite right, you didn't. Can you also have them locate my travel machine that I described to you and have it brought here? We may have a use for it.'

'Certainly. The tubeway link should be open now,' Green-8 said. 'It will not take long to bring your machine here.'

'But even with the TARDIS we can't evacuate all the scavengers,' Peri said. 'I saw the sort of weapons Judd has on the files the same as you. A few robot guards aren't going to stop tanks. They could hardly stop one dumper truck!'

Kel interjected. 'This Judd is enemy of my father's father?'

'More or less,' the Doctor agreed.

'And he is coming to fight?'

'Yes,'

'We can fight also!' He held his spear aloft. Raz and Nerla cheered and waved their knives.

Peri smiled sadly at their futile show of bravado. They didn't understand half of what was going on, but they had guts. 'I'm afraid you're going to need better weapons than those to fight Judd.'

'Perhaps we have such weapons,' Green-8 said.

They all looked at him. 'What do you mean?' the Doctor asked.

'Peri Brown has given me an idea. We have weapons of a sort – but I hesitate to use them. We talked of morals when we first met, Doctor. I disabled robots in the garden knowing they were not sentient, but is it ever right to inflict injury, perhaps death, on sentient beings, to prevent greater harm being done to others?'

'That is an eternal dilemma,' the Doctor said gravely. 'The answer is sometimes yes, if it is the last resort. But it is never a decision to be taken lightly.'

'In your opinion, have we reached the last resort?'

The Doctor looked at the expectant faces around him. He took a deep breath. 'Yes, I think so. Judd may cause immediate harm to the scavengers and if left unchecked may destroy the lives of millions of others.'

'Then I will proceed. It may bring you time to find some more complete solution.'

'Ahh, I see,' the Doctor said.

'But what's he doing?' Peri asked.

The Doctor looked mildly disappointed. 'Peri, just think for a moment. Meanwhile, we must assess our resources and see how they might be applied to stopping Judd, or at least convincing him that there is nothing here of value.'

Peri tried to match the Doctor's outward composure. 'Don't

forget Dynes. He'll be sending more of his drones to replace the ones he lost. He wants to record the battle from both sides. Whatever we do has got to take care of him as well.'

'I shall bear that in mind. Now, what are our assets?'

'Three young cavemen, a few robots and these APS things,' Peri summarised. 'Can they fight?'

'Not very effectively, I imagine.' The Doctor pulled a lens-studded sphere from his pocket. 'That's an APS projector. It couldn't apply much actual physical force for long or it would drain its battery and have to recharge.'

'I don't suppose some holo-trickery can hide the whole Palace?'

'Rather a tall order, I'm afraid.'

'Maybe we could use the APSs as scouts?' Peri suggested. 'At least we'd know where Judd was.'

'That is an idea.' The Doctor turned to the control board. 'I'll activate this unit and send it down the spaceport road.'

'Luci Longlocks didn't seem keen to go into the night side.'

'She didn't want to enter one of the gardeners' workshops either. Probably programmed against it. I'm sure I can adjust that. Green-8 and I viewed a range of simulations earlier, including animal forms. Something four-legged might be appropriate. It should be less conspicuous and naturally move rapidly. As long as we can maintain its data link…'

A library of images flashed across the screen until the Doctor stopped at one of a large dog. 'That should do.' He checked the projector unit for its code number and assigned it to the APS sub-programme. 'Now we put this on the floor and stand back…'

'Are you sure you know what you're doing?' Peri asked.

'Of course. I'll just activate the programme…'

The sphere rose into the air. The lenses glowed and the form of a large dog materialised around it, wagging its tail and lolling its tongue realistically.

Kel gasped. 'Magic!'

'Applied science,' the Doctor said firmly. 'Now, I'll just tell it what to do –'

The dog suddenly yelped and contorted, as though it was trying to bite its own back. Its form blurred and shimmered. There was a frightened scream and then the figure of a young woman in a flowing dress was crouched on the floor in front of them.

Oralissa had been suspended in the limbo of a nightmare.

She was consciousness without form; deaf, dumb and blind, yet tormented with the sense that all around her was pulsating activity she could not see or hear. She had cried out soundlessly for release from the eternity of nothingness to which she had been consigned, but no answer came.

Was this death?

Then in the distance she thought she saw a faint light. By some means she could not explain she moved towards it. Dimly she sensed motion and sound and substance at its core and longed to experience those things again. She moved closer. Something was twisting her body, but she fought back with all the force of her will, shrieking her defiance.

Suddenly she could hear her own voice and feel her own body about her. Sobbing uncontrollably with relief yet fearful of what she might find, she opened her eyes…

She was crouched on the floor of a strange chamber ranged about with incomprehensible furnishings. People were watching her. Four ragged youths, a mechanical, a strangely dressed man…

Her eyes fastened on the man. A familiar face… She pointed a trembling finger. 'I saw you at the banquet… you climbed into a mechanical…' She looked about her. 'What has happened to me? Where is my family?'

The man frowned in irritation. 'You shouldn't be here.'

'Doctor, can you be a little less insensitive!' one of the ragged women scolded.

'I... I am the Princess Oralissa of Aldermar,' Oralissa said. 'I demand... I beg, you, tell me what has become of me?'

'It's all right, we aren't going to hurt you,' the young woman said, laying a reassuring hand on Oralissa's shoulder.

Her hand passed through Oralissa's flesh without the slightest sensation.

'Oh... of course,' the woman exclaimed, recoiling.

Oralissa wailed in horror. 'What have you done to me! God save me, I'm dead... dead!'

The Doctor's hands were passing rapidly over the strangely illuminated panel before him. 'I'm putting you back in your proper place... there!'

Oralissa screwed up her eyes and clasped her head in her hands. She could feel her form melting away, but she would not go back to the terrible void of darkness.

'No! Not that – please!' she begged.

'You're hurting her, Doctor!' the young woman shouted.

The Doctor frowned. 'That should have worked, unless... of course!' He passed his hands across the panel again, saying urgently: 'Oralissa! I'm opening some data files... some books, for you. Read them, then you'll understand. Read them –'

Suddenly Oralissa's image was gone and the projector dropped to the floor of the control room. As the others looked at him in surprise the Doctor rubbed his chin thoughtfully.

'What did you do?' Peri asked.

'You kill ghost girl?' Nerla said.

'No, at least I hope not,' the Doctor said. 'Her programme is back inside the computer. Hopefully, I've given her a chance to learn what she really is.'

'Which is what?' Peri prompted.

The Doctor worked the keyboard. A bar chart appeared on the

screen, with names allocated to each block. *King Edrin, Queen Celestina, Prince Benedek...*

Most did not fill half the space available, Peri saw, except for one, which rose off the top of the chart. *Princess Oralissa.*

'That is the memory space allocated to each character sub-programme in the interactive play in which Oralissa starred,' the Doctor explained. 'Enough for simulated intelligence, and some random storage space to compensate for minor variations in the play caused by viewer participation. Every time the play repeated they would be wiped. However...'

A schematic diagram of computer system programmes appeared. The Doctor pointed.

'Look, a narrow data bridge has formed between Oralissa's memory block and the computer's general data files. You might say she exists partly outside the play. Every time it ran she's built up memories, mostly repetitious, that weren't erased when the programme reset.' He looked at Green-8. 'And now I think she's sentient.'

Peri, glancing at Green-8, asked doubtfully: 'Doctor, isn't this sort of thing happening twice on one small world a bit much?'

'It is not such a great coincidence as it may seem. The special circumstances here have played their part: time, repetitive behaviour, programmes unchecked for errors. Green-8 developed his sentience partly through unsupervised repair work. This computer system was not designed to support sentience, but through repetition the Princess's character, as defined by her original sub-programme, has formed its own self-sustaining matrix within it.'

'So what's she doing now?'

'Since her consciousness actually exists in the computer, she should be able to access the data files I opened very rapidly. I hope the information will help her come to terms with what she is.'

'I always knew I was a machine,' Green-8 said. 'But she believed she was a person. It may not be easy for her.'

Peri shook herself and looked at her watch. 'Hey, we're getting sidetracked here! In case you've all forgotten, we've got a heavily armed megalomaniac coming this way and we've still no idea how to stop him!'

The glow of scientific discovery faded from the Doctor's face. 'I had not forgotten. This does have a bearing on our future actions concerning Judd. I said we might have to destroy this control complex to keep certain knowledge from him. We cannot now do this without effectively killing the Princess.'

'Oh… I see,' Peri said slowly. 'That could be a problem –'

Without warning the APS projector rose into the air and Oralissa appeared.

They looked at her uncertainly, but all trace of fear and confusion was gone, replaced by a quiet composure. She smiled pleasantly.

'Forgive my earlier outburst. I am quite all right now.'

'Are you sure you understand what you are?' the Doctor said.

'I do,' Oralissa said simply. 'I know that this world is not Esselven but a royal world estate situated amongst the stars. Also that the reality I believed in was an illusion; a fiction of times past created for the entertainment of those who dwelt here. I have come to terms with all this and also how I came to exist. I have cried for those I thought were my family, and know now why they could not answer my questions…' She gave a sad, wry smile. 'I am reconciled. This state of being is strange, but it is greatly preferable to the madness or hell to which I imagined I had been consigned. Now, may we be properly introduced?'

The Doctor made the introductions. Oralissa seemed to accept the oddly assorted group perfectly calmly.

'You look like you've got yourself together pretty quickly,' Peri said, trying to adjust to Oralissa's change of character.

'Within the machine it has seemed as though many days have passed since I first saw you all here,' Oralissa explained. 'I spent a long time reading the files the Doctor made accessible to me.

Much was beyond my understanding at first, but there were other references to make things clearer. And it seems I do not forget anymore, which is a great aid to learning.'

'Did you read the file on Glavis Judd?' the Doctor asked.

'Yes, and the history files and Palace records. Do I take it he threatens this world also?'

'He's probably on his way here right now,' Peri said. 'We've been trying to work out how to stop him.'

'I would like to help you if I can,' Oralissa said. 'I have seen King Hathold's last message. It is very… moving. There are recordings of his family stored in the general files. I understand Judd is indirectly responsible for their premature deaths.'

'Well thanks for the offer,' said Peri, 'but I'm not sure what you can do. The Doctor says APSs can't fight.' She turned to the Doctor. 'What about it, Doctor? I think we're about done with characters popping out of plays, messages from the past and history lessons. We've got an hour, maybe two at the outside. How are we going to stop Judd?'

The Doctor beamed brightly at the ring of expectant faces, then gradually his smile became fixed.

'At this moment,' he said, 'I honestly don't know.'

Chapter Twenty-seven

Judd's armoured column had travelled almost seventy kilometres when the warning came through from one of the drone scouts.

'Sir, activity in the woods to the east!' the operator reported. 'Large vehicle detected… no, two vehicles… three vehicles…'

'Stand by all gun crews!' Judd ordered. 'Cannon only. Save the missiles for when you have a clear shot.'

Now it comes, he thought. They waited until almost the last moment, but we're ready for them.

The external cameras relayed images to the sealed and armoured cabins. Indistinct slab-sided shapes were moving through the tangled trees towards them.

Gun turrets spat fire, lighting up the gloomy forest.

Soft fungal growths exploded in clouds of steam and flame. Severed boughs dropped to the ground. Energy bolts splashed off hard metal hulls. Deep in the woods something exploded in the blue-white flash of a ruptured power cell.

But still they came.

Then the last line of trees crashed down and the attackers were upon them.

For a second Dynes almost laughed aloud. The angular forms of eight or ten mechanical excavators, dozers and dumper trucks lumbered out of the forest onto the road, each with an empty control cabin.

Gunfire raked the oncoming machines, tearing off plating and exploding tyres. A dumper truck, its cabin blazing and remote controls destroyed, veered round in a crazy circle and plunged back into the trees again. The engine of an excavator was blown apart by a volley of armour-piercing rockets and it ground to a smoking halt.

But the rest of the makeshift war machines rolled on. A scout drone was crushed under their whirring tracks. They were heavy vehicles built for rugged conditions and very little stopped them.

They smashed into the armoured column.

A burning dozer rammed a tank and drove it off the road and onto its side. An excavator rode up over an APC, pounding it into the soft ground. The forest road became a churning melee of grinding metal enveloped in smoke from blazing tyres and melting powerpacks. Judd was thrown against his chair harness as a dumper truck crashed into his own APC with a squeal of tortured metal.

'First squad, disembark!' he ordered. 'They're not armed – disable those things at close range.'

Troops in battle armour poured out of the hatch and advanced on the defenceless vehicles, riddling engines with gunfire from point-blank range and tossing grenades into cabs to destroy their controls. One by one they reduced the great earthmoving machines to inert, burning hulks.

Dynes watched the images relayed from his drones with considerable satisfaction. The battle of the forest road would make a novel opening sequence to the final assault. As long as he had cameras there to record it.

He turned his attention to the reserve DAVEs on their way to the Palace. The one he'd sent on from the village was almost there, he noted with relief. It had followed the course Peri Brown had taken and was even now speeding along the road parallel to the wall enclosing the Palace grounds. The gateway Peri had entered so spectacularly was not far ahead.

Dynes took manual control of the drone and sent it hopping

over the wall and into the shelter of some shrubbery on the other side. From recent experience he knew that guard robots were watching the gate and were adept at shooting down drones. But if he avoided them and followed the drive it would presumably lead to the Palace.

Making a detour round the gate area, he struck the drive some way down and sent the DAVE winging along it. The artfully sculpted and perfectly maintained grounds flew past. He hoped whatever lay at the heart of it all would be equally impressive.

The rolling landscape gave way to more formal gardens and lights appeared through the trees. Dynes slowed the drone down, guiding it from one piece of cover to the next. What had to be the Palace came into view.

Dynes gazed approvingly at the confection of soaring spires and towers drawn straight from ancient pre-spaceflight history. It was perfect; and expensive recreation that was practically made to be attacked.

Then he blinked, peering closer to the screen. A spire had just vanished leaving a shorter turret in its place. Even as he watched, a nearby tower grew a pointed roof and shifted sideways. Dynes edged the drone closer along a garden path, realising that windows were flickering in and out of existence and changing shape. What was going on?

Then his view was obscured as a figure stepped out in front of the DAVE. It was a blonde girl in a long white dress. She bent down and peered right into the camera lenses.

'Hallo, who do you belong to? My name is Luci Longlocks. Do you want to play?'

A tank and an APC had been completely destroyed by the attacking earthmovers, while three other vehicles were damaged but still serviceable. Eleven men had been killed and five others badly injured. Judd assessed the losses, redistributed his troops amongst the remaining vehicles and the column continued on.

The attack had been improvised so the defenders must be short of conventional armaments. All credit to them, Judd conceded. They had made good use of what they had to hand, but it had only delayed his advance.

The forest avenue ended in a junction where a gravel road crossed its path. Opposite was an ornate gateway set in a high wall that extended in either direction until it vanished over the horizon. The tall ironwork gates were closed, but a couple of shots from the leading tank destroyed the supporting pillars and the column rolled over the mangled remains and onto a long winding drive.

Energy bolts lashed out from the shadows of trees and bushes, burning pits in their armoured hulls. Turret guns returned fire. Sheltering tree trunks were shattered, shrubbery burnt away. Humanoid forms advanced on the column, firing rifles as they came, and were blasted into fragments by the far more powerful guns of the invaders. From the remains Judd recognised them as basic sentry robots, effective against infantry and light armour only. The defenders were truly desperate now.

They were still in the dark hemisphere of the tiny world, though the glow in the sky ahead of them showed the sun was now only just below the horizon. The road wound on through ornamental night gardens filled with illuminated pools and fountains and softly glowing fungi that had been cultivated in many delicate forms. Even Judd was momentarily distracted from his objective to admire the beauty about him. Perhaps, when this was over, he would make the world his private retreat.

'I'm afraid things are not quite right in the Palace today,' Luci Longlocks admitted candidly. 'Even I'm not feeling well…' her form seemed to shimmer disconcertingly for a moment. 'I was going to complain to the Lords. Would you like to meet them?'

Dynes said cautiously through the drone's speaker: 'Thank you. That would be most convenient.'

Luci set off towards the Palace.

Obviously she was some sort of simulation, Dynes realised, though quite what her function was he had no idea. But anybody, or anything, that could get his drone safely inside the Palace right now was not to be ignored. Judd might be there at any minute.

Luci entered the Palace through a garden door and led the way along a corridor whose walls were flickering with transient decorations, pictures and hangings. They reached a large hall and took a lift down to an underground vestibule with three doors leading off it. Luci went to the one on the right, saying:

'I've talked to them before but they don't seem to take any notice. Perhaps you can make them understand…'

She pulled open an outer door. A second inner door slid aside and the light came on. Dynes gaped at the makeshift morgue within.

Luci strode briskly between the racks of bodies waving her finger and saying: 'You can't just lie here and do nothing. There's work to do outside. Are you listening…?'

The red sun climbed over the horizon. Silhouetted in its rosy glow was a large structure capped with graceful spires. Judd smiled. His goal was literally a Palace. One of Hathold's private indulgences, no doubt. Then he noticed that the outline of the building was flickering, as entire segments appeared and then vanished. The improbable sight was so unexpected that Judd halted the column.

Was it a kind of subtle trap or form of defence? But how was it meant to function?

Even as he pondered, figures swarmed out from behind every bush and tree, springing from nooks where it would seem they could not possibly have been concealed. There were animals and people in period costume, some waving swords. All threw themselves wildly at the column, shouting, screaming or growling as they came.

The gunners blazed away at the incredible ragtag hoard by reflex. Bolts of energy that should have severed limbs seemed to pass through them without effect. Then a running man was struck in the chest by a bolt. Something exploded in a shower of sparks and he vanished. Suddenly Judd understood.

'They're just mobile simulations,' he announced. 'Ignore them.'

The hoard began clambering over the vehicles, too close for the external guns to bear on them, and threw themselves over the camera lenses and viewing portals. In seconds the drivers were blind.

Judd contained his growing anger. Somebody with only pawns left on the board was still playing a desperately clever end game.

In the crew compartment behind Judd, a soldier opened a hatch in an attempt to clear the simulations that were clinging to the vehicle with his hand weapon. A small bear-like creature wearing improbable red boots dropped onto him from the roof. There was a flash and the simulation vanished. The soldier was dragged back inside the vehicle with a smoking hole in his body armour and the hatch was rapidly shut again.

The simulation had shorted out its power cell with the force of a small grenade.

Then came the clangs of objects too solid to be simulations against the hulls. They could hear powerful drills whirring, probing for gaps in the armour, working at wheel hubs or links in caterpillar tracks.

'All crews,' Judd roared over the command channel, 'prepare for close quarter combat! Exit your vehicles on my mark... now!'

They burst out into the low red sunlight.

Service robots were clustered round their vehicles, trying to cut into them with power tools fitted to their arms. The soldiers opened fire, blasting heads and limbs from the robots. The simulations threw themselves at the soldiers. The air was filled with flying shards of metal, sparks and bolts of fire.

Judd stood shoulder to shoulder with his men, shooting down robot and simulation alike with cool precision. Nothing would stop him now he was this close to his goal.

'You see, they never listen,' Luci confessed miserably, closing the door on the room of corpses.

'Isn't it always the way?' Dynes said sympathetically. 'What's behind the other doors?'

'Oh, you wouldn't want to go in there. It's just a control room.'

'I might. Could you open it for me… please?'

With an indifferent toss of her head, Luci opened the door and ran inside.

Dynes saw a room banked with displays and control panels. A tall, oddly detailed blue box was standing in a corner. Peri Brown and an unknown man in a multicoloured coat were hunched over a console while Kel, Raz and Nerla looked on anxiously. A service robot stood inside the door as though on guard.

Under cover of Luci's entry, Dynes slipped the drone into the room over the guard's head and parked it unobtrusively in a corner.

'Hallo, do you want to pay a game?' Luci said brightly as she ran up to the others.

'Go away!' Peri shouted at her. 'See, they're going crazy, Doctor. Can't you do something else?'

The man did not resemble the Doctor that Dynes recalled from their encounter on Gelsandor. Had he had a total body makeover? But the blue box was familiar – their shuttle pod, or something. Odd design…

'It's not working! Peri said, her voice shrill with panic.

'I'm doing the best I can,' the Doctor snapped back.

'Well try harder. Judd will be here any minute!'

'Perhaps if I try this...' he tapped out another combination on the keypad.

The three young scavengers gasped in alarm, looks of horror frozen on their faces. Their bodies seemed to dim, then fold in upon themselves. For a moment three APS projector spheres hung in the air where they had stood, then dropped to the floor with sharp cracks, rolled over and lay still.

Luci screamed. Peri gazed at the motionless spheres in stark disbelief.

'They... were APSs!' she choked out. She clutched at her forehead. 'Doctor, what's happening?'

The Doctor looked equally astonished. As though in a daze he turned back to the keyboard. Text scrolled across the screen.

'"*Adventures in Primitive Cultures*"', he read. 'It's another interactive APS programme, part of a prehistory educational simulation. It must have been activated at the same time as the period play that gave rise to the stories of Lords still living here. They were all APSs like Luci.'

'But I could touch them! They seemed so real.'

'We know simulations can interact with physical objects to a limited extent. You must face the truth, Peri. Everybody we've met, apart from robots, were photonic illusions!'

A warning alarm sounded on the control board and lights flashed angrily. A clipped clear voice said: 'Warning: secondary systems failure imminent.'

Banks of lights began to go out. Luci gave a feeble cry, faded and vanished. As her emitter bounced to the floor, the robot on guard waved its arms about wildly, spun in a circle and keeled over with a crash.

'They're all dying,' Peri wailed.

'No,' said the Doctor, taking her firmly by the shoulder. 'The last people who died on this world are the ones in the freezer out there. We haven't won – but Judd won't either. There's nothing left to fight for here. Come on, Peri, let's go.'

Peri allowed herself to be led across to the blue box. Both of them slipped through its narrow door which closed behind them. Even as Dynes looked on curiously, a breathless, pulsating sighing filled the air, growing steadily louder. With it the blue box faded and was gone.

Out in the garden the remaining robots writhed and collapsed, the glow dying from their eyes. The simulations winked out and projector spheres dropped out of the air.

Judd's men looked around in surprise, suddenly deprived of their enemy. Judd didn't know what had happened to the defenders, but nothing was going to distract him now.

'Forward!' he commanded, and set off at a determined, power-assisted jog towards the Palace, his surviving troops fanning out on either side of him. The building had been shorn of all its illusory architectural trimmings to reveal a large but less ostentatious residence. Was Hathold still there? It didn't matter. He couldn't hide for long on such a tiny world. Judd would open the shield and bring reinforcements down and search until he found him.

There was no sign of resistance from the Palace. As their boots crunched across the gravel courtyard, Judd saw that one of Dexel Dynes' camera drones was waiting for them on the steps leading up to the main entrance.

'You'd better see this,' it said with Dynes' voice.

Judd stomped along the aisles between the desiccated corpses in the underground cold room. He examined the face of each male figure, trying to reconstruct the features of the man as they must have appeared in life. Finally he stopped before one in plain grey overalls and stared at it intently.

'Yes… this looks like Hathold.'

He strode back into the control room, watched in silence by his men. He prodded the fallen robot with the toe of his boot and kicked one of the emitter spheres aside.

'What happened here, Dynes?' he demanded of the DAVE hovering attentively before him.

'I'm not certain, Protector,' Dynes said through the drone.

Judd seated himself at the controls and began working the keyboard. 'There may be records that explain what happened here…' Images from APS programmes scrolled past as though taunting him with their illusions. 'How did you die, Hathold?' Judd muttered, half to himself. 'And where are the others?'

Suddenly a screen came to life displaying the Esselvanian coat of arms, then faded to reveal Hathold's haggard features.

'This is my last message to you, my dear wife and children…'

They listened to the recording in silence.

'… remember we were trying to reinforce the shield… something went wrong… we were irradiated… reprogrammed the robots as best we can. I hope the systems were not too badly damaged. They will maintain and defend the Palace until it is safe for you to return. Meanwhile let the reserve ship take you to other worlds who will fight Judd's tyranny with you… last words of Hathold, King of Esselven…'

The screen went blank.

Judd was a rigid mask as he fought the frustrated rage within him. Hathold had escaped him forever and his family had gone on to some other hideaway. Meanwhile, Judd had wasted valuable men and equipment fighting robots and illusions obeying a dead man's orders. This would be a humiliating chapter in the history of the Protectorate. Then a small detail rose to the surface of his mind…

Judd worked the keypad. Information appeared.

'That recording was made only weeks after Hathold left Esselven. Yet now this system's timebase shows the current date to be five hundred and eleven years ahead of what it should be.'

His men looked baffled. Through the drone Dynes said: 'So when I thought you'd been delayed in orbit…'

'Precisely,' said Judd. 'Five minutes became the equivalent of almost two days down here. It is also consistent with the state of the spaceport and ship in the hangar. Their attempts to strengthen the shield must have altered time itself. The continuum must be highly distorted on this world… yes, it makes sense. The shield was a virtual time/space stasis!' Eagerly he crossed to the shield control bay and started examining the readings. 'If we can duplicate what they did, Hathold may have unwittingly given the Protectorate a powerful weapon –'

'Warning!' a clipped computer generated voice said from the main console. 'Unauthorised use of shield controls. Antihandling trigger and timed destruct sequence activated.'

Judd sprang to the main console, scanning the readings intently. 'Computer: cancel destruct sequence!' he said.

'Voice pattern not recognised,' the computer responded. 'Enter proper access code to cancel and reset.'

Judd had drawn his handweapon and pointed it at the computer before he realised it was a futile gesture. That would only trigger what he was trying to prevent. If he had time he could bring his specialists down and they could bypass the security devices. But to do that had to open the shield first…

'Access code has not been entered,' continued the computer, after a pause. 'Timed destruct sequence activated. Nuclear reactor safety systems disengaged. Power grid and shield generators will be destroyed in one hour. Shield discontinuity now open for egress only. This system is closing down…'

All the panel lights went out except for those on one small

display which showed the numeral: 60.

Judd trembled with rage. Hathold was dead, yet still he denied him his final triumph! Judd's armoured fist smashed into the control board, splintering the plastic panel and sending fragments skittering across the floor.

His men shifted uneasily, uncertain what was to come next.

Judd took a deep breath, then opened the channel to the lander and said tonelessly: 'Bring the ship over. Prepare to evacuate advance party…'

Dynes watched the lander lift off from the spaceport even as he recorded Judd's men trudging out of the Palace.

As he prepared the *Stop Press* for take off, headlines were running through Dynes' mind. A WORLD LOCKED IN TIME, perhaps. Yes, he could play up both the scientific and sensational aspects of the story. He had some good action scenes… but it was a dead end as far as his coverage of Judd's progress was concerned.

Suddenly he felt it would be wise to leave Judd alone for a while and file the story personally at INA central on Plexar. Judd would only try to find out where the second ship carrying Hathold's family went, and that was a cold and very un-newsworthy trail by now. Neither would this latest setback help Judd's temper. He might lose control completely and it might be dangerous to be in the vicinity when it happened. It was probably fortunate that Dynes hadn't mentioned Peri Brown, the Doctor or their unlikely blue box.

Now they were characters that would be worth closer investigation. Who were they anyway and how did they come to be here? And how had they just vanished into thin air…

By the time the *Stop Press* lifted into the sky, Dynes was cursing himself. He'd been blind! What sort of story had he let slip through his fingers? To hell with Judd and his obsessions! Why didn't the man get back to invading planets like he used to and give him some decent newscopy.

You couldn't trust anybody these days!

Chapter Twenty-eight

With a final deep sonorous note and a dull thud, the TARDIS materialised once again in the palace control room. The Doctor emerged and made straight for the shield controls. Peri followed him, saying; 'Oscar winning performance or what?' Kel, Raz and Nerla cautiously exited the TARDIS, looking around them in wonder and delight.

One of the APS projectors lying on the floor rose into the air and Oralissa appeared. 'I believe we were successful,' she said.

'Those simulations you made of Kel, Nerla and Raz were perfect,' Peri complimented her. 'And Luci did a great job leading Dynes down here.'

Green-8's eyes glowed and he levered himself up off the floor.

'I only hope all this destruction was necessary,' he said solemnly. 'How many of Judd's men died in the attack?'

'I don't think there was any other way, Green-8,' the Doctor consoled him, still working at his keyboard. 'They suffered because they came prepared to use violence in an evil cause. Besides, Judd would never have believed our deception if he had been allowed into the Palace unopposed. In the same way Dynes had to think he was secretly observing us so he would accept what he saw as the truth.'

'Then the objective was achieved,' Green-8 said. 'They left convinced that everything of value here would shortly be destroyed. The modification of King Hathold's recording together with Miss Oralissa's computer warning were most convincing.'

Peri frowned. 'But if Judd hangs about and the shield doesn't go down, won't he get suspicious? He'll just start all over again. And if it's open, he might come back anyway. The same goes for Dynes. We can't have him snooping around again or he'll blow everything.'

'Don't worry,' said the Doctor. 'It was only necessary to persuade them to leave this once. That will be enough.'

Peri looked at him closely. There was an odd look on the Doctor's face, half grim, half mischievous.

'Doctor, what are you up to?'

'Just preparing to bring time here back in synchronisation with the rest of the galaxy,' he said casually. 'Of course, things have to balance out, you know... Look at the screen. Two ships are about to enter the discontinuity. I can't detect any more so Judd must only have brought one down... I think Dynes' ship is in the lead. Apparently he's in a hurry.' He pressed some keys. 'A stitch in time... There, that should do it!'

He sat back from the controls and beamed at them in satisfaction.

'That's it?' Peri asked doubtfully.

'Yes. Judd and Dynes will not be troubling us again.'

'You haven't... killed them?'

'Nothing so cold-blooded, I assure you. Just don't give them another thought.' He looked at Green-8 and Oralissa and the scavengers. 'You have many more immediate concerns.'

'Such as, Doctor?' Green-8 asked.

'For a start, educating our young friends here, and their fellow scavengers, about their true origins. I think Oralissa will be particularly good at that. Meanwhile you must repair the old spacecraft in the forest. You have the manufacturing facilities, and all the technical data is no doubt in the computer files somewhere. By the time you're ready to return to Esselven, I think you'll find the Protectorate's control will not be as secure as it was. The planet will need a leader. Perhaps young Kel will be up to the job.'

Kel goggled. 'Me… a chansor?'

'A king, even higher than a chansor,' Peri said. 'And of course you'll need a queen – but don't look at me, I'm a republican!'

Nerla looked expectantly at Kel. Kel slowly grinned back. Peri sighed in relief.

'Well, Green-8,' the Doctor said. 'You wanted things to change and an opportunity to travel. This is your chance. I don't say it will be easy, but will you accept the challenge?'

'I will, Doctor… if Miss Oralissa will help me.'

Oralissa smiled. 'A chance to do something different, something worthwhile. Yes I'd like that.'

'Then why don't you all go outside and make some plans?' the Doctor suggested. 'It's a lovely morning.'

'But there is no morning here, Doctor,' Oralissa said.

The Doctor smiled. 'You can still think of it as the dawn of a new day.'

When they had gone he looked at Peri and raised an enquiring eyebrow. 'Well, would you like to stay here for a while? Do a bit of gardening, perhaps?'

'No gardening!' Peri said firmly. 'And first a bath – for a week!'

The Doctor smiled indulgently. 'Each to their own, I suppose.'

Peri started towards the TARDIS, then looked back at the Doctor. 'You're sure Judd and Dynes won't give us any more trouble?'

'Perfectly,' the Doctor said. 'As sure as I am that history will look after them exactly as they deserve.'

Epilogue

DYNES recovered from the effects of the passage through the shield discontinuity as the *Stop Press* rose into space. He didn't try to make orbit but headed on out, knowing Judd was close behind him.

As he laid in a course for Plexar, Dynes automatically opened the link to the INA newsnet. To his surprise there was nothing but static on the channel. He checked the receiver but it seemed functional. Where were all the regular broadcasts?

Then he realised something else was missing. He scanned space behind him. Where was Judd's fleet? They had been in such close orbit about the tiny world that they were practically touching. But they wouldn't leave without their leader. What could have happened to them in the relative few minutes he'd been down on the planet?

A horrifying thought struck Dynes. No, it couldn't be…

Suddenly he felt very alone.

The captain of the Esselvanian Astrocorps quietly entered the audience chamber. It was the afternoon period that the royal family spent informally together. However, this was a rather unusual circumstance.

The garden doors of the chamber were open and the children were playing chase with their nanny, their shrill cries mocking the normal solemnity of the room. The Queen was gardening while the King was lying on the grass, laughing and urging them on. The

Chancellor was standing in his usual place by the throne, watching indulgently.

The captain crossed over to him. 'Your pardon, Chancellor.'

'Captain?'

'We have just brought in a person captured by the outer system patrol. He was with a handful of men in an antique warship travelling on emergency hyperdrive. They resisted boarding. Only he survived. He's claiming he is... well, Special Order 178 applies.'

'I understand. Please have him brought here. His Majesty will want to see him.'

A few minutes later a small compact man was escorted in by two guards. His hands were cuffed in front of him. His sunken, shadowed eyes darted about the chamber, as though trying to make sense of his surroundings.

The King was now seated on the throne. 'I am Kel the Third of Esselven,' he said. 'I believe you wanted to see me?'

The man blinked, then managed to focus on Kel. 'Do you know who I am?' he said sharply.

'I know who you claim to be.'

'I'm Protector Glavis Judd!'

'That is most unlikely.'

The man raised his hands to his brow for a moment, screwing up his eyes, as though trying to hold onto a thought. 'There was an accident in time... I am Judd... this is my world!'

'This world belongs to the people of Esselven. By their will I represent them in matters of state. Glavis Judd disappeared over 500 years ago, and his Protectorate disintegrated shortly afterwards. Everybody knows that.'

The man shook his head. 'No! The Protectorate was a perfect creation. It was efficient and productive. All were equal...'

'Some more than others, perhaps?'

'How can you dare say such a thing!'

'You're right,' King Kel said with unexpected candour. 'The concept of royal privilege is not logical, however it seems to be what the people want. There must be room for such idiosyncrasies in life. Protector Judd never understood that.'

'Don't tell me what I understood!'

'Then tell me why the Protectorate fell.'

'I don't… it couldn't…fall.'

'But it did! The Protectorate was a cold, heartless creation. That was why it fell.'

'Never!' With a surge of berserk strength the man threw off his guards and made a lunge for the throat of the young king.

The Chancellor's hand caught him by the collar and lifted him off his feet like a child. The stranger kicked and punched with desperate strength, but it was no frail old man like Dhalron who wore the chancellor's chain of office now.

The guards recovered and grabbed the stranger who was snarling with frustrated rage. Spittle rimmed his lips and there was a mad light in his eyes. 'You can't do this to me! I'm Judd the Protector! Where are my warriors?'

'Take him away,' the King said sadly. 'See that he is cared for appropriately.'

When the man's cries were lost in the distance, the King looked quizzically at the impassive face of his Chancellor. 'Well, Greeneight, my good conscience. Is this the end of the old matter?'

'I believe it is, Your Majesty.'

The King realised small faces were watching them and turned with a smile. 'It's all right, children, the excitement's over. Back to Nanny Oralissa. She has some lessons planned for you…'

As he went back out into the garden, Chancellor Greeneight contacted the central administration office via his internal radio.

'Please cancel Special Order 178. I do not think it will be needed again…'

* * *

Dexel Dynes sat in the office of the Editor-in-chief of Stellmedia, the company that Interstellar News had become 500 years on.

'That's quite a story, Dynes,' the Editor said. 'Of course we'd like to feature your return exclusively on our network. How soon will you be ready to give an interview?'

'But when will you run the story?'

The Editor shifted in his chair. 'The trouble is everybody who studied history knows what happened to Protector Judd. Of course, your report will fill in some of the details. It could make a fascinating documentary –'

'A documentary!'

'Look, Dynes. You're a man from the past with a unique insight into the way things were in the old days. If you want to keep working in the media, maybe you should consider presenting historical programmes.'

'Historicals? I report what's happening now,' Dynes protested. 'I make the news!'

The Editor shook his head sadly. 'To tell you the truth, your style of reporting is no longer popular. That sort of sensationalism just isn't acceptable any more.' He shrugged. 'Face it, Dynes: you're history!'

The attendants led Judd, gently but firmly restrained in a force jacket, along the calm, pastel coloured corridor.

'You can't treat me like this!' he said, his voice now harsh with shouting. 'Don't you know who I am?'

'Of course we do, sir,' an attendant said in kindly, condescending tones. 'Your room's just along here. We'll make you quite comfortable. A doctor will be along soon to talk to you about your treatment.'

'I don't need any treatment. I'm the Protector, do you hear! I'm Glavis Judd!'

A voice sounded from behind one of the many doors that lined the corridor: 'Judd? I'm Glavis Judd!'

'No!' cried another unseen voice, 'I'm Glavis Judd!'

'Don't listen to them!' Judd sobbed. 'I'm Judd, I tell you. I'm… Glavis Judd…'

But he no longer sounded quite so sure.

About the Author

Christopher Bulis was born and has lived most of his life in Sussex, on the south coast of England.

He was a science fiction fan from an early age, but only took to writing SF as well as reading it after working as an artist and designer, amongst other things. He still draws and paints when he has the opportunity, which is not as often as he would like. He has just calculated that, somewhere around the very end of the *Palace of the Red Sun*, he passed the milestone of one million published words of *Doctor Who*- associated fiction.

ALSO AVAILABLE

QUANTUM ARCHANGEL by Craig Hinton ISBN 0 563 53824 4
BUNKER SOLDIERS by Martin Day ISBN 0 563 53819 8
RAGS by Mick Lewis ISBN 0 563 53826 0
THE SHADOW IN THE GLASS by Justin Richards and Stephen Cole ISBN 0 563 53838 4
ASYLUM by Peter Darvill-Evans ISBN 0 563 53833 3
SUPERIOR BEINGS by Nick Walters ISBN 0 563 53830 9
BYZANTIUM! by Keith Topping ISBN 0 563 53836 8
BULLET TIME by David A. McIntee 0 563 53834 1
PSI-ENCE FICTION by Chris Boucher 0 563 53814 7
INSTRUMENTS OF DARKNESS by Gary Russell ISBN 0 563 53828 7
RELATIVE DEMENTIAS by Mark Michalowski ISBN 0 563 53844 9
AMORALITY TALE by David Bishop ISBN 0 563 53850 3
DRIFT by Simon A. Forward ISBN 0 563 53843 0
ESCAPE VELOCITY by Colin Brake ISBN 0 563 53825 2
EARTHWORLD by Jacqueline Rayner ISBN 0 563 53827 9
VANISHING POINT by Stephen Cole ISBN 0 563 53829 5
EATER OF WASPS by Trevor Baxendale ISBN 0 563 53832 5
THE YEAR OF INTELLIGENT TIGERS by Kate Orman ISBN 0 563 53831 7
THE SLOW EMPIRE by Dave Stone ISBN 0 563 53835 X
DARK PROGENY by Steve Emmerson ISBN 0 563 53837 6
THE CITY OF THE DEAD by Lloyd Rose ISBN 0 563 53839 2
GRIMM REALITY by Simon Bucher-Jones and Kelly Hale ISBN 0 563 53841 4
THE ADVENTURESS OF HENRIETTA STREET by Lawrence Miles ISBN 0 563 53842 2
MAD DOGS AND ENGLISHMEN by Paul Magrs ISBN 0 563 53845 7
HOPE by Mark Clapham ISBN 0 563 53846 5
ANACHROPHOBIA by Jonathan Morris ISBN 0 563 53847 3
TRADING FUTURES by Lance Parkin ISBN 0 563 53848 1

THE MONTHLY TELEPRESS
The official BBC Doctor Who Books e-newsletter

News – competitions – interviews – and more!

Subscribe today at
http://groups.yahoo.com/group/Telepress